BEST
OF
BEST
WOMEN'S
EROTICA 2

BEST
OF
BEST
WOMEN'S
EROTICA 2

Edited by

VIOLET BLUE

CLEIS
PRESS

Published in the United States
by Cleis Press Inc., 2246 Sixth St., Berkeley, California 94710.

Printed in the United States.
Cover design: Scott Idleman
Cover photograph: Douglas Menuez/Getty Images
Text design: Frank Wiedemann
Cleis Press logo art: Juana Alicia
First Edition.
10 9 8 7 6 5 4 3 2

ISBN 13: 978-1-57344-379-1

The following stories are reprinted from *Best Women's Erotica 2006*: "Just Watch Me, Rodin" by Cate Robertson; "The Upper Hand" by Saskia Walker; "Another Assignation with Charles Bonnet" by K. L. Gillespie; "Heat" by Elizabeth Coldwell; "Paid for the Pleasure" by Adrie Santos. The following stories are reprinted from *Best Women's Erotica 2007*: "Chill" by Kathleen Bradean; "Becky" by Kay Jaybee; "Call Me" by Kristina Wright; "Voice of an Angel" by Teresa Noelle Roberts; "Worth It" by Alison Tyler; "Animals" by Rachel Kramer Bussel. The following stories are reprinted from *Best Women's Erotica 2008*: "Mercy" by A. D. R. Forte; "Wet" by Donna George Storey; "Lost at Sea" by Peony; "Penalty Fare" by Jacqueline Applebee; "Rear Window" by Scarlett French. The following stories are reprinted from *Best Women's Erotica 2009*: "Fly" by Valerie Alexander; "The Bitch in His Head" by Janne Lewis. The following stories are reprinted from *Best Women's Erotica 2010*: "Amy" by Heidi Champa; "On My Knees in Barcelona" by Kristina Lloyd.

CONTENTS

INTRODUCTION:
MY BODY, MY HEART, MY BONES

I've broken many bones: ribs, toes, fractures under the knee, my right ankle, my nose, once. My heart is not a bone. It breaks, though, too. When it breaks it feels like it will never mend. If it were a bone, things would be easier. But just as hearts can break, they can be filled, treasured, even stolen. Not long ago, while someone I once loved was asleep I whispered in his ear that if he gave me his heart, I would keep it safe: I would put it in a beautiful precious box and bury it in a place only I know about near the most beautiful flowers in all of Golden Gate Park, and I would make sure nothing bad ever happened to it.

He never gave me his heart. But I learned this: the only things in life worth having are stolen.

Stolen glances in a circle of friends, when a little pull in your chest makes your eyes return to that one person—and he meets your gaze yet again. A stolen kiss when you least expect it. A turn of your head, an unexpected meeting of lips, and that thing you desire most comes along in one heartbeat of space; someone says, "I want you so recklessly I don't care anymore." You rip off each other's clothes, nuzzling, licking, biting with that frantic raw edge of desire found only in the stolen moment of absolute *yes*. It's fleeting, and it must be taken and savored.

The last time this happened, I'd been watching the boys playing their instruments onstage, all the pretty girls dancing, many just watching *him*. I love to watch the girls—and the boys—watch him, photograph him, dance for him, try to get close to him. I've watched them for years. He went away for a couple of those years, in prison for a while for something stolen. But he was back with the band now, even more like Steve McQueen than before: bigger muscles, more sway, a quiet strength with a boy's smile.

His shirt came off, as all the clothes eventually do when the band plays. Afterward, in the green room, I picked up his trumpet on the couch. The last time I'd seen him, he'd stolen a kiss; an electric spark that was our secret. I looked up, and there he was to collect his trumpet. The chaos of the band and dancers was all around me; everyone was half naked, drinking, still dancing, splayed and gyrating in the tiny green room backstage in the old, legendary San Francisco jazz club. Sexy dancing girls were letting me take pictures of them with their legs nastily and playfully spread; horn players and drummers were toasting me, tickling me while I tried to take pictures, flirting with me, asking to see a little more skin. I got plenty of theirs in return, and it seemed like the party would never end.

Looking up at him at that instant flipped a switch inside; I recalled the same feeling when I was a kid and jacking food from a store and had a hair-second to get it in my sleeve or pocket or be caught, or have to give up the prize and keep going. I met his eyes, extended my long fishnet-stockinged leg up off the ratty couch, and put a gloriously spiked black lacquer high heel on his stomach. He smiled and leaned over to get his trumpet.

I leaned into him for a split second and said, "Come back to my place and let's make out."

"I have to give people rides home," he replied.

I said, "Okay, good night."

I'd been home for ten minutes when there was a knock at my door.

All lanky and long, he leaned, filling the doorframe, with a sly smile. He had a beer bottle in one hand. I laughed, bit my lip, and led him slowly up the stairs to the kitchen, still in my fishnets and sweat and beaded dance costume, up to the table for a game of long-awaited cat and mouse.

The seats kept us too far apart, he insisted. I told him he'd ripped my fishnets during the show. Stealing his hand into my purse, he fished around and came up with the switchblade he knew I carried. "It's very sharp," I told him as he flicked open the blade.

The neighbors in the house behind me have a fantastic view. It also includes my kitchen. They were stealing something, too.

He took his time, sometimes using the tip of the blade, sometimes the sharp serrated saw at the base. Cut, cut—kiss. Cut, cut—kiss. Salty boy. Big hands. I shuddered with each cut, so close to my skin, especially when he reached between my legs. Our mouths locked for longer and longer, my heart beat up into my throat like I was going downhill too fast, driving a car with no brakes. Mid-kiss, he set down the knife and lifted me up, all the way off the ground like a doll. I held on tight, and then we were drowning in our own drunken hearts and kisses in the place where I rest my body, my heart and my bones—my bed.

After five years of secret desire, we fucked now like we wanted to tear each other's skin off, like we wanted to hold each other tight against the gale force of all the things we'd broken; like we wanted to get inside each other in every possible way, to wrap each other in desire and wet sex and the kind of passion that breaks you in half and heals you all at once. There was never a space between us. We licked and sucked and fucked and held each other tight all night, without sleeping, kissing every exposed part whenever there was movement.

When the light poked through the blinds, and he said that leaving me made him want to quit his job, I laughed.

He forgot to kiss me good-bye.

Being the editor of the *Best Women's Erotica* series for five years has been like that night: Cut, cut—kiss. So much desire, so many stories, and a fucking thrill every time I check my email for more submissions, the whole process a thrill to fuck by. I've often read submissions aloud to lovers, with the desired result of needy mouths and swollen bits grasping to take what they need.

Every year, I've culled from upward of three hundred stories for each volume. I've whittled it down to around twenty-two for each collection, and it's never been easy, though it's always been raw and filled me with passion for the craft of these incredible authors. The result of taking all five years' final selections, over one hundred stories, and choosing the very best—the ones I couldn't ever get out of my head, the ones that turned me (and others) on almost dangerously fast, like a match to gasoline—was worth the wait. Like that trumpet player.

The perfect opener is Rachel Kramer Bussel's "Animals," where in a fast and crazed moment of pure lust, a girl opens herself to her boyfriend—heart, mind and body—in a fuck that will leave you as breathless as the two lovers, and as alive as the marks on their skin. In Kristina Wright's wonderful and hot "Call Me" an accident leads to a furtive fantasy come true when an obscene phone call goes delightfully awry.

Teresa Noelle Roberts brings us the unforgettable "Voice of

an Angel," which culminates in one hell of a stolen moment backstage at the opera, but as with many of the complex stories in this collection, the journey is just as erotically enveloping as the sweet notes sung at the destination. Cate Robertson's fierce young female protagonist takes the upper hand in "Just Watch Me, Rodin"—another story that followed me around the streets of San Francisco as I remembered fragments of the girl's increasing erotic one-upmanship with the older, sexually dominant male artist who paid her for the pleasure of drawing her.

Everything about K. L. Gillespie's "Another Assignation with Charles Bonnet" sends the senses into overdrive, like that long-awaited fuck, but this time there's a twist (and a turn) when we rocket through sexual desire from behind the eyes of the sightless. "The Upper Hand," by Saskia Walker, not only shows why Walker is one of the hottest explicit erotic authors on the scene, but also what happens when two naughty young boys think they can play games with a neighbor who's got a firmer hand than Mrs. Robinson.

When I think of the hottest, most graphic and furious moments I've read in sex writing, I think of Elizabeth Coldwell's "Heat." Here, a barmaid decides she's not putting up with her asshole boss anymore, though the tables turn more than once before everyone gets to the boiling point of being hot, hard, and uncontrollably wet. To dispel the fire, Kathleen Bradean's "Chill" follows up with the most unique and compelling female sexual fetish I've ever seen written out, and the tale is so well-crafted that by the time you get to the very unusual point of orgasm you'll find your muscles cramping in sympathy, and likely in shared ecstasy.

Sometimes the price you pay for getting caught stealing is the whole reason for transgressing in the first place, as we see in the daring, lip-smacking oral encounter in Jacqueline Applebee's

"Penalty Fare." Janne Lewis's "The Bitch in His Head" is so much more than a complex relationship between a control freak corporate king with a very pernicious phobia, and his made-to-order (but very sneaky) call girl. It's an outrageous example of turnabout as fair play, but with ropes and the skilled use of special sex toys.

Kay Jaybee's "Becky" takes the office job well into the realm of nasty tongue-in-cheek fantasy within the first few paragraphs, as a wide-eyed (but not so innocent) Becky learns that spilling coffee in the break room gets you way more than a reprimand in an office where corrections involve canes and paddles. And for those of us who graze Craigslist for erotic fodder, Adrie Santos's nervy, cautious "Paid for the Pleasure" scratches more than one itch as a girl decides to let a man pay her—to receive oral sex.

Just when you think you have gender play all wrapped up in a nice and tidy bow, Lee Cairney's "Cruising" takes you trolling with a lesbian late at night in a park where she doesn't belong. What happens to her anonymously in public is as surprising as it is incendiary. Meanwhile, across town, Scarlett French is looking out her "Rear Window," watching her male neighbor and his trick provide full, explicit service for her to enjoy.

Peony's "Lost At Sea" is the most lyrical and rapturous of the bunch, more a tone poem of raw passion than a tale; it's complex, beautiful, and impossible to get out of your head. Then the legend of erotica writing Alison Tyler gives us one of the edgiest and most intense encounters of her writing career (so far) in "Worth It," in which a woman wants her fiancé to do the nastiest thing that he can think of to her—to see if she is indeed, "worth it."

In Heidi Champa's "Amy," a girl receives mysteriously mailed DVDs made expressly for her voyeuristic pleasure: each video portrays yet another girl submitting to one man's rough pleasure and punishment in the place where our narrator once kneeled for the camera (and the man) herself. A woman makes a snap decision and takes what she wants in "On My Knees in Barcelona" by Kristina Lloyd, where a sweaty summer vacation evening in a Barcelona bar turns into a pay-for-play slippery oral encounter.

A. D. R. Forte's "Mercy" is merciless when it comes to taboo sex; male and female high-power business associates decide that the hazing ritual for a sexy new male employee is to see how far he'll go, culminating in an intense bisexual first-time three-way. Another story made for masturbation and intense memories of the places it takes you afterward is Donna George Storey's "Wet," in which an American woman immerses herself in Japanese culture, fantasizing about submission and rough sex in the baths—and gets more than she asked for, much to everyone's slippery delight. The first time I read (and the next several times I reread) Valerie Alexander's "Fly" I realized that some stories are perfect when they leave you wanting more. When Tiger Lily tops Wendy and comes all over Peter's face as the start of her evening, you know it's a win for everyone. As Tiger Lily takes what she wants (just as Peter has in stealing Wendy) we truly learn that the only things in life worth having are stolen.

When you find that raw fuck, that passion; when you want to breathe in that stolen moment of pure sexual being until you drown, whether for a minute or an hour—take it. Take it with your body, your heart, and your bones.

With every ounce of passion for a series I love,

Violet Blue
San Francisco

ANIMALS

Rachel Kramer Bussel

"I want you to hold me down and fuck me hard. Don't treat me like myself, or like a woman at all—treat me like an animal," I told him, the last such pronouncement I would make. Aidan was the kind of guy who always made me feel depraved, and he had a special knack for making my pussy tighten so fiercely I worried that it would stay that way permanently, the way parents warn their kids their eyebrows will stay furrowed if they keep on frowning. I'd been lusting after him for almost a year, but had finally broken through my own fear and told him what I wanted from him, only to find he felt the same way. I'd never asked anyone anything of the sort—a little spanking, a few minutes of bondage, a few dirty words thrown my way, but that was about it. This was different. This was real, raw. That's how much I wanted him. At first, I wasn't sure if he got what I was saying—I didn't want him to hold back, *at all*. I could tell that he had been holding back, just enough to make me long for more, to make me feel slightly put off, as if he thought I was too fragile to take what he could really give me.

Maybe it's because, outside the bedroom, I'm his boss at our small town's indie record store. I'm the girl all the wannabe guitar players drool over—five nine, long jet black hair often tinged with green or red, eyebrow ring, purple lipstick, powder-pale face. My clothes, some mixture of black, tight, and sexy, usually paired with imaginative stockings and combat boots, never fail to make at least one set of eyes turn at the store. But Aidan, unlike most of the guys who passed my way, caught my gaze immediately. He was smart, not just some snot-nosed punk looking to steal CDs when he thought I wasn't looking. Aidan could talk as easily about Dorothy Parker or Bukowski as he could the Buzzcocks or Braid or even the Beatles. He didn't lord his intelligence over anyone there, either, it just came out if you provoked him enough and stayed hidden, like a turtle under its shell, if you didn't. He was more clean cut than the other guys, so you had to peer a little more closely to see his edge, to catch a sneer or raised brow, to see the smirks that were gone almost before they'd even formed. He had plenty of scars and dreams and fantasies, but they were wrapped up so tight I didn't know if he'd be able to let go, even though it was clear from his rock-hard cock and the look on his face, eyes half-lidded and wet mouth slack, that he wanted me.

I was sick and tired of lying back and letting some guy rock his cock inside me as if we were on a seesaw, gliding gently upward, pausing, then zooming downward at the most predictable pace imaginable. Even at twenty-five, I knew that sex should take you out of the everyday, should make you as wild and ferocious as a rabid dog—in heat. The guys before Aidan had been cute enough, but they just couldn't give me what I most craved, what I dreamed about, squirming against my slithering fingers as the walls of my bedroom shook with the latest single the store had sent our way.

"Are you sure that's really what you want, Tina? You already drive me so crazy with that sweet ass of yours, twitching it the way you do when you walk, like you're moving each of those cheeks separately, taunting me with them so I just want to grab you and smack them till they're bright red." Just hearing the normally sly, sarcastic Aidan saying those words, thinking those thoughts, made a tiny trickle of liquid slide down my thigh. Since somehow finding ourselves wedged together behind the counter last week during closing, we'd been fucking like rabbits until every moment seemed suffused with his scent, his touch. Even when we weren't together, my pussy was working overtime, as if asking when he'd be back.

We were standing in the doorway of my tiny kitchen, part of the so-called bargain I'd scored to live in the East Village, meaning I got a minuscule doll-sized set of three rooms, rammed right up against my neighbors' identical layouts. But I didn't care, because how much room did I really need to get fucked into oblivion?

Aidan was behind me, his back against the front door, while mine was slammed against his hard cock. I could feel it pressing between my asscheeks as I pushed back against him, and I leaned down, showing off my flexibility by wrapping my wrists around my ankles, making my already short black latex skirt ride up my unusually bare thighs. I was sure my tiny, wet red thong barely covered my pussy lips. He growled, and I knew I had him right where I wanted him. He tugged upward on one side of the thong, making it dig into my cunt lips until I whimpered, tears of joy forming in my eyes. *More*, I thought, *I want more.* Then he let go, but immediately grabbed my hips and slammed me hard back against his dick. I heard the metallic twang of his zipper being undone, and then his warm cockhead was tracing the contours of my slit, tapping against my opening as if he was testing out the right key to unlock my door. Except Aidan knew after only a week together that he could have me anywhere and everywhere, could take me when I least expected it and I'd be wet and ready for him. He was simply that kind of guy. Just as I was getting used to the feel of him rubbing against me, making me ache more than I would have thought possible, he stopped.

He pushed me roughly forward, and I had to scramble to place my hands on the floor in front of me to steady myself. Then he shoved the remaining fabric of my skirt well over my hips and reared back, slapping my right asscheek hard. The sting traveled throughout my body, seeming to leave my mouth in a whoosh of air. I had to really focus not to tip over, and then he did it again, the sound echoing through the room. He tugged on my thong, harder this time, keeping it there so it bisected my lips, letting them fall on either side of the thin piece of fabric. "You want me to treat you like an animal, T? I hope you're ready for me." *I am, I am,* I mouthed to myself.

Then he let out a growl, mimicking several animals at once as he brought his hand down and spanked me again, this time using his hand to get at both cheeks at once. He leaned down, and before I knew what was happening his teeth had sunk into my skin, the fleshy underside of my ass, his mouth moist, his teeth sharp as I got what I'd asked for, got the fangs and claws as his nails dug into me, his teeth nipping down my ass to play at my thighs. When he moved us into the other room, carrying me over to the bed and laying me down on the mattress, my body pressed flat against the crisp sheets, all of me bared, open, waiting, I sneaked a peek behind me and almost didn't recognize him. Like the best actors, he'd become someone else, gone to his own primal core as he scowled, his features contorted into a wild snarl of pleasure and passion and lust and sadism, his eyes sparkling with excitement as he whacked my legs apart. I went limp, a willing rag doll, as he pounced on me. His weight pushed me deeper into the bed, his cock pushing against my slit.

I felt deliciously, delightfully small, a little girl to his hugeness, as his hands raked through my hair, then clawed down my back, the red lines burning as he did his best to mark me, brand me his wildest animal. He reached beneath me, pinching my clit hard, until it hardly even felt like my special nub, but something else entirely. He ground my hard pink button between his fingers, so tight I felt almost numb, a blaze of heat wicking its way upward and inside, then petering out just as quickly as it started. I'd wanted something, certainly, when I'd asked for this treatment, wanted to go farther than I ever had, shed some layer of skin that's essential for daily life but feels like a cloak during sex, even when I'm naked. I'd wanted something vaguely urgent, something like the Nine Inch Nails line, something like what I'd seen in those porn videos where the girl screams and screams and screams until you don't quite know what's happening to her, only that she cannot live without it. But whatever I'd wanted, whatever I'd dreamed about, Aidan had torched completely. My meek little fantasies were child's play compared to this, were like going to first base when he'd simply upended the whole ballpark. With just his bare hands, his voice, his cock, he *became* an animal for me, one who wouldn't take no for an answer because he didn't even speak any language, let alone English. He became exactly what I hadn't known I needed until then, his paws digging at me, burrowing deep inside, stretching not only my pussy but my boundaries as he bit and dug and pinched and thrust.

My cunt was so perfectly sore, so raw, so hot, that when he finally slammed his cock into me, I went wild. The sounds I let out now were inhuman ones, bubbling up like some deep ancestral wail, coiling forth from my stomach, my cunt, my gut, my memories. My body was pinned beneath him, as much by shock as by force, and I let the tears stream down my cheeks, let him overtake me as his cock seemed to fill my entire body, coursing through me like blood, like power, like magic. Later, I would laugh at how truly out-of-this-world this was, how far removed from our petty punk politics, our little scene, the endless rounds of gossip. Whereas other girls might tattoo their sluttiness across their arms, or their asses, or their chests, the way Aidan fucked me went deeper than any ink ever could. It marked me inside, until I thought I might explode, combusting right there, his prey through and through. He speared me, plunging inside me with all the force he'd been holding in for years, forever possibly, going farther than I'd have thought possible, literally and figuratively, smashing me into the floor while my body tried not to escape but to mold to his, to fuse against him so I could feel what he was feeding me forever. As he plundered me, as he fucked me like the animal I'd become, he gave me so much more than his cock, so much more than simply his body. Aidan gave me his darkest self, like a werewolf or a witch, the kind that only came out at night, under the coveted safety of the dark, a self meant not for public viewing but for me alone. His dark side became mine as we growled at each other, shaking with need until I crumbled first, howling, baying, barking, making noises that were neither animal nor human, but somewhere caught between the two, my body twisted beneath him as I let his power crash over and then through me. I was still quaking when he came, his semen shooting into me like a rocket launching.

And then somehow, after many minutes of silence, of mouths opening and then closing, of words and thoughts gently tiptoeing back into our heads, pushing us over to what humans do best, we smiled at each other. He tumbled onto his back and pulled me on top, and we laughed, while a few errant tears raced down my cheeks. "I think I know what your next tat should be," he said, doodling his finger against my right bicep. "Wild Animal—because you are." Later, he sketched it for me, somehow managing to recreate the essence of what we'd done with elaborate gothic letters, a forest surrounding them, danger signs lurking amid beaded eyes and sharp teeth. For now, I'm just keeping his sketch in my pocket all day, so I can pull it out and look at it and be reminded of him, of us. There are some things I want the world to know about, things I can't stand to have assumed and so must emblazon them prominently, but Aidan and I together, well, that's something else entirely. Besides, anyone watching closely enough when I smile just so, making my incisors gleam and my eyes flash, should be able to see the animal in me. And if they don't, they're just not looking closely enough.

CALL ME

Kristina Wright

Claire dialed the number before she lost her nerve. The phone rang and she switched hands to wipe her damp palm across the sheet.

"Hello?" It sounded as it he'd just woken up.

"Hi," she said, trying for a sultry voice. "It's me."

"Bad connection," he mumbled. Static crackled across the line.

She frowned. That wasn't what he was supposed to say. She tried again. "I've missed you."

"You have?"

"Yes. And this is an obscene phone call."

"Really?" He sounded more awake now, but not quite himself. "Sounds intriguing."

"Mmm...I promise you won't be disappointed."

"Well, sweetheart, where do we start?"

Something wasn't right. The static on the line made it impossible to hear him clearly. "Sam, let me call you back. This is a lousy connection."

"Who's Sam?"

"Oh, my god—" It wasn't Sam. She had just propositioned a stranger.

"Hey, no, it's okay," he said quickly. "Don't hang up."

She hung up.

Claire stared at the phone, waiting for it to ring. She shook her head and picked up the receiver, carefully dialing the number Sam had given her. The phone rang twice.

"Change your mind?" There was humor in his voice. Humor and a warm familiarity that reminded her of late-night radio deejays.

"I'm sorry," she managed to say. "I'm trying to call someone else."

"So I gathered."

"My boyfriend, actually."

"Lucky guy."

"I'm sorry," she said again, feeling like an idiot. A horny idiot.

"I'm not." He chuckled. "So tell me, do you make a lot of obscene phone calls?"

She laughed. "Hardly. This is my first."

"You mean we're still on?"

"What? Oh, no, I meant I was trying to make my first one. I botched it, huh?" She absently rubbed her fingertip across her nipple. It was puckered, rising up from her breast. She stroked the opposite nipple until she had a matching set.

"I don't know," he said. "I'm willing to give it a go."

"Really? Do you get many obscene phone calls?" She smiled, wondering what he looked like. She decided it didn't matter. She liked his voice.

"Actually, I'm hoping this will be my first one."

"Please tell me you don't have a sleeping wife or girlfriend lying next to you."

"Well, I do have a girl next to me, but she's a ten-pound ball of fur."

"Cat or dog?"

"Cat. Please, no jokes about men with cats."

"No, no," she said quickly. "I think it's sweet."

"What can I say? I like a little pussy."

She laughed at his lame joke. "You're cute."

"You don't know that. You haven't even seen me."

"True," she agreed. "But you sound cute. You sound…"

"Sexy?"

"Yeah, you do. Very sexy."

"Mmm…you sound pretty sexy yourself," he said. "What are you wearing?"

She laughed. "Is that a standard question with men? 'What are you wearing?' Why does it matter?"

"I don't know. I want the visual, I guess."

She could almost see him shrug. "Would you be shocked if I told you I'm naked?"

"I'd be aroused."

She kicked her legs out from under the sheet. "Well, I'm naked."

He groaned. "Well, I'm aroused."

"But are you naked?"

There was some rustling and then finally, "I am now."

"Are you touching yourself?" she asked, shocked at her own boldness.

"Oh, hell. I wasn't, but now I want to."

She stretched out on the bed, phone cradled between the pillow and her head. She closed her eyes and imagined she could see this stranger with the sexy voice in front of her. He stroked himself up and down while he watched her. She slid her hands over her body, tugging gently at her nipples, caressing her breasts and stomach for him. She spread her legs a bit and felt the cool air glide over her fevered crotch. She gasped.

"What is it, hon?"

"I spread my legs. The air feels good."

"Are you wet already?"

"I haven't touched myself yet," she confessed.

"Are you playing with your breasts?"

"Mmm, yeah." She rubbed her fingertips lightly over her nipples again. "They're so sensitive."

"Pinch your nipples for me," he said. "Tell me how it feels."

She grasped her nipples between her fingers, as he requested, and pulled on them. She felt a corresponding tingle in her clit. "Oh, god, that felt nice. I could feel it right between my legs."

"I bet you're soaked. I wish I could see you."

"Tell me what you're doing."

He laughed, a breathy sort of laugh that let her know he was aroused. "I'm running my hand up and down the shaft, slowly. Up over the head, then back down. Real slow."

"You like it slow," Claire said. "I like that."

"Yeah? I'd love to touch you like this, this slow. Run my hands over your body, so slowly until you begged me to be inside you."

"Mmm..." she breathed into the phone, hearing an echo of herself. Instead of being embarrassed, she was decidedly more aroused. "I'd like that."

"Touch yourself for me," he murmured.

She slid a fingertip over her engorged clit and gasped. "Oh, I'm so wet."

"Beautiful. Show me how you get yourself off."

Claire slid two fingers inside herself. She was so wet she was sure he could hear her. "Oh," she whimpered, using her thumb to rub her clit.

"That's it, hon." His husky voice urged her on. "Fuck yourself."

She could see him, see his cock. She whimpered. "I wish you were here. I wish you were inside me."

"Me, too. I'd slide into you slowly so you could feel every inch of me." His words teased her, driving her higher. "I want to feel your wetness around me. So tight and warm."

"Oh, god. I want you to fuck me hard." She arched her back off the bed and raised her hips as if to meet his thrusts.

He groaned. "I'd fuck you hard. I'd bury myself so deep inside you."

She slid a third finger inside herself, wanting to feel it just as he described it. She moaned, pumping her fingers into slick wetness while she rubbed her clit faster. It wasn't her fingers she felt as the pressure built, it was him.

His breath quickened and she knew he was close. Her cunt clenched her fingers. She wanted to come with him.

"Oh! Yes, now, please! Come inside me," she moaned, thrashing around on the bed, fucking herself the way she wanted him to fuck her.

"Oh, god," he gasped. "That's it, yes."

She could almost feel him throbbing inside her. She bucked against her palm, coming hard, riding the wave of her orgasm while his deep moans filled her head.

Her fingers slowed as her orgasm faded. Her cries became soft coos of pleasure as she teased her sensitive clit.

"That was nice," she whispered. "Thank you."

His quiet chuckle tickled her ear. "I should thank you. What a great way to be woken up."

She felt the postcoital pull of sleep and yawned.

"Tired?"

"Mm-hmm." She yawned again. "Sorry."

"Don't be. I'll take it as a compliment."

She smiled in the quiet darkness of her room. "I don't even know your name."

"Oh, I don't know if I can tell you that. It seems so... personal."

They laughed together, then he said, "Michael Rossetti."

"Hello, Michael." She hesitated. Did she dare give him her real name? It hardly seemed to matter. "I'm Claire."

"Sweet dreams, Claire."

"You, too. Good night." She untangled herself from the sheets and hung up the phone. As tired as she was, sleep was a long time coming.

It seemed only minutes later when the phone startled her awake. She pushed her hair out of her face and fumbled with the receiver. " 'Lo?"

"Good morning, sleepy girl."

She glanced at the clock. 7:45 a.m. "Hey, Sam. What's up? How's your trip going?"

"I'm fine. I was worried when you didn't call last night."

"I'm sorry, sweetheart. I tried to call, but I think I wrote the number down wrong," she said, feeling only a fleeting sense of guilt.

"That's all right. I'll email it to you later. Everything all right?"

"Fine." She yawned. "But I need to get in the shower. I'll call you later, okay?"

"Sure thing. I love you."

"Love you, too." No sooner had she hung up than the phone rang again. She picked it up and said, "Forget something?"

"You've got the wrong person again."

A shiver danced up her spine. "Sorry, Michael." His name slid so easily off her tongue. "I wasn't expecting to hear from you."

"Amazing thing, Caller ID. I hope you don't mind."

She shook her head, amused and turned on at the same time. "Seems only fair, since I woke you up last night."

"Busy?"

She looked toward the bathroom. She needed to take a shower and get dressed. She was supposed to be in a meeting at nine thirty. She snuggled back under the covers and spread her legs. "Not really."

"Good. Because this is an obscene phone call."

VOICE OF AN ANGEL

Teresa Noelle Roberts

Jessie was hired for the costuming job at the Berkshire Opera because she had a great portfolio and several years of theatrical costuming experience.

Her knowledge of opera, however, was limited to what she'd learned from classic "Bugs Bunny" cartoons.

It didn't really matter for the job. As long as the directors could explain their vision for a production and point her in the right direction for visual inspiration, she didn't need to know that much. But plunging into a new world full of beautiful but unfamiliar music had piqued her curiosity. Most people in the company were glad to answer her questions, but she'd found a particular friend in the set designer. Nelson, a fiftyish self-described "flamboyant opera queen," was delighted to have someone new to convert to his passion, and she often found his nonmusician's explanations more comprehensible than those of the people with conservatory degrees.

So it was to Nelson she turned when the early discussions

of a production of Handel's *Giulio Cesare* left her confused. "I have no problem with crossgender casting. If the director wants Nora Murray to play Ptolemy, I'm glad to make the costume. But aren't they going to have to transpose the part for her?"

"A lot of the Baroque repertoire is written for a castrato voice. Yes," Nelson continued, seeing her wince, "it means exactly what it sounds like. Disturbing thought, but supposedly it produced a lovely voice, high but powerful. Mutilating boys for the sake of art is frowned on nowadays, though, so women usually get those roles."

"If it's a choice between cutting some poor kid's balls off or making someone built like Queen Latifah look manly, I'll take on the extra costuming challenge."

"I'm glad that's your department, not mine—talk about engineering! On the other hand, I do envy you getting to fit Daniel Gwynn."

"The one coming up from New York to play Caesar?"

"A countertenor, and one of the best. A male alto or soprano, to oversimplify vastly," he added, seeing the blank look on her face. "They're rare, of course, and great ones rarer still, but Daniel sounds like you'd imagine an angel would, and he's utterly gorgeous to boot. The idea of getting paid to have your hands all over that man and maybe see him in his underwear... my dear, I am terribly, terribly jealous."

Jessie immediately imagined some pretty, fey, androgynous creature, Boy George with more class. Nice to look at, fun to costume, but not her type. Just as well, really.

When Daniel Gwynn actually walked into the first cast and crew briefing session, though, he wasn't at all what Jessie had imagined. For one, he was tall, six two or six three if she estimated correctly (and after several years of fitting bodies of all shapes and sizes for costuming, she usually did) and nicely built. He wasn't a broad-chested fantasy figure off a romance novel cover, but lean and leggy and gracefully strong like a great cat, not at all the androgynous sylph she'd pictured.

He wasn't pretty, either, but handsome in an almost stern way, all about high cheekbones and chiseled features and pale gray-blue eyes that looked cold and remote until he smiled. He was dressed all in neutral colors—black jeans, charcoal gray sweater, lighter gray turtleneck under it to protect his throat against the chilly spring air.

When he smiled, his severe good looks were transfigured into something otherworldly yet very sexy, something like the way she'd always imagined Tolkien's elves (the cute college-boy appeal of Orlando Bloom notwithstanding). Jessie melted—right along, she figured, with everybody in the room who fancied men. His speaking voice astonished her even more than his looks: rich, resonant, lower than she expected.

"Aren't you a countertenor?" she blurted out when they were introduced. "I'd expected your voice to be higher." Then she bit her tongue, realizing that she'd sounded like an ignoramus.

He gave her one of those blood-igniting smiles. "Only when I want it to be," he replied in a much higher register, still backed with all the power of years of vocal training. "My natural speaking voice is lower than my singing voice," he added, in the deeper tones she'd heard at first. "That's not uncommon."

She felt herself blushing. "I'm sorry. I can't believe I said that. I'm new and still have a lot to learn. The regular members of the company are used to my dumb remarks by now, but I should have spared you."

He laughed, and even though Jessie was convinced, after her faux pas, that it was at her rather than with her, it was still a glorious sound. "Don't worry about it. You're a costume designer, right?" he said. "I don't understand how you do what you do, either—I'm color-blind, I've got the design sense of a wombat, and I can't sew on a button—but I do appreciate someone who dresses me up and makes me look good." He winked. "I'll look forward to chatting with you more during fittings. Maybe you can finally teach me to sew on a button."

Then he wandered away to talk to some of the other singers, leaving Jessie still flustered and repeating to herself firmly that the wink meant absolutely nothing. She would not, repeat would not, get a crush on him, although he was just as good-looking as Nelson had claimed.

She managed to keep that resolution for a couple of days.

Then she actually heard Daniel sing.

As the costumer, she wasn't expected to attend most rehearsals, but in the early stages, when the company was still working out its vision of the production, she found it useful to sit in on a few before she got too committed to costume sketches that just wouldn't work. Besides, she was intensely curious about this particular production, and, to be honest, about what a countertenor sounded like.

She scrunched down in the front row of the theater—forlorn and curiously stale-smelling now with no sets, no costumes, no special lighting—and prepared to take notes on any costume ideas that popped into her head. In Handel's day, it was perfectly manly to wear brocade and lace and accepted practice for heroes to be played by high-voiced castrati, but in the twenty-first century the male soprano emperor and the female Ptolemy had a hip, gender-bending quality, at least on paper. Might she be able to work some of that contradiction into the costuming?

As soon as Daniel began to sing, though, she understood there was no real contradiction.

The story was purely a coat hanger for the music, the glorious music.

And the music was designed to show off a voice like Daniel's.

He sounded as otherworldly as an angel, yet sensuous. She'd heard boy sopranos singing in a similar range, but their voices were light, innocent, almost disembodied. Daniel's voice was definitely bodied, and in a pretty damn amazing adult male body, and although it didn't sound "masculine" in any of the ways she was used to, it unquestionably was. That should have seemed weird, but instead it was hot, as if he were turning the whole notion of gender on its head in a way that made Jessie even more aware of his body and hers.

This music didn't carry the raw emotion of some of the nineteenth-century opera she'd gotten to know earlier in the season, let alone the gritty, let's-get-down passion of rock. There was no mess involved. It was all about technique and elaboration. Yet its beauty, and the implausible glory of Daniel's voice, seemed to go straight between her legs and vibrate.

As she sat transfixed, listening to that gorgeous voice coming from that gorgeous body, Jessie could feel her nipples perking. Her labia were swelling, throbbing, pressing against the seam of her jeans, and she could feel her panties getting sticky.

Male yet not male. An emperor yet a soprano.

She would dress him in lace and brocade, drawing on the wildest extravagances of the Baroque era, but in a way that showed off the strength and power of his body. Make the breeches the more fitted ones that became popular shortly after this opera was written, to show off his long legs; make the coat really full-skirted and over-the-top—maybe a loud but glorious brocade lined with Imperial purple—but make sure it emphasized his shoulders.

And Nora...Nora and the other women playing male roles

would dress like Baroque drag kings, with obviously padded crotches, and blatantly fake mustaches and goatees. Make them all strange and beautiful, partaking of both male and female, to support the beauty of the music and play up the aspects that to a modern observer seemed strange.

As she made notes, Daniel kept singing and she kept getting wetter.

As she began to make some sketches, Daniel and Fritz, a baritone, had a brief song exchange.

She'd always liked Fritz's deep voice, thick and golden as caramel syrup, but with Daniel's angelic tones weaving around it, soaring and trilling in ways Fritz could not, it sounded grounded, mundane. Just a guy after all, though a guy who could sing better than most men could dream.

The director came forward. "Thanks, Fritz. Daniel, Mei, I want to hear your first duet now." Mei Wong, who was playing Cleopatra, stepped forward, looking even tinier than she actually was next to Daniel's height.

Jessie set down her pencil and closed her eyes to listen. She'd been wondering about the romantic duets, how the two voices would blend. Until she'd actually heard Daniel, she'd thought the two high voices together in a love song might seem strange, at least to people who weren't aficionados of Baroque opera. She wanted to hear Daniel and Mei together the first time without visual cues.

Shame not to see Daniel, though, she thought as they began to sing. It must be his good looks that were affecting her so.

It wasn't.

If anything, the voice's soaring beauty seemed even more striking without his face and body distracting her. And the way it wove in and out with Mei's—astonishing! They were roughly in the same range, but with entirely different timbres to their voices.

It was as if Mei was being courted by a beautiful being from another world. Love among the aliens.

Make that lust among the aliens, because if anything the duet was tickling her clit more than the solo had. That voice...that voice!

Jessie opened her eyes to see Daniel gazing down at Mei. He wasn't trying to act the role yet and didn't look particularly romantic or lustful. (To be honest, Jessie wasn't sure where the opera picked up the story. Was this even a love duet or was Cleopatra saying something more to the effect of "Get out of my country, you great oaf of a Roman"?) But she still envied Mei for being the subject of his attention, his gaze.

His singing.

Jessie shifted in her seat, bit her lip to stifle a moan. This was more than she could stand. Quietly, she gathered her things and crept away to the bathroom.

Safely in a locked stall, Jessie peeled her jeans down, leaned on one shabby gray stall wall. One hand slipped between her legs.

She was slick as a seal, hot as an oven, and all without being touched.

She couldn't hear Daniel's voice from the bathroom, but with the memory fresh in her ears, it only took a few flicks of her fingers against her swollen clit to bring her over the edge.

Music soared in her head as she clenched on herself and muffled a betraying groan.

Afterward, as she zipped up her jeans and composed herself, Jessie scolded herself for being even sillier than a teenage girl lusting after—whoever teenage girls lusted after these days. (Justin Timberlake? Aaron Carter?) For heaven's sake, she was supposed to be working with Daniel Gwynn. Costuming him. Dressing him up to be even more striking than he was in street clothes. Measuring him. Fitting him. Touching him.

Curiously, while that thought gave her a pleasurable shiver, it didn't compare to the thought of hearing him sing again.

Jessie tossed and turned that night, Daniel's voice echoing in her head, enough to inflame her. Finally she grabbed her favorite vibrator, hoping it would end her torment.

As soon as she turned it on, though, she knew it wouldn't work. That whirring noise—it was so ugly, so intrusive, drowning out the sense memories of Daniel's singing.

Disgusted, she shut it off and went into the living room, rummaged around until she found some CDs Nelson had loaned her that, as yet, she hadn't had a chance to play. He hadn't had *Giulio Cesare,* but he'd passed on another Baroque opera, *L'incoronazione di Poppea,* by Monteverdi.

She skimmed the liner notes, figured out who the counter-tenors were, and selected an aria to put on repeat.

Then she settled back on her comfortable couch, spread her legs, and imagined Daniel.

Oh, this voice wasn't quite right—glorious, but not quite right. For all she knew, this singer was better. He was someone famous, after all, someone who'd sung at the Metropolitan Opera and La Scala, not the young, up-and-coming talent that Daniel Gwynn was.

But he didn't have the same effect that Daniel did. She felt a thrill of pleasure listening to the music, but an aesthetic thrill, not a sexual one that helped with the throbbing frustration between her legs.

Finally, she cursed and got the vibrator. It wasn't what she wanted, wasn't what she needed, and its noise fought with the strains of the music, but its familiar shimmering touch stirred her. That, and the music, and the vision of Daniel worked in concert. (Luckily, the upstairs neighbor was away and the downstairs neighbor worked the night shift, or she might have been the first person ever to get the cops called on her for playing Monteverdi too loudly.)

If Daniel were here now, singing for her, he'd get quite a show, she thought. What would he think if he saw her like this, naked and splayed-legged on the couch, a vibrator pressed against her clit and two fingers working in and out, moaning, "Sing for me, Daniel"?

Would he like her breasts with their tidy maroon nipples, the line of her hips, the wet sheen of her shaved pussy?

She could picture those pale, astute eyes studying her, and felt herself flutter in response to the idea, one step closer to coming. Would he like what he saw? No way of knowing, but hell, it was her fantasy.

She imagined him stopping in midsong to enter her, imagined Daniel's face, his hands, his cock—his voice in her ear, making sweet music of her name.

And with that, she exploded.

The next day, Jessie sneaked a small tape recorder into rehearsal and taped Daniel.

The sound quality was ghastly when she played it back at home. It sounded as though he was singing five miles away through a pair of old socks. Unaccompanied and unmiked, he was scarcely audible. Yet every night, she played it over and over again, coming and coming.

Thus armed, she was able to maintain some kind of professional demeanor during the preliminary work on Daniel's costume, although it certainly wasn't easy. Daniel smelled good, a bit musky, a bit like raw silk, and like the big, handsome cat he was, he seemed to enjoy being the focus of attention while he pretended to take it all for granted. Jessie's skin pulsed whenever she got near him, but she took a deep breath, looked ahead to an evening with her vibrator and the recording, and tried to think of it as a particularly torturous, drawn-out form of foreplay.

It worked until it came time to perfect the fit for his satin breeches. Doing the muslin for these had been trying enough, but she'd had an intern with her then, writing down measurements, handing her safety pins and chalk, asking questions, and generally forcing Jessie not to give in to the temptation to make a pass at him. (Jessie was half-convinced that Ayesha knew that her distraction value was higher than her value as an assistant that day. Some of her questions were too dumb, and some of her timing was too handy, to be entirely artless.)

But Ayesha had the flu and had been out for most of the week already, and the older Polish woman who also helped out in the shop had been called away for a family emergency. They were already a little behind schedule—what else was new?—and finally, she decided to go ahead with this, the third attempt to do Daniel's fitting. It was definitely easier with help, but she had to get on with things.

Even if it meant being alone with him.

On her knees in front of a man she lusted after, separated from his flesh only by a thin layer of fabric that she would be tweaking so it fit snugly. It wasn't just that she would be able to touch his thighs, his glorious butt; she was obliged to touch them in order to get her job done.

Jessie's heart was racing as if she'd gulped down four double espressos in rapid succession, and her stomach jittered to go along with it. She was one Daniel-smile away from having the shaky hands to complete the too-much-coffee illusion, and that, considering that she was working with pins, would just be bad.

And, of course, he had to say something. "You seem a bit

anxious, Jessie. Is anything wrong?" It was hardly sexy banter, but in Daniel's amazing voice, it was good enough, or bad enough.

Some adolescent bit of her thought, *He cares. He cares enough to notice!*

Her nipples perked up. Her clit quivered. And predictably, her hands started shaking.

"I'm fine," she lied. "Late night, last night, and a little too much coffee this morning, that's all."

"Good. I think I'm nervous enough for the both of us."

"You'll be great," she replied. "And I'll make sure you look fabulous, which should close the deal. The big companies will be beating down your door after opening night." While the Berkshire Opera didn't have the fame of some of the big-city opera companies, it was watched very closely by those same big companies. Making a splash here in a leading role could take Daniel from up-and-coming young singer to—would a male diva be a divo?

He gave her a devastating smile. "Thanks, Jessie. That helps."

Something about the way he said it suggested it hadn't helped enough. Oh, well, he knew she was hardly an expert on opera, and how many nervous performers ever listened to a mere costumer about their worth anyway? Their fashion statement, maybe, but not their worth.

The only way Jessie was going to survive this fitting was to pretend that Daniel was a mannequin. No more talking, she vowed. In silence, she went to work, smoothing and stroking the satin of the breeches against his legs, marking with chalk where she'd need to adjust the fit. She focused on the luxurious, smooth fabric, trying to shut out the heat of his body, the scent of his skin.

It might have worked, too, if she hadn't needed to double-check that she'd gotten the placement of the buttons at the fly just right.

She'd been trying desperately not to look there, but she had to check—it would hardly do for the breeches to fit perfectly everywhere but there. And when she did, she saw Daniel had a hard-on.

A hard-on that suggested if his voice hadn't been pure gold, Daniel could have found work in the porn industry.

A hard-on so nicely outlined by the tight, slightly stretchy fabric that she could see the mushroom shape of the head, even the way it was throbbing. The buttons were straining, and she was pretty sure he wasn't wearing underwear under the breeches.

That explained the nerves: he was also concerned about getting through this very intimate fitting.

There was only so much a woman could take. Jessie set down her pins and chalk, took a deep breath and reached out. "May I?" she breathed, and Daniel nodded frantically.

Her fingers fumbled at the buttons, and she cursed the impulse that made her use this historically correct but currently inconvenient closure, instead of something more expedient, like a zipper. (It wasn't as though it would show much under the voluminous coat!)

Then she forced herself to slow down and make the best of necessity by playing with the teasing possibilities. With each button, she paused for a few seconds, stroking at the little bit of him now revealed, driving them both a little crazier.

By the time the breeches were open, though, Jessie was done with playing. She took him in her mouth.

He groaned, a deeper, more animal noise than she could have imagined him making, even in her wildest fantasies. She could already taste a bit of precome, salty and delicious. He was thick as well as long, not a candidate for deep-throating, but great to play with. She closed one hand around his base and began to stroke in time with her sucking, cupping his balls with her other hand.

Her sex was flooding. Lovely as it was to have him in her mouth, she wanted him inside her, fucking her. In a little while, she'd probably beg for it. But not yet. Now she was just enjoying the taste of him, the way he stretched her mouth a bit.

His balls tightened under her hand. "If you don't stop—" he choked out.

She backed off but left her hand hefting his balls. They felt so right, there. "Thanks for the warning. Not that I'd object to you coming in my mouth, but I'd had other hopes for that cock of yours."

He grinned, not the practiced performer's smile, but the cat-with-the-canary smirk of a man who'd stumbled into sex he'd hoped for but hadn't really expected. Then he caught her up and gave her a kiss that tickled down and touched places that shouldn't have been reached by lips and tongues coming together.

Even while they kissed, she was peeling out of her clothes. The yoga pants she favored for crawling-around-on-the-floor days might not be elegant or sexy, but they had one advantage under the circumstances: they were easy to take off. Daniel's clothes were a little trickier, especially the still-basted breeches, but one thing she'd learned in her years as a costumer was how to help someone undress quickly.

Normally, Jessie would want more kissing, some serious time spent toying with her nipples, some reciprocation for her oral teasing. But she'd been fantasizing about Daniel for so long that she was wet and eager.

She looked at the project on the cutting table (one of Mei's gowns, a heavily boned confection of heavy gold-on-white brocade designed to look like something a person of Handel's era might imagine Cleopatra wearing) and was briefly tempted to sweep it onto the floor.

No, it would wrinkle, and expensive white fabric and floors were a bad combination. Dancing internally with impatience, she took a few seconds to drape it neatly over a chair, out of harm's way.

Then she hopped up on the table and lay back.

Proving his worth as a gentleman, he bent down to lick her, but she stopped him. "No," she muttered. "I want your cock. Please."

Again that smug grin.

Lucky guess. A table the right height for cutting wasn't a bad height for fucking either (provided, at least, you had a partner as tall as Daniel), although it took a little fussing to get everything properly aligned. The extra perhaps thirty seconds this took was excruciating, and when he finally pushed inside her, Jessie almost screamed with relief.

He filled her pussy the way he'd stretched her mouth. She couldn't move much in the position she was in, which was both exciting and frustrating. Exciting because it put her at Daniel's mercy, depending on whether he stroked in and out slowly or pounded to the finish line, and frustrating because, at the moment, he *was* stroking slowly. All right, she should give him credit for realizing that when you're well hung, you need to take a little extra time and make sure your lover's opened up and ready for you. But she was ready, dammit, more than ready.

Jessie grabbed his ass with both hands. "Please. Harder." She pulled him forward as she did, pushed with her hips as best she could, trying to get more of him inside.

Daniel began to pump faster.

Yes. That was what she'd needed, a good, primal fuck, one that would leave her a bit sore afterward but right now felt really good.

Her abs fluttered. She could feel her pussy clamping down, making him feel even more deliciously huge inside her. Her nipples felt sharp and hard as blades. Yet she couldn't quite come. This was just the kind of fucking she'd thought she needed, and it felt great, but it wasn't quite doing it. New partner nerves, maybe?

She moved one hand to her clit, planning to give herself that extra little boost she needed to break the dam and let loose the orgasms she could feel were ready to pour out with a little more stimulation.

Just at that second, Daniel's eyes widened. He pumped into her wildly for a few seconds, let out a small sound of surprised pleasure—a much smaller one than she would have expected, given the power of his voice—and ground against her. She could actually feel his cock jump inside her as he came, a tiny but delightful movement that still didn't quite push her over the edge.

He spent about fifteen seconds looking happily dazed and smug before the smugness gave way to embarrassment. "Sorry. It's been a while and I've been thinking about doing this with you way too much lately, but that's no excuse."

"It's all right," Jessie said feebly, trying to be polite. Damn, and she'd been so close!

"No, it's not. I pride myself on a good performance." He gave her the stage smile again, but with a playful wink. "You wouldn't let me lick you before. Will you now? I'm told I'm quite good with my tongue," he added in a teasing voice. "I think it's from learning to sing in Italian."

Tempting. Very tempting. A few licks right now ought to do it, and she had no doubt that Daniel's tongue was skilled. But the mention of singing suggested another idea—one that the sudden contraction of her pussy told her was a good one.

"Would you sing for me?" Jessie begged. "Sing for me while I touch myself? Please? Your voice turns me on so much."

First Daniel blushed and looked bewildered, but another look, sexy and mischievous, replaced it. "Only if I can touch you instead. I want to feel you come on my hand while I sing for you."

Just the thought of it made her spasm a little.

He settled two fingers on her clit. Circling it gently, he began to sing.

His voice poured over Jessie's bare skin, caressed her all over, circled around her clit following his fingers.

She spread her legs wider, picturing the song slipping inside her—and jumped as Daniel's fingers slipped in instead. Still wet and open, and slick with his come, Jessie took his index and ring finger inside her easily. He seemed to know exactly where to touch, where her G-spot was, how fast to pump her (quick and forceful as industrial dance music), how much pressure the other hand needed to put on her clit (delicate, gentle as a waltz.)

Or maybe everything felt so right because his voice was also working its magic on her, intimate as his hands, yet impersonal as an angel on high.

He hit a particularly lovely high note and trilled it, a technique that she knew had a name if she'd had enough brain cells left to care. She didn't.

It worked like a musical vibrator.

Jessie contracted. Her hips bucked up, pushing her harder onto his hands. The room spun as she cried out "Ohgodoh-godohgod."

The orgasm was a long one, and he kept playing with that note the whole time. Finally she flopped back on the table, feeling, if not quite sated, then damn content.

He kept going, though. Kept singing. Kept touching her.

Suddenly she understood. He wasn't done with the piece of music, and if he'd finished prematurely before, he wasn't going to this time.

One of the things she'd picked up about Baroque opera was that an aria could be ornamented and varied for as long as the singer's invention and lung-power allowed.

She'd learned from sitting in on rehearsals that Daniel had plenty of both.

That was the last coherent thought she had for a while. Occasionally her brain would kick in long enough to admire some lovely trick of his voice, but then some equally lovely trick of his hands would set her coming again and her cries almost drowned out his voice. Or maybe it was the other way around: she focused on the hands, but the voice triggered the orgasm.

She lost count at five, but it seemed that there were more.

Finally, she caught his voice faltering, at about the same time she was starting to get almost too sensitive. She grinned wearily, clapped, and croaked, "Bravo!" while pushing him gently away.

"What, no encore?"

"You need to save your voice for rehearsal later," Jessie said, amazed she could form so coherent a thought. "And I'm worn out. But I'd definitely like an encore sometime."

He grinned. "And to think," he said, his voice a little shaky, "that some people think Baroque music lacks passion."

JUST WATCH ME, RODIN

Cate Robertson

As he has instructed, I knock and enter.

Glancing up from his cluttered, battered old desk, he impatiently motions me in.

"I wish you could be on time for once, Camille," he says wearily. He doesn't want to know why I'm late because he has no interest in me as a person with any kind of life beyond the walls of this skylit loft.

I know better now than to protest his calling me Camille. I undress in a corner while he watches me from his desk. Unlike some other men I've worked for, he offers no screen or private space for this part of my job, and undressing in front of him always feels provocative, like stripping. He mentioned once that watching me peel off sparks his muse.

I try not to shiver. It's not that he can't afford to heat the place. No, I'm sure he keeps it cold deliberately, to make my nipples stick out hard.

He points to the bench, sleek brushed steel and buttoned-down black leather, the single piece of decent furniture in this bright but spartan space. "Do you remember the position? On your back," he says quietly.

How could I forget? Last week, after several sessions of sketching me in an exhausting variety of positions—on, over, around, and even under the bench—he'd finally settled on a conventional fetal pose because, as he said, "It makes your cunt look like a split peach." Besides, any pose must be comfortable enough to hold for forty minutes or more without a break.

I'm just not very comfortable with it right now, hunched here with my forearms clasped lightly around my shins and him stalking around the bench, staring. He goes to the easel, tilts his head; narrows his eyes at me, then at the canvas; then returns to adjust a wrist or thumb here, spread a knee there, untuck the fullness of my left breast from my upper arm.

His fingers on my skin convey energy, like a current or a hum.

He pushes a lock of hair off my forehead and smiles down at me. "Very good, Camille."

By the time he settles at the easel, my cunt is aching.

The canvas is larger than life, four feet high by six feet wide. He paints actively, jabbing and diving and whirling, dancing with it, teasing it, flirting with the paint and the surface. He's all art. Me, I'm just raw material, ore. The diamond-hard point of his gaze drills into me and extracts my essence, claims it for himself, pours it out in an image.

Of me. The way my arse tilts up. He's painting me wide open. I wonder what possessed me to take this job. This is what I get for dallying in a bar with a cute older guy who turns out to be a big-shot artist. "I need a model," he said. "Want a job, Camille?" Fuck. In for a penny, in for a pound.

The odd thing is that when I close my eyes, I feel the touch of his paint-laden brush on my flesh like a caress. He sees and traces it all, the incurve of my cheek, the contours of my petals, the puckered vortex of my anus. I'm squeezing inside just thinking about it.

Finally, he swirls his brushes into the water: "Time for a break."

In a kitchenette at the back, he makes coffee while I walk around, bend, stretch, jog on the spot, try to dislodge the yawning ache in my cunt. Four times I've been here, naked all afternoon, and he's never offered me a blanket or robe. He brings the mugs and sits beside me on the bench, leaning back, long legs stretched out straight.

I glance at his length, feel his energy close. Clench gently, dewily. Pray that I'm not wetting the leather, or maybe that I am.

He nods at the easel. "Go on. Have a look. It's almost done."

No photo-realist, he's made the splayed, upturned cleft between the creamy thighs fill the canvas with brash, wild color. At first glance, you'd hardly be able to tell that it wasn't the gash of a pitted peach, dripping with juice. Look again, and it's wet, throbbing, joyful, and oh so in your face. My cunt.

For once, I'm speechless. He chuckles. "You like the first in my new series?"

"Series? There's more?"

"Oh, yes. I thought I told you. This is just the beginning. Each painting in sequence will go deeper into eroticism. Here, you simply display yourself. In the next one—" He pauses. I hardly dare to breathe. "In the next one, you'll touch yourself. And so on."

I try to swallow but my mouth is dry because I'm picturing myself masturbating in front of him. "How many paintings will there be?"

"That depends on you, Camille. How far you can go." His voice is quiet, and he's looking at me now without a trace of a smile.

Yeah, well, you just watch me, Rodin.

After I strip, he says, "No painting today, Camille. Just drawing. Get on the bed. Sit cross-legged. Face the camera."

The bench has been pushed aside for a king-sized platform bed made up with a fitted sheet and a pile of pillows in a soft rose pink. I want to question him about the video camera on the tripod, but I keep my mouth shut. He doesn't pay me for small talk.

Bracing his sketchbook on his thigh, he sits on a high stool at the foot of the bed and puts me through several poses, his eyes glued to me, his hand moving as if by remote control, charcoal pencil scratching rough paper.

First, I must throw my head back, cup my breasts and draw out both nipples between thumbs and forefingers. He wants them very erect and red.

"Pinch. Pull harder. Harder," he murmurs. When I wince, he seems pleased.

For the second pose, I lie back on a pile of pillows with my knees bent and spread. On command, I draw my lips apart. I rub and knead. I insert two fingers and then three. I circle and expose my clit rhythmically. He draws nonstop, in patient detail.

I gradually become engorged and very wet. When he stands, I notice the ridge in his jeans and the wet spot just below his belt.

He says, "This last pose may be difficult. If you don't want to do it, I can get someone else."

No damn way, Rodin. "I can do it."

On all fours, I have to present my arse to the camera and

press my chest against the bed so that my back is uncomfortably up-arched. Quite the view.

"Spread your thighs," he says quietly. "I'm going to touch you."

With one knee on the bed, he dips his fingers into my cunt and strokes the juices slowly up my crack behind. I swallow to keep myself quiet, hoping against hope that he's going to fuck me now.

But—"Give me your hand." He slips my middle finger into his mouth and sucks it. The one I had up my cunt. Can he taste me? Can he smell me? Then he pulls my arm back at an awkward angle and places the tip of my wetted finger on my anus.

"Press," he says, showing me how. "I want your finger inside up to the last knuckle. Your other fingers should splay against your cheeks like a starfish."

My anal ring tenses, then relaxes at my finger's intrusion. I slide in all the way. I'm breathing so hard that he says, "Move it if you need to, but only slightly." I rock imperceptibly and work my clit with my other hand until my ooze dribbles cool down my inner thighs.

How can he hold back when he sees how much I want it?

But he does. He draws endlessly, while I squirm in misery. Then I hear him get up. Does he move away? I can't tell. With my face in the pillows, I'm not sure where he is, but I sense his presence, and if he's not drawing, what the hell is he doing?

I hold the pose because this is what he pays me for. My thighs are trembling.

In a few minutes, his voice slices through my tension. He sounds breathless, almost winded. "That's enough. Enough for today."

When I know he's gone to make the coffee, I bring myself off hard right there, convulsing with a hand in front and my finger plunging behind. I don't care if he hears my moans.

He brings the mugs. His erection is gone. He clicks the camera off and smiles pleasantly at me.

"You were good today, Camille."

I hope he wanks himself blind when he watches that video.

I almost didn't come back. When I got home and thought about how he made me masturbate in front of him and then jacked off secretly, I was hopping mad. But he sent flowers, no less. With a note on his letterhead. Inside, five twenties. Five times what he pays me per hour. He wrote: *Camille, if I pushed you too far, I apologize for any embarrassment I caused you. Please accept the enclosed as extra payment for the video. I was remiss in not paying you for that up front.—R.*

How could I not come back after that?

I've arrived on time this week. When I hold up my hair behind so he can buckle the velvet choker around my throat, I feel his breath. I swear he caresses the nape of my neck, but maybe I just want it to be a caress. His nails strike sparks off my skin.

He's produced two paintings from the video session, for which I am to pose briefly for final detailing. So I'm here on his bed, reclining into pillows with my clit caught between my right fore- and middle fingers, and my left thumb and forefinger "offering"—that's how he describes it—my right nipple.

"I'm the viewer," he says. "Look at my face. Think, 'I am beautiful. I am me...' No, not like that, Camille. Don't look seductive. This isn't porn. Give me a level gaze. Open to me... That's it! Good girl. Now hold it."

I watch him, at his easel at the foot of the bed, watching me. This isn't porn. This is the body spread open and translated. The luminous essence of flesh, my flesh, in thick, slippery paint. I try to picture him watching me on the video. His face contorted in *le petit mort.* His spunk spewing from the tip of his cock.

During the break, he switches canvasses, cleans and recharges his palette.

Casually: "Do you have a boyfriend?"

"Not right now."

"Fuckbuddy?"

"No. I wish." I roll my eyes: a joke. He doesn't smile.

"Too bad. It would be easier. For the next group of paintings—" he trails off, selecting his brushes. The silence vibrates: I hardly dare breathe. Then his eyes lift and take mine, bore into me. "Would you be averse to posing with a naked man?"

What? Oh, god. I don't know. I stammer. "I don't—think so—who?"

"A friend of mine, another artist."

I gulp. "You want me to fuck him."

He shrugs. "Not necessarily. It's just that it could happen in the poses I want. I'll pay you well."

"I can do that." He shows me the second canvas, tall and narrow, almost finished: me kneeling, from behind. All soft sweep of thighs and intricate cunt-spread curving and shifting into shadow. Lines and planes rise and converge at the still point, just above center. Where my fingers fan open like a sunburst around the middle one, which is buried deep.

Something, some ground inside me, caves in and liquefies. How does he find in an image so outwardly gross a delicacy and fineness so sharp it slices your heart to shreds?

I take up the position on the bed.

He invites me to meet him and Peter for lunch. Café Malu, no less. He introduces me as Camille. Peter is cute and talkative, and wears a wedding ring. For some reason, that reassures me.

When we are back in the studio, it's pen and watercolors, and

Peter's good humor is taking a beating. The minute I undressed, he horned up, and he's been stiff ever since. Well, he would be, with the positions Rodin's put us through. But so far the contact has been all external.

Now he wants us doggy-style. For real. He wants a close-up of the entry: how the cock pries the lips open, how the lips wrap around it. The way he talks about it makes me seep. We've all agreed that Peter won't actually fuck me but simply hold his cock at the required depth.

"Need lube?"

"No. Thanks."

Peter kneels close behind, opens my cunt with his fingers, and guides himself gingerly in. Halfway, and Rodin says, "Stop. There. Hold it."

I fight the urge to push myself back, to take him all inside.

Long minutes pass. The pen races, the brush swipes. Page after page. Peter's sweat drops onto my back. His cock is throbbing and I can't help clenching and I know that must drive him mad but I can't stop. We're both trembling, straining to hold back the jungle rhythm in the pulse.

He starts to pant. "Jesus. I'm gonna come."

"Pull out," says Rodin. He passes me a cloth to dry my streaming thighs. "Don't dry your cunt," he says.

Peter fetches three beers from the fridge. "Fuck. I almost blew then, man. I'm gonna get you back for this." He's done this before, I can tell.

After the break, Rodin wants one last position: on a wooden chair, me splayed on Peter's lap with my back to him and his cock securely rooted. He holds my arms, steadies me sweetly, his chest hair soft on my shoulder blades. Rodin kneels right in front of me with his sketchbook. He barks out commands and the pencil flies. No time to think. Just respond.

"Pete, pull her nipples. Perfect... Pinch her clit.... Grab her hips.... Dig your fingers into her thighs. Higher... Camille, where he enters, touch his shaft. No, a circle with your thumb and forefinger. Good... Cup his balls... Now play with your clit. That's it. Good girl."

My nipples ache and all I can see is the bulge in his jeans. By the time we finish, my juices drip drip drip off Pete's balls. A little puddle on the seat.

Leaving, I stop at the door and turn. "Can I ask you a question?"

He's cleaning up. He raises an eyebrow. "Sure. Shoot."

"It's probably a stupid question. I just wonder—why do you make me pose live like that? You have a camera. Why can't you just take photos?"

He nods. "It's not a stupid question, Camille. It should be asked more often, in fact. The answer is simple. The camera sees only with one eye. It has no depth perception and it distorts the image very subtly. With two eyes, I have depth perception. I can see what's beneath and behind the surface. I see the whole image, as the camera cannot see it. I bring out the invisible."

As he explains this, something predatory and angular rises inside me, a sharp and bladelike craving. I want to push myself into him.

"And what is invisible?" I ask.

He hesitates. Warily? He wonders where I'm going with this. "Heat. I paint heat."

"Heat? Whose heat?" I press on recklessly, feeling lucky. I want to make him say it. *Say, 'Your heat. I paint your heat.' Say it, you fucker.*

Even across the room, his eyes pin me down. "Mine," he says. "I paint my heat."

* * *

For the next several weeks, he paints nonstop, always a couple of canvases going at the same time with several more roughed in. Some days he calls me in to pose, but often he just wants me to be there while he works. Calls me his muse. Right. I feel more like an ornamental house-pet, lounging around on the bed, reading, listening to music, even napping, and always naked. It feels normal. He talks rarely while he paints, but when I make coffee, he takes a break and chats.

One day, he shows me some of the finished work: props the canvases up along the wall.

It's always a shock to see myself painted like this—in feverish color, with frenetic brushstrokes, everything vibrating and glowing together. The throb in my cunt radiates from the paint. His work is electric. It looks like fucking feels.

Looking at the paintings, he says, "What do you see?"

I stammer. "Me, but not me. Me, in your eyes." I'm breaking a sweat with the effort.

He says, "Exactly. You in my eyes. How I see you." Now he's looking at me. I can smell him, his sweat, his coffee breath. Did my nostrils flare? No doubt he can smell more than coffee off me.

"Camille, look at me." His face is lined, his eyes magnetic. He's probably my father's age. "I never thought anyone would do what you've done for me. You took on my challenge. And you've performed just as I'd hoped." He pauses. "But—"

Always a *but,* yeah. "I want to push you further."

"How much further?"

"Until you beg me to stop. Until you hit the wall."

I shrug. "What do you have in mind?"

The way his eyes drill into me, I feel my nipples prickle up. "A game. Play a game with me. A game of bondage and domination. Could you do that?" He gives a casual smile, but an undercurrent of tension hums in the air between us.

He wants this. Desperately.

Damn. Damn him. "Sure. I can do that."

When I arrive for the next session, he's laid out some nasty-looking equipment on the bench. I can barely look at it for fear of caving in: handcuffs, a collar, a red ball gag? A blindfold.

A purple butt plug. Something that looks like a small riding crop.

Nipple clamps? Jesus. What have I got myself into?

The video camera is pointing at the bed.

He smiles. "Are you afraid?"

"Yes."

"Good. You should be. It's going to hurt. It has to. But I promise I won't cut you or make any permanent marks on your body. And we'll do this only once. I'll cam it all. And of course I'll make it worth your while."

"Okay." So he's going to pay to tie me up and whip me in front of a camera. Have I now definitely crossed the line from model to whore? Or is this all still for art? I'm not sure anymore. He beeps the camera on.

He buckles the collar around my neck and the cuffs around my wrists. I lift each foot to the bed for him to buckle cuffs around my ankles.

"Kneel on the bed. Facing me, so your hands hang by your ankles."

When he clips the wrist cuffs to the ankle cuffs and I try to move but can't without spreading my knees, I have a revelation: restrained, in this position, my body is automatically designated a sexual object. My raison d'être is crystal clear.

With just a few buckles and clips, he's made me into a fuck toy.

"Now listen. This is important. You won't be able to talk with the gag. We need a safe signal. If you want me to stop, for any reason, stretch out your fingers. Like this. Okay? Good. Now open your mouth."

The ball, though soft, feels huge on my tongue. By the time he buckles it securely in place, my jaw joint is already sore with the strain.

The blindfold is next. Everything goes black and I'm operating by touch and sound. He is quiet for a few seconds. I strain to hear his breathing. Then—"Now I want you to turn over with your face and shoulders on the bed." I obey. Upended. His favorite position for me, but he doesn't say that.

"Are you ready to be spanked?"

I nod, my cheek flattened against the sheet.

Without another word of warning, he hits me with his bare hand, and just after the force of his blow sends fire streaking through my arse and the gag stifles my scream, I wonder if he wonders: how fast will I hit my wall?

I chomp down on the gag. Just watch me, Rodin.

It begins with his hands: slow swipes. Forehand, backhand. With each fiery stroke, I drive my fingernails into my palms and clench the gag in my teeth. Between each pass, he strokes my hips gently, almost lovingly, feathering my skin with his fingertips until I relax with relief, when the next blow knocks me sideways.

I lose count.

"Are you okay, Camille? You're glowing now."

I nod. My face feels flushed and my arse is blazing. His fingers coax sensation back, cool on my cheeks and down over my thighs. Then they creep between my legs and begin to rummage insistently among my petals. He grunts approvingly. I'm oozy and engorged. All that extra blood flow. Everything he's done to me, over so many weeks, all coming to fruition now. I try, but fail, not to rock in response.

He steps away, returns. Something hisses and swoops in the air behind me, makes me startle. The crop. He chuckles. "I want some nice red stripes on this rosiness."

And just like that, he strikes me. *Swoop. Swoop.* Each stroke forces a mangled moan from my lungs. My fists clench and unclench at my ankles as I consider signaling for safety. Again I lose count. But just before I hit the wall, he stops.

I'm struggling to breathe because my nose is so stuffed up. The blindfold feels wet on my cheeks. What is that sound, that muffled sobbing?

Me.

He rolls me onto my back and caresses me, his voice low and soothing, until my breathing steadies and strengthens. "Darling, don't cry. My god, you're beautiful like this. You'll see. I'll show you how lovely you are."

He presses his mouth to my forehead, my cheeks, my breasts. His chest hair brushes me, his cock slides hard and satiny against my thigh. I realize: he's naked. Since when? Since the blindfold? My nipples prick up between his fingers.

"Have you ever had them clamped?"

Before I can shake my head, something bites into the tender, tumescent flesh. One. Two. The pressure is savage and I scream but the sound is strangled. The twin throb of my pinched nipples ignites a relentless pulse down through my clit that makes me buck and grind helplessly. I'm desperate. My body is pleading for release. Begging him.

"Good girl." His voice is tense.

A swipe of thumb between my pussy lips spreads my syrup

down and behind. Is that his finger, opening my back hole? Oh, sweet fuck. Yes. One. Two. Probing, stretching. I melt down onto him, whimpering. Oh, dear god, dear Jesus.

"The butt plug," he murmurs just before he nudges it in. It's solid and it feels huge. My sphincter hugs it so tight I almost explode. But not yet, not until he rolls onto me and and shunts into me rough and deep. When his cock stuffs me full and everything goes numb, I realize I'm dying because I just can't breathe anymore. I hit the wall.

At that instant: the gag is yanked out, the blindfold off. He releases the clamps and fire surges through my nipples and my clit. I'm flung screaming and singing and soaring headfirst through cascades of fireworks into the endless night sky.

I don't know how long I lay there in his arms: until my sobbing and trembling finally petered out and I lay still, shell-shocked. Until evening purpled the studio and hunger won out over exhaustion.

At Malu, my ass throbbed on the chair. I could feel each welt where he'd beaten me.

Where he'd beaten me. Not a sign of the sadist now, in this attractive, middle-aged man of the world sitting across the candle flame from me, stirring his coffee and considering me carefully. Just hours before, this man had cleaved me to my core, ripped apart everything that I thought was me, and put me back together.

"What made it so intense?" I finally asked him. "Was it the blindfold? The gag?"

He lifted an eyebrow and shrugged. "Possibly. Sensory deprivation. When you can't see, your other senses go on high alert. Everything intensifies. When you can't vocalize, everything is bottled up inside. The release was powerful, no?"

Powerful? It was nuclear. I never came so hard.

* * *

"Stay the night," he says.

He plays the video and when it is over, he says, "Did you see the beauty in that? How you exploded under me. I want to capture that in paint."

I answer the tense note in his voice with my thigh over his. He fucks me warmly and companionably this time, but sleep is fitful until the gray half-light when he drags me from my dreams to prop me on all fours and slam into me from behind, our bodies clapclapclapping an accelerated applause.

Then a sound sleep, then startling awake at ten thirty-five with a midmorning sun baking the bed. Untangling from him and the sheets, fumbling for clothes: "I've got a class at eleven!"

"Easy, darling. I'll give you a lift." Over a cup of his strong coffee, he passes me a thick envelope. Hundreds. A thousand.

"What's this?"

He smiled. "Payment for your services."

"Services? I didn't do anything. All we did yesterday was fuck."

He keeps smiling until it dawns on me.

"If I take this from you, I'm a whore." I put it on the table.

"No. If you take this from me, you're my whore. A whore in the service of art."

He raises a finger to silence my protest. "Camille, listen. Nothing has changed. I pay you to do what I want. What I want changes from day to day. You know that. I've had you masturbate for me. Fake-fuck Peter. In different positions. You've fucked me. Tomorrow I may want you to fuck two men while I watch. But this I can promise you: I will always push you to your limits and I will always want to paint you there."

He offers the envelope again. "You can stop anytime you want. It's all up to you. How far can you go?"

How far? I see the walls stacked three deep with canvases of me, me as sexual energy made flesh, all dark raw wild beauty. Who knew such an erotic creature existed inside me? He draws it out and breathes life into a part of me I never knew existed. Where can he take me? What can he unearth inside me? He's given me a taste.

A taste for more.

I take the envelope with a grin. "Just watch me, Rodin."

ANOTHER ASSIGNATION WITH CHARLES BONNET

K. L. Gillespie

The smell of rubber tickles my nose and it feels good as I stretch the elastic band out and allow it to snap back on my fingers over and over again. Each time I do it, the rubber band releases a fresh flood of aroma and reminds me of stolen moments from my teens devoted to fumbling and fucking under an old oak tree in the woods behind my house with Jonathan, the boy next door.

The rhythmic snapping hypnotizes me like a metronome and the hubbub of my office blurs into white noise as I lose myself and my inhibitions once again under that old oak tree. The sun warms my face and birdsong fills the air. His hands are on my body and his breath is moist on my skin. He pulls out a condom and I can remember its smell and the way it felt between my fingers as if it was yesterday. I help him peel it on and...

Trng-trng...trng-trng...

The phone starts to ring, ripping through the rose-tinted, sentimental memories of my youth and a sigh begins in the pit of my stomach and escapes from between my lips as I reach out and pick up the receiver, elastic band still in my hand.

It's my mother; she worries about me constantly and phones me often. I struggle to put all thoughts of Jonathan from my mind and hers at rest as she bombards me with a thousand questions. I can understand why she worries, so I tell her I'm fine and pretend I'm going out with friends tonight. She seems satisfied by this and after a few minutes of general chitchat she hangs up.

As soon as I have replaced the receiver I hold the rubber band to my nose and try to recapture Jonathan, but my memories are playing hide and seek with me, teasing me from around corners and mocking me for not being able to picture his face. The harder I try the farther away he gets until I am left with nothing but a pile of work to get through before the end of the day.

Five o'clock arrives and I leave the womblike confines of my office and step out into the great big wide world.

The West End's noisy today and even though I've lived here for five years, if I'm not careful I'll get lost, so I cement a thousand-yard stare on my face and make a beeline for Charing Cross Station.

The traffic fumes sting my nose and the streets are full of obstacles to overcome. A police car, with its sirens blaring, half circles me as I wait to cross Shaftesbury Avenue and a group of Italians chatter away quickly to my left while to my right an American lazily notices the obvious. A rickshaw whines by and as soon as it has passed I take my life into my own hands and step into the road with a babel of voices ringing in my ears.

The next thing I know a bus whistles past me, taking me by surprise, and as the wind catches my face I gasp, lose my balance, and stumble backward.

As I prepare to collide with the pavement I feel arms around me, fingertips pressing into my shoulders, and a distinctive scent enters my nose. Cinnamon. Sweat. Leather. Tobacco. A unique aroma that announces his presence with a bang. I breathe him in deeply, trapping every drop of his essence in my olfactory canal and savoring it slowly before committing it to memory.

This is love at first smell and I am overwhelmed. Suddenly my life becomes a compulsion to make this strange man mine. Unable to resist, I brush my fingers over his hand and a network of nerve endings dance over the surface of my skin, registering the soft warmth of his body and the faint pulse of his life force.

My senses are racing toward overload as I fancy I can taste his strong scent in the air; my mind wanders and I find myself imagining him in my bed, naked and sleeping off a wild night of sex. I would trace his entire body with my fingertips and then I would...

I am dragged back to reality when he removes his hands from my shoulders and I pray that now he has lifted me to my feet he isn't going to just walk away. I still need to hear the sound of his voice to complete the picture and I urge him to speak to me under my breath.

"Are you okay?" he eventually asks, thank god, and his words vibrate gently in my ears. His voice is deep and warm, like butter at room temperature, and as he speaks to me the rest of the world fades into the background and his utterance fills my head.

I repeat his words over and over in my mind, and I can feel him looking at me, waiting for an answer. My face starts to burn and I break the silence by mumbling something incoherent—but I have no idea what because all I can think of is him, stripped bare between my legs, submitting to my every whim.

Once again my fantasies are cut short when he hands me my white stick and my heart sinks as I sense myself through his eyes for the first time. Out of pity he offers to see me across the road and I hate myself for accepting, but I need more to create him fully in my mind.

I know time is running out so I run through a mental checklist—smell, touch, taste, sound, all accounted for—and then the foreplay is over. He makes his excuses and disappears into the throng but that's London for you, faceless, especially when you're blind.

Nevertheless as I walk away I lift my hand to my lips and I can still smell him on me. He is under my nails and on my skin and I can't wait to get him home.

My train pulls into the station and I search out the nearest door with my stick. I enter an invisible carriage and wait behind a gray curtain for the doors to close and sever my connection with the buzz of the outside world.

As soon as the doors shut I am alone. Everything disappears into a wall of silence, but I'm used to living in an invisible world. I know there are people all around me; someone to my left is eating a burger and the woman in front of me is wearing Poison, but I can't see them and unless I can hear them or touch them they might as well not exist.

I submissively let someone lead me to a seat and count the stops as they pass until the tannoy announces that I have reached my destination. Only another 438 steps to go.

When I arrive home I head straight to the bedroom and begin searching my memory for him but his smell is fading and time is running out so I quickly set about slipping out of my clothes.

As I'm undressing I begin to wish I'd had the courage to run my fingers through his hair and over his face, but I tasted him in my mind after all and as I position myself on the bed I am sure that will be enough to bring him to me tonight.

The soft satin of my bedspread embraces my body as I sink back and recall the sensation of his hands on my shoulders and the taste of him in the air. I lift my hand to my nose again and inhale his odor deep into my lungs, trapping it there until I can hold it no longer. Cinnamon. Sweat. Leather. Tobacco. I run through the memory like a mantra and in the blank darkness I search inside myself for him.

I part my legs and my eager fingertips seek out the triggers that open up the most dormant part of my mind. Quivering with excitement, I conjure him and he appears before me, by the window.

I know he is smiling as he climbs onto the bed behind me and wraps his arms around my naked body. I can feel his sweet breath on the back of my neck like a cinnamon-scented breeze. His pulsating life force warms my skin and as I collapse into him, I place his hand on my breast and shake with delight as he squeezes my nipple between his thumb and index finger. His warm voice murmurs sweet nothings into my ear and I can feel him planting tiny kisses on every notch of my spine.

I can feel his cock hardening in the small of my back and I press myself against it as his hungry hand searches out the cleft between my legs. I arch my back and he slides his fingers into me, holding me tightly by the base of the spine with his thumb. I shiver with anticipation and hold my breath to intensify every flutter and gyration.

As I reach the peak of my pleasure I whisper the secrets of my darkest desires to him and he takes my vulva in his mouth and parts my swollen lips with his tongue. I wind my fingers into his hair and pull him closer until his nose nudges my erect clitoris.

Gently, I rock his head toward me, increasing the rhythm at my body's whim until I am fucking his face with abandon and my senses shift ceaselessly, evoking sight out of sound, smell, and touch. I am about to come but the orgasm is secondary because a miracle is happening.

As I writhe in his arms the gray curtain that shrouds my life begins to disappear and he transports me to a world of light. With a cry of ecstasy I come out of the uncharted void, and for a few seconds colors whose names I don't even know fill my mind and I can snatch them from the darkness. They pulsate in concentric circles like a kaleidoscope and I stare at them in wonder as they shift like curtains in a breeze before my eyes. And they are bright, so bright that I have to narrow my eyes to look at them, but they are the most beautiful things I have ever seen and I drink them in greedily while I can because I know they won't last long, they never do. Then, with a shudder I am plunged back into the darkness.

Sex is my way of seeing and my imagination has a luminous eye. Passion gives color to my mind and for a few seconds I cease to be imprisoned by my own identity. Every time I do this it ends in a little death and part of me feels sad—because it was such a short affair, like the life span of a mayfly, destined to expire. But tomorrow is a new day and who knows who I will bump into then.

Sleep comes easily. I don't dream but when I wake up my mind is still reeling from the night before. On the way to work my senses are on hyperalert and I realize I am searching for him in every person I pass. I can't concentrate on anything and my appetite, usually so hearty, has jumped ship. Maybe I'm coming down with something. My mother phones and with three questions she has diagnosed my problem. I am in love. It makes no sense in my head but my heart understands, and an hour later I am back on the street where we met, in exactly the same spot, 173 steps from my office and about to cross the road.

I'm still there forty minutes later, sniffing the air, desperate for a hint of cinnamon or a whiff of leather. Waves of musk, citrus, clove, and Brylcreem assault me from every angle but I don't find what I am looking for. He doesn't show and I go home alone.

I'm not hungry so I go straight to bed. For almost an hour I try to conjure him before me again but he is just a shadow that lingers outside my window and refuses to come in. I know he is watching me though, and this quickens my pulse and I slip my hands under the sheets and slowly start to run my fingertips over my naked body. I know the contours of my body better than anything else in the whole world and within seconds I am rushing headlong into seventh heaven. I shut my eyes and will the colors to come, but I orgasm in the dark and it leaves me feeling emptier and lonelier than when I started.

I can't sleep so I put the radio on for company and wait for the morning. The velvet tones of the nighttime presenter rock me gently but my mind is racing, chasing after the cinnamon man of my dreams. I try to imagine running my hands over his face, tracing the contours of his lips, running my fingers through his hair. It's driving me mad and I know I have to do something about it. I have to try to find him again, starting first thing in the morning.

Sunrise drags its feet and I count the minutes one by one until the alarm goes off.

I rush through work on autopilot, determined to leave early; I was too late the day before and that's why I missed him. It never crosses my mind that he is a tourist, or was just passing by—something deep inside tells me that we will meet again, it's just a matter of time.

It's getting late and I've been waiting so long that my feet are numb. I'm beginning to feel faint and my mind has started playing cruel tricks on me. Every now and then I can smell leather or sweat or tobacco but never together, never in that evocative combination that identifies him.

There's a war going on in my head and I'm beginning to listen to my own logic. I know I'm being stupid but rational rules hold no sway over my heart so I continue to stand there, smiling sweetly at every good Samaritan who offers to see me over the road; feeling like a fool but refusing to give in.

Suddenly I start reeling with hope and my sixth sense kicks in, forcing me to turn round.

Cinnamon. Sweat. Leather. Tobacco.

He's here. He's nearby. I've been given another chance.

I take a deep breath and turn in his direction. I hear myself saying hello; it doesn't sound like me but I know it's me because the words came out of my mouth. The next few seconds seem to stretch out for hours. I can feel my face burning up and I wish the ground would open up and swallow me.

What have I done? My mind is spinning: Did he hear me? Is he ignoring me? Is he as embarrassed as I am? Is he still here?

Then I hear it, the same warm, buttery voice that melted my heart. He remembers me, he asks how I am, he tells me his name: Charles. I smile and I know he is smiling back. He asks me how I am and if I plan on throwing myself in front of a bus today. I laugh. He laughs. It's all going so well.

He asks where I am heading and I reply; he's going to Charing Cross too and he offers to walk me there. I accept and I know that by the time we arrive I'll be 438 steps away from seeing again.

THE UPPER HAND

Saskia Walker

Thwack. Lucinda inhaled sharply and counted to ten while she resisted the urge to stand bolt upright. Heat flared through her flesh where the missile had hit her left buttock. She bit her lip and continued to tend her flowerbeds.

"Bloody kids, you'll be sorry," she muttered to herself.

Her neighbor probably had her sister's children over. There'd been laughter and shuffling from over Diana's fence earlier and the missile, whatever the hell it was, had definitely come from that direction. She moved along the flowerbed with her buttock on fire, and then eased upright as gracefully as she could. She wasn't about to let them know they'd hit home, oh, no. With kids you couldn't let them get the better of you. Besides, hopping from foot to foot would provide them with no end of amusement.

She collected her gardening basket, pulled her halter bikini top straight, and headed indoors. Once inside, she gave her buttock a quick rub and ran upstairs to the back bedroom, where she had a good view of next door's garden and could spot the little blighters for later public identification. Easing the venetian blinds open a crack, she peeped out.

"I'll be damned...." It wasn't kids at all. Instead it was two rather attractive young men that she spied over the fence. One of them was sprawled in a deck chair looking like a reject from a metal band. Wolf lean, shades on, with baggy shorts and T-shirt complete with offensive slogan, he had straggly hair to his shoulders and a stack of empty beer cans at his side. The other was on his knees, foraging through the undergrowth to spy through a gap in the fence.

"Checking out your target, hmmm," Lucinda murmured. "Well, I caught you red-handed, you naughty boy."

Because he was bent over in the bushes, she couldn't see too well what he looked like overall, but his rear end was looking pretty good from this angle. Sensing fun, she smiled, her hand going to the exposed part of her buttock, where she'd been hit on a tender spot beneath her high-riding, frayed denim shorts. With a brisk rub of her hand she freed a frisson of sexual pleasure while she took time to observe the view. When the kneeling figure emerged to report to his buddy a moment later, she let her eyes roam over his naked torso. This one was built and built solid. His hair was shaved close to his head, a zigzag pattern delineating the shape of his skull.

"Very interesting indeed," she murmured when she watched him rubbing his hand over the bulge in his jeans, while speaking to his buddy and laughing. They'd obviously been getting off on the view of her rear end while she'd been bent over doing her gardening.

After a good fifteen minutes' observation—during which time she came to the realization that Diana's son must be home from university and he'd obviously brought a friend—she began to formulate her plan to take the upper hand with these two lads, because Lucinda wasn't about to let them get away with it, oh, no. She hadn't had the pleasure of meeting Diana's son before, but he was about to find out that his target wasn't shy or easily embarrassed. Star of several explicit art-house movies in the late eighties, and currently director of a South London alternative theater, Lucinda was the type of woman who could envisage the full entertainment potential of a situation like this and had no trouble going after it.

Before she left the upstairs room she hauled her video camera out of the wardrobe and set it up on a tripod, making sure it would catch any activity on the lads' side of the fence, and then she headed back down to the garden, grabbing her sunhat, lotion, and shades on the way out.

The August afternoon heat was simmering; the faint hum of insects in the flowerbeds accompanied her own humming as she strode down the garden. She hauled a sun lounger across the lawn and positioned it just about level with the area of the spy hole. Sitting down, she squirmed into her seat deliberately and began rubbing sun lotion into her arms, alert for signs of attention from beyond the fence. By the time she had covered her arms and shoulders in lotion, she picked up a scuffling sound in the bushes beyond the fence. Smiling to herself, she moved to her legs, kicking off her sandals with panache, being sure to apply the lotion in a seductive and suggestive manner. She thought about having the two lads doing this job instead—one on each thigh. Oh, yes, she could just picture it, she could almost feel it. Her hand slid up the length of her inner thigh, massaging as it went.

A suppressed comment emitted from the other side of the fence and a muffled conversation followed. She ignored it, because she didn't want contact yet, she was making this an investment for later. The camera upstairs was whirring and so were the visuals in her mind—they'd be clamoring for a view, she'd be willing to bet on it. Would they both be able to see, she wondered, or would they have to fight over one spy hole, like two young bucks infected with midsummer madness?

She set her bottle down and reached for the ties on her halter neck. When she dropped it she heard another sound. She avoided looking directly at the area of their peephole, but a cursory pass-by under cover of her sunglasses definitely showed movement, and a moment later she caught sight of the crown of the shaved head moving at the top of the fence. They were getting sloppy in their eagerness to see what her breasts looked like. That amused her greatly and knowing she had their full attention, she made a big display of squeezing another puddle of lotion into her palm from a height, dribbling it out slowly. Dropping the bottle, she spread the fluid between her hands and then moved to her breasts. Her nipples were already peaked and she sighed loudly as she spread the creamy liquid over the surface of her breasts, massaging it deep.

They'd be aroused and hard now, cocks pounding, had to be.

Her breasts ached with pleasure and an answering thrum in her groin drew her hand lower, across her abdomen and down, into her shorts.

A stifled groan reached her.

They were watching all right. She wasn't about to stop now.

She decided to watch the video just after sundown, savoring the idea of it while she showered and slipped into a sarong. A large glass of Châteauneuf-du-Pape in one hand and the remote in the other, she settled down on the sofa and flicked the video on.

The camera angle was just right, with just a clip of her in one corner as a reference point. She could see her legs from midthigh down and she chuckled to herself as she watched the action begin. The shaved head was clued in to her reappearance by the time she was creaming her thighs and gestured for his buddy to join him. The long-haired one clambered out of his deck chair and over to the fence.

They stood still at first, as if disbelief had them in its grip. Then they were jostling for the best view. As time passed their expressions grew serious, tense. Shaved head turned to say something to his buddy as he pulled his cock free of his fly. They whispered and nodded agreement, then began to hunt around. A moment later it seemed as if they located another peephole and they were both stationed close to the fence, eyes trained on the view, cocks out, occasionally turning to each other to pass comment. They were both masturbating vigorously in the bushes, unabashed by each other's presence.

Fascinating, reflected Lucinda, as she toyed with her nipples through the thin sheath of her sarong.

Shaved head was soon gone on it, rubbing at his cock vigorously, face taut with concentration, eyes narrowed as he squinted through the fence. She took a long draft of her wine and sighed. What an absorbing sight that was and how hot it was making her. She slid off the sofa and onto the floor, closer to the screen, legs akimbo on the rug. She flicked her sarong open, her fingers stroking over her tummy and down, remembering how it had been in the garden, when she'd known she had an audience. She'd always been a bit of an exhibitionist but this was different: they didn't know she knew they'd been watching. Now this was her voyeuristic journey into their arena, their secret wanking, and their laddish camaraderie over the slut next door.

She'd been brewing for another wank and she fingered her slit, imagining it was their eager young male hands on her, as driven as they were over their cocks right now on the screen. Shaved head was stroking himself fast, concentration honed, and then his head went back as a jet stream of come ribboned into the air and splattered on the fence. The toes of her left foot stroked down the side of the screen while she watched wolf-lean one trying to watch through the gap in the fence and wank himself off. What a sight it was when he finally came.

"Oh, boy," she murmured, and thrust harder, her clit bound in pleasure under the pressure of the palm of her hand, two fingers inside, slick and moving frantically. Her sex was on fire, her hips bucking up from the floor. The whirring of the video and the sounds of her pleasure-fueled sex filled the silent room. And she had the remote; she could fast-forward and rewind just as much as she wanted. Knowing they were so hot for her and being able to watch it over and again was a heady intoxicant and she eked out her pleasure that evening for just as long as she could bear another self-inflicted orgasm.

Diana enjoyed cut flowers. Lucinda preferred to see them growing in the beds, but for the sake of her project she cut an armful and took them round to Diana's the next day. She'd waited until late afternoon, when the lads had taken up residence in the garden and had already downed a few cans of their favored brew.

"They're beautiful, thank you, dear," Diana said as she took the bouquet and ushered Lucinda inside after her while she put them in water.

In the oak and marble kitchen Lucinda gravitated toward the window that overlooked the garden. "It's another glorious day," she commented. Out in the garden the two lads were stretching like waking tomcats, reclaiming their territory, sprawling in the summer warmth. "Oh, is that your son home from uni?"

"Yes, that's Jamie. And the one with the hair," she rolled her eyes, "he calls himself Man, although I don't think that's his real name."

"Man, ay." Lucinda smiled as she watched Jamie cavorting in the sun. He was definitely the showman. And Man was the quieter, long-haired, wolflike one. She was determined to find out what they would be like in closer proximity.

She turned back to her neighbor. "It must be great having two strapping lads around, to help you out with chores and such."

Diana gave a derisive laugh. "Well, I daresay they'd help out in an emergency but they aren't ones to put themselves forward for any task that doesn't instantly appeal to them." She smiled over the flowers, now stashed in a vase. "The garden and the beer seem to have held their attention pretty solidly these past few days. I was out yesterday and when I got home Man had somehow picked up a rash from the bushes and both of them were in danger of getting burnt from overexposure."

Lucinda enjoyed her secret thoughts for a moment. "Are they going to be around for long?"

"Until next week, then they're off to some rock festival in Wales."

"Hmm, in that case would you mind if I borrowed them for an hour or two? I've got one of those self-assembly shelf units that I need a hand with."

"Feel free, I'm sure the offer of a beer or two might sway them."

"I'm sure you're right," Lucinda replied, and smiled. "I'll take your advice and offer plenty of tempting bait."

And she knew just what sort of bait they liked best.

Up close they were just as attractive, if not more so. "Hello, boys," she said, trying to suppress her grin as she noticed Jamie's eyebrows shoot up at the sight of her on this side of the fence. Man shielded his eyes against the sun for a better look. "If it's not too much trouble, I'd like to drag you away from your afternoon sun-worship."

"This is Lucinda, our neighbor," Diana explained. "She needs a hand with some bookshelves; can you two make yourself useful and help her out?"

"I'll make it worth your while," Lucinda interjected.

The two men glanced at each other for support. After a moment they got to their feet.

Once she'd led them round to her place and got them inside, she pointed out the Ikea flat pack in the sitting room and told them she'd get them some beers. Like two hungry hounds that had been thrown a scrap from a plate but sensed the real juicy meat was being kept somewhere nearby, they worked with the chore they'd been given while looking forlornly in her direction.

The floor was soon covered in packaging, but when she got back their eyes were trained on her. Not surprisingly, she was as provocatively dressed as yesterday, if not more so. She had a great figure for a woman knocking forty years and she knew how to show it off to its best advantage. And she was enjoying every moment of their lascivious eyes on her.

"It's so hard for a single woman to manage a big erection," she said, idly, as she handed them their drinks. Jamie nearly dropped his can; Man swore under his breath and two patches of color appeared on his gaunt cheekbones.

Nice to see we're all on the same wavelength, even if they don't know it yet.

"I really appreciate you two helping me out."

"Any time, Lucinda," Jamie offered, grinning widely, glancing over at his friend and winking conspiratorially.

That was enough of that, she was in control here. She walked over to the sofa and lifted the remote. "Carry on," she said. "I want to see what you make of it." She flicked the video player on.

Dutifully, they turned back to the job they had been assigned to. Lucinda smiled; they were pleasantly malleable and that suited her well. She fast-forwarded through a rather fine BBC production of *The Merchant of Venice* until she felt it was time, and then casually swapped over the videos.

The two of them floundered to a standstill when they caught sight of themselves on the TV screen.

"You were watching us," Jamie murmured.

"I was, but then *you* were watching *me*. Fair exchange is no robbery." Her eyes flicked back and forth from them to the TV. "Quite a sight, isn't it?" she added, raising her glass to them.

"Oh, shit," Man declared, flushing when he saw himself wanking on-screen.

"Oh, please, don't be coy. You've got nothing to be ashamed of."

Jamie was a little more in touch with what might be on offer, weighing up what he saw on the screen and what she was showing him: a knowing smile, an enticing glance, a hand nonchalantly linked over the belt of her low-slung shorts, fingers tapping over the zipper.

He set down the assembly instructions he had in his hand. "You knew all along. You went along with it, and filmed it?"

She nodded.

"So why have you brought us round here, really?"

She purred. "Oh, I liked what I saw and I think you owe me a closer look…in the flesh, as it were." She couldn't keep the dirty smile off her face. "You wouldn't object to giving me a repeat performance, up close, would you?"

Jamie grinned. "I'm up for it." He put his hand on the bulge in his jeans. He really did love that cock of his! He turned to his friend. "Manfred?"

Man flicked him a disapproving glance at the use of his full name, but nodded. His lean, hungry looks matched the expression in his eyes.

A bolt of sexual power hit her, pure and powerful. She moved, kneeling up on the sofa. "Right then, I'm sure you won't mind me having a more active role, this time around...?"

They both shook their heads. Man had a wild look in his eyes.

God, this was good! The power rush alone was getting her wet. And they were both sloping closer, hounds with their eyes on the main dish. She had a split second to decide, but she was a very naughty girl at heart and she couldn't resist. She reached into her pocket and pulled out the condom she had stashed there. Flipping it toward the strewn packaging and abandoned shelves she said: "Whoever finds that gets to fuck me; the other has to give me a show."

They stared at her, open mouthed, for a whole five seconds and then reacted, the pair of them scrabbling amongst the cardboard and bubble wrap to find the packet. Lucinda couldn't help chuckling, wishing she had her camera.

Man jumped up triumphantly with the prize in his hands.

Perfect!

"Oh, bloody hell," Jamie muttered. "That's not fair."

"It is fair; besides, you have no right to complain about anything, since you smacked me on the arse yesterday!"

He pouted.

She pulled her top off, squeezing her breasts in her hands right at him. "Stay where you are. Man, come round here, I want you to fuck me from behind...while Jamie watches." She wriggled her shorts down her thighs, leaning over the back of the sofa.

Jamie's eyes were black with lust. He had his zipper open. He grunted his disapproval when Man took up his position behind her, but started wanking almost immediately. What a sight! A dribble of moisture followed her shorts down her thighs.

"Oh, yes," she moaned. Man had dipped his fingers tentatively into her slit and was stroking his way back and forth from her clit into her wet hole. "Keep going, you're right on target!" He did as requested for a few moments before he cursed under his breath and she heard the sound of the condom being ripped open. She pushed her bottom back, inviting him in, her eyes on the incredible tightness of the muscles on Jamie's arms and torso while he rode his cock with his fist, his hips arched up, his mouth tight as he watched.

Man plowed into her, his cock filling her then rolling in and out, bashing her breasts against the back of the sofa with his urgency. Moments later his fingers groped and hit her clit; she arched again, and his balls hit home. She contracted on him, her body on fire. She groaned and pressed her nipples hard on the sofa, moaning loudly as she hit the jackpot.

"Come closer," she urged Jamie, as she surfaced. He shuffled forward. She stuck her tongue out, and licked the drop of come from the end of his prick. She was starting to come again. He moaned, his eyes frantic. "Come on my tits, baby," she said. He did, a split second later, just as Man exploded inside her.

"You are one hot lady," Man said when he collapsed on the sofa beside her.

"Yeah," Jamie agreed. "I hope you have plenty more *bookshelves* for us to *erect*," he added, with more than a hint of suggestive sarcasm.

"Loads," she confirmed, winking at him approvingly. "But next time I really must film you *getting it up*."

"You drive a hard bargain, but it's a deal," he replied, and Man nodded, laughing.

Not bad for a day's work, Lucinda reflected, and made a note to buy more videotape for her new personal video collection: the upper hand in action.

HEAT

Elizabeth Coldwell

When I think of Ian, I think of heat. The heat of the sticky days of summer and sweaty sheets. The heat of the flame that draws in the moth. The heat of passion, and shame. I think of that sultry August night, and the things he did to me, and I still hate him—and I still want him.

I took the job at the Red Mill because I needed the money. We've all done it—poxy jobs for poxy pay that kill your self-esteem but keep the nasty letters from the bank manager at bay. Trouble is, most of us do it when we leave school, or to help us get through a degree course, not when we're knocking thirty, like I was. You don't need to hear the sob story; all you need to know is my nice, safe marriage and my nice, safe job in retail management bit the dust at roughly the same time, and I found myself living in a rented bedsit with damp in the kitchen and a DIY-fetishist landlord who spoke a dozen words of English and whose idea of fun was drilling holes in the walls at eleven at night. Bar work at least got me out of earshot of Costas and his home improvements. I didn't know it would bring me into the orbit of Ian.

You could quite easily walk past the Red Mill and never know it was there. It's a bizarre little pub, set into a long terrace of Victorian houses, with a polite notice taped on the door asking drinkers to keep the noise down as they leave for the benefit of the neighbors. With its sun trap of a beer garden out the back, bar billiards table, and jukebox packed with albums from seventies dinosaur bands, it attracted what Cameron, the fat, fortysomething landlord, called a "select clientele": mostly bearded real ale drinkers and their aging hippy girlfriends, and the sort of football fan who wanted to discuss the result of the match with the opposition supporters afterward, rather than glass them over it. The only concession Cameron made to the younger drinker was to stock a range of sickly alcopops in Day-Glo colors. But I quickly came to love the atmosphere, the feeling that you'd somehow been invited into the landlord's front room for a pint. Within days, the Red Mill became the stable center of a world which, for me, had been so thoroughly tipped on its axis.

So when Cameron announced that he and Jean, his wife, were taking a couple of months off to visit her elderly, ailing mother in New Zealand, my first thought was to ask how it would affect me. "The brewery'll send a temporary manager, Stella," he told me blithely. "You'll be fine."

And that was how Ian Todd appeared on the scene, and from the moment I saw him, I knew I wouldn't be fine at all. I turned up for work on the Monday lunchtime, and there he was, bringing a crate of mixers up from the cellar. It was too soon after Martin had walked out on me to be assessing another man sexually, and yet with Ian, I couldn't help it. As his gaze met mine, my pussy clenched with a sudden spasm that was almost painful. It was a reaction no one had garnered from me since Martin. No, make that including Martin.

I don't go for men like Ian, I never have. My ideal is a swarthy, cuddly little bear of a man, just like Martin. Ian was just the opposite: tall and lean, with dishwater blond curls falling to his shoulders, and eyes of a green so pale it was almost colorless. When he spoke, it was with a Liverpool accent, which immediately raised my hackles. It isn't a rational prejudice, but that's the one accent I simply can't stand. It goes all the way back to my old comprehensive school, and the art teacher I had then, Mr. Prior, from somewhere on the Wirral. I was never going to be in the top stream for art—to be honest, most of my efforts gave the impression I just about knew which end of the pencil to draw with—and he was one of those teachers who took great pleasure in ridiculing the less able pupils in a class in front of all the rest. I dropped art as soon as it was no longer compulsory, but even now the sound of those flat Scouse vowels was enough to bring memories of my frequent humiliation at Mr. Prior's hands flooding back.

"You'll be Stella," Ian stated. It wasn't a difficult process of deduction. Cameron only employed two barmaids on a regular basis: me, and an Australian girl called Gill. With her pale, freckled skin, beaky nose, and seventies dress sense she was as far from the "Neighbors" stereotype of the antipodean beach bunny as it's possible to get, but she had a good rapport with the customers and she worked hard. As did I. Or so I thought till Ian launched into his spiel.

"I don't know quite how much you've been getting away with before," he said, "but I don't stand for any shit. You turn up on time, you don't slope off early because you need to pick up your kids from the babysitter or your period's come on, you don't accept drinks from customers and you make sure the tables in this place are always spotless. No dirty glasses, no full ashtrays. And no slacking. And if you don't like it, tough. Bar staff are ten a penny, and if you don't pull your weight, I can get rid of you like that—" He snapped his fingers contemptuously.

Part of me wanted to tell him to stick his job. Part of me wanted to tell him to stick his fingers in my knickers. What I did was just shrug, and say, "Well, there's nothing like knowing where you stand."

"As long as we understand each other," he said, and turned his back on me to go and fetch another crate of bitter lemon. *Oh, I understand you,* I thought. *You're a shit and you get off on being a shit. It's not big, it's not clever, but I love working here and I'm not going to let you spoil it for me.*

Keeping that resolve wasn't easy. It seemed everything I did, everything I said rubbed Ian up the wrong way. Even though I was there from well before my shift started till well after it ended, I always had the feeling he had one eye on his watch as I walked through the door. If he caught Gill and me chatting together, in that first, dead half hour after opening time, he would glare in our direction until one of us went to wipe the already clean tables, or fill bread rolls with cheese and ham and wrap them in clingfilm, ready for the lunchtime rush. We kept smiles plastered to our faces for the benefit of the customers, even when we were calling Ian every name under the sun beneath our breath. And we never, ever gave him the satisfaction of letting him see just how badly he was getting to us.

At the end of the week, he would hand us our pay packets without a word of thanks for our efforts, and I would bite back the urge to tell him not to expect me the following day, since I would be looking for alternative employment. God knew I could find it easily enough: as Ian himself had told me, bar jobs were ten a penny round here. The sensible option would have been to go down to the Internet café on the high street and spend half an hour updating my CV in an attempt to get another management post—something I should have done long before now, in truth—but I was determined that Cameron and Jean would not return from New Zealand to find me gone without an explanation.

What made it more difficult to hold on to my composure was the fact that I was constantly aware of Ian's eyes on me, whether I was stretching to take a shot of whiskey from one of the optics, or bending to load a rack full of dirty glasses into the dishwasher. It was the beginning of August, stiflingly hot, and I was dressing for work in skimpy little vest tops or short, flimsy rayon dresses in a vain attempt to keep cool. As I moved, as Ian watched me, I was sure that he was hoping to catch a glimpse of flesh—a bare, tanned thigh or a small, braless breast—through a gap in the loose fabric of my clothes. And sometimes I would catch his gaze, his expression a mixture of disdain and something darker, something greedier.

If Ian had come on to me, I could have coped with it. Years ago, when I had been barely out of my teens and working as an assistant in a shoe shop, I'd had a boss who had taken delight in brushing up against me in the stockroom, "accidentally" touching my breasts and making suggestive remarks. Not knowing how to react and fearful of getting the sack if I spoke to anyone about what was happening, I had stupidly put up with it, even the time he had pressed his hand to the bulge in his regulation black twill trousers and groaned, "You're making it hard for me, Stella." What I should have done was squeeze his balls till he was begging for mercy, pink slip or no pink slip; instead, I put up with his lecherous advances for the next three months, before leaping at the chance to be transferred to the Gillingham branch. I'd already let one man drive me out of my job; perhaps that was why I was so keen it wouldn't happen again. Or perhaps I was just waiting to see whether Ian would finally make the move that proved he wanted me as much as I thought he did, before the tension between us became as unbearable as the heat that assaulted me every time I stepped out of my front door.

Gill didn't seem to have picked up on the situation, but then she was too busy inventing endlessly imaginative ways of torturing Ian, the mildest of which involved stripping him naked, smearing him in honey, and staking him to an anthill. If he'd shown any interest in her, she would have been pretty much oblivious to it anyway, wrapped up as she was in her latest boyfriend, Steve, a burly prop forward for the local rugby team. She described their marathon sex sessions with the same graphic relish she used in her never-ending plans for disposing of Ian— indeed, a couple of them featured the same kitchen utensils. And then Ian would shout across the bar and ask us why we were gossiping when there were customers to be served, and I would go to refill glasses, leaving Gill to wonder aloud just how long it would take Chip and Lemmy, the beer garden rabbits, to nibble Ian to death after she'd shoved carrots in all his orifices.

Although she hated him as much as I did, Gill was openly pleased with the fact that, unlike Cameron, he never let anyone drink in the pub past closing time. Most Friday and Saturday nights, Cameron would have a lock-in with four or five of the regulars, drinking till the small hours of the morning, and he would expect Gill or me to stay behind and join them, at least for an hour or so. Ian wanted us off the premises as soon as possible so he could count the takings, and that suited Gill, who was usually itching to get home to Steve and his amazingly versatile tongue.

I just appreciated the chance to get an extra hour in bed—or at least, that was the plan, until the night I was woken by what sounded like crockery smashing downstairs. Startled, I switched on the light and squinted at the bedside clock. Just gone one in the morning. Through the floorboards, I could hear loud, angry voices. Costas and his wife, arguing. It was a regular occurrence: they would fight, and then they would fuck, the second part of the process being just as noisy as the first. Usually, I would reach for my personal stereo, using music to block out the unwanted sounds of their coupling, but that night I found my hand straying down to part the curls of my bush, a finger slipping inside my pussy to find it moist and wanting. I frigged myself in time to the banging of the bed below me, and in my mind I pictured Ian pressing me down against the mattress, thrusting so hard into me that the breath was forced from my lungs. My fantasies were never this brutal; normally, I imagined myself being stroked and caressed by gentle hands, a soft mouth moving down to tongue the folds of my sex and suck on my clit. Ian, I was sure, would fuck me without these preliminaries, just yank down my knickers and shove his cock into me, while I moaned and begged him to take me, use me like a cheap whore. I was mouthing the words silently as my fingers moved faster, slithering in the wetness that spilled from my cunt. "Use me, Ian, take me, fuck me." My movements speeded up as the creaking and groaning in the other room got louder and faster, and then Mrs. Costas gave a howl and came, and my own orgasm was triggered by her wild, unearthly cries. In my fantasy, Ian shot his load inside me, then wiped the sticky length of his cock in my hair and walked away.

Needless to say, I didn't mention to Gill that I was fantasizing about being used and abused by Ian Todd; that sort of revelation would not have gone down too well with her. And I certainly couldn't talk about it to the man himself. I mean, how did you tell a bloke you couldn't stand that you got wet at the thought of him holding you down and fucking your brains out? It would have implied I had a personal life, for a start, and Ian never discussed anything even remotely personal with anyone. I didn't even know if he was single: there was no ring on his wedding finger, but for all I knew he could have had anyone waiting for him at home, from a heavily pregnant wife to a garage mechanic called Barry.

We could have gone on like this until he finished his stint as stand-in pub manager, rubbing along together in this unhealthy mix of desire and mutual loathing, but on the last day before Cameron came back, everything went weird. The heat wave was at its height, with that thick heaviness to the air that usually means a storm is on its way. When Ian opened the door of the Red Mill to Gill and me, he was in a truly foul mood, like nothing we had seen from him before. He didn't even acknowledge us as we stepped past him into the already humid interior of the pub.

"Someone's got out of bed the wrong side this morning," I muttered to Gill.

"That guy doesn't have a bed," Gill replied. "He hangs upside down in the wardrobe."

We barely saw Ian during the lunchtime session; the pub was fairly quiet, and he disappeared into the upstairs quarters, muttering about having some paperwork to attend to. Free of his lurking presence, Gill acted like she often did when Cameron was around, flirting outrageously with the customers and putting all her favorite songs on the jukebox. I kept an attentive ear out for Ian's tread on the stairs, but by the time he finally rejoined us, Gill had persuaded the final couple of stragglers that we would be open again in a couple of hours and they could finish their drinking then. He paid us as much attention on the way out as he had coming in.

We opened up again at five; when Ian let us in this time, his hair was wet, as though he'd just come out of the shower. A vision came to me: Ian soaping his lean, naked body as water beat down on him; his hand straying to cradle his cock and start to rub it, steadily—I shook my head: the man would be out of my life in a few hours. It wasn't worth wasting any more of my thoughts on him.

He was still brooding about something, only this time he chose to do it downstairs, glowering at us as he leaned by the till.

"What's eating him?" Gill asked as she passed me, half-a-dozen dirty glasses dangling from her fingers.

Me, I wish, murmured the small, disloyal voice in the back of my head. I just shrugged. "Frankly, Gill, I'm way past caring." I'd been asked for a whiskey and green ginger, and I reached past her for the bottle of ginger wine that nestled with all the other rarely used liqueurs at the back of the bar. As my fingers closed round the neck of the bottle, still sticky from the last time it had been used, Gill took a step back from the glass washer and bumped into me. The bottle slithered from my grasp to shatter on the bare floorboards, spattering my sandaled feet and bare shins with liquid.

"Shit!" I exclaimed.

"Don't move, there's glass everywhere," Gill ordered me, hunting under the bar for the dustpan and brush we kept there for incidents such as this.

"You know that's coming out of your wages, don't you?" Ian said. They were the first words he had spoken to me all evening, and something in the tone of his voice, after a day of contemptuous silence, made me snap.

"You've been waiting for this, you bastard," I yelled at him, oblivious to Gill beginning to sweep up the glass fragments and the hapless bloke on the other side of the bar waiting to pay for his drinks. "You've been wanting me to make some mistake so you could bawl me out in front of everyone. Tell me, just what kind of kick do you get out of humiliating your staff? Do you go home at night with a hard-on, knowing you've made someone feel completely worthless?"

The words were falling out of my mouth too fast for me to stop them. Rage was blazing in Ian's eyes, and I knew I'd gone too far, but it felt so good to finally tell him what I thought of him. Gill was getting to her feet, looking at me with something that veered dangerously close to respect, as Ian's hand shot out and caught hold of my wrist.

"That's enough, Stella," was all Ian said, as he yanked me from behind the bar, past a knot of surprised drinkers, so fast my feet were almost pulled from under me. I struggled in his grasp, but he was stronger than he appeared, and that strength alarmed me. I'd intended to provoke some kind of reaction from him, but not this. He dragged me out onto the balcony, slamming the French door behind him, and then he let go of me. It was surprisingly quiet with the noise of the pub muffled; even at the height of summer, the neighbors went to bed early here, ready to rise at six for the following morning's commute. There was enough light for me to see the expression on Ian's face: anger and lust fighting to get the upper hand. Even though there were people sitting less than three feet away on the other side of the door, chatting and laughing over the beat of the music from the jukebox, I suddenly felt vulnerable and very alone.

"Come here," he said, in a low voice that was as threatening as it was sensual. I knew what was about to happen; every moment of our time together had been leading up to this. I needed it— and yet still I feared it. I backed away as far as I could, until I felt the cool wrought iron balustrades of the balcony against the backs of my legs.

"Don't make this difficult for me, Stella," he said. "You want this as much as I do."

And then his hands were on me, lifting me up till I was sitting on the balcony rail, limp as a rag doll in his grip. I knew I shouldn't have been so passive, but arousal was drugging me, making my limbs heavy and fueling my desire to give in.

His mouth met mine, tongue pushing insistently at my lips, forcing them to open and let him in. He tasted of peppermint and lime juice, and I found myself responding, my hands snaking up round his neck, fingers tangling in his messy curls.

He yanked at the neck fastening of my halter top, pulling it apart in one swift movement, baring my breasts to the night air. I broke the kiss in my urge to protest. "Please—someone might come out..."

"And if they do?" Ian's reply was almost a sneer. "Come on, Stella, you know half the blokes in there want to see your tits. Everything you wear shows off those big nipples of yours, you little slut." As he spoke, he took one of my nipples between his fingers, pinching it gently at first, then squeezing it until a moan slipped from my lips, part pleasure, part pain. I could feel my pussy opening against the white cotton of my underwear, the slow pulse between my legs more powerful than that of my heart.

I wanted Ian's fingers in my knickers so badly, but if I asked him to put them there, I knew it would prove me to be the slut he'd already called me. My legs were wrapped round his arse, and I used the backs of my calves to push him a little closer to me, so that his cock was resting against my cunt, hot and vital even through the layers of clothing which separated us.

For a moment, I almost came to my senses, and a voice that didn't sound like mine murmured, "Gill's on her own in there. Won't she start wondering where we've got to?"

"Let her wonder," Ian replied. "She's a big girl, she can look after herself. What are you hoping, Stella, that she might have some problem with a punter and come out here looking for me?"

An image flashed through my mind: Gill's freckled face peering through the French door, in the moment before she framed some question. I knew she wouldn't see too much; though I was as good as topless, my seminaked state was obscured by Ian's broad back. And yet a small, shameful part of me hoped she would realize what was happening, and come closer to take a look at my small, uptilted tits with their unmistakably erect nipples. Maybe she would even reach out and pinch one, just as Ian had done—

His next words made even that image seem strangely innocent. "Let's give her something to see if she does come out. Something that'll make her realize just how long you've been starved of cock for."

I heard the metallic rasp of his zip being undone and looked down to see him freeing his cock from his fly. It stood out pale against the black shirt and jeans he wore, long and slender but stiffening as he stroked it. Watching him made me want to reach out and take over, but he was setting the agenda here, so I settled for caressing my own bare breasts.

Ian reached up my skirt and tugged at my knickers. They snagged against my bum and I lifted it slightly, conscious of my precarious position on the balcony rail. The limp white cotton came away in Ian's hand, smelling so strongly of my juices that my cheeks flushed with shame. He let my sodden underwear fall from his grasp, fluttering down like a flag of surrender to land on the picnic table below.

"Oh, Stella, you're so easy," he crooned. "You'll let me do anything, won't you?" As he spoke, his fingers were pushing up into the furnace that was my cunt. His thumb settled on my clit and began to rub. I groaned, no longer caring if anyone heard me.

"Please, Ian, fuck me." The despairing words were so close to all the dirty fantasies I'd woven around him, though I had never pictured myself quite like this, naked except for a couple of rucked-up strips of cloth and my sandals, my legs splayed to give him access to every intimate part of me as I begged for his cock.

He pulled his fingers out of my sex, leaving it gaping and desperately empty. And then I felt a juice-slicked fingertip pressing at the entrance to my arse, and whimpered. Martin had never touched me there—it hadn't been part of our nice, safe sex life—and I wondered how it would feel if Ian decided to thrust up past the tight ring of muscle.

I didn't get the chance to find out. Tired of toying with me, of seeing how willingly I was responding to his depraved little games, he just took hold of his cock and guided it up into my pussy, hard. My cry at being filled to the hilt rang out in the still night air, and I felt sure someone would come out to see what was going on.

My hands were clasped tight round Ian's neck as he began to thrust, my bum slithering on the varnished wood beneath me, even though he was holding my bare cheeks in his hands. With all the tension, all the need that had been building up between us, I was prepared for it to be quick. I wasn't expecting Ian's next words.

"Do you trust me, Stella?" he panted.

"What?" I replied.

"It's a simple question. Do you trust me?"

"I..." The honest answer was no. I didn't trust him; I didn't even like him, and yet he was buried up to the balls in me, fucking me with a purpose and a skill my husband had shown all too rarely over the years of our marriage. "I don't know."

"Well, you're just going to have to." And with that, he reached up a hand and prized my fingers apart. Startled, I found myself falling backward into nothing, and yelped. "It's all right," Ian soothed. "I've got hold of you."

And he had. He was still gripping me tightly, my legs were still wrapped round him and I was still balanced on the balcony rail but my head was pointing down toward the flagstones on which the picnic table stood, thirty feet below. He wouldn't let me drop, I told myself. He couldn't. I felt sick, I felt scared, but most of all I felt horny. The blood was rushing to my head, intensifying every sensation I felt as Ian's hot, thick length continued to pound into me. The situation must have been getting to Ian, too, because his thrusts were faster, less coordinated, and he was grunting with effort.

As Ian's cock jerked inside me and my stomach clenched in the first spasms of orgasm, I let myself go. The rush was like nothing I had known; the blood was singing in my ears and my heels were beating a wild tattoo against the backs of his thighs. That should have been the moment at which the storm broke, fat raindrops beating down on us as we both came. But the thunderclouds continued to hang heavily above us, and as the pleasure began to ebb and reality kicked in, I was left feeling weak and dizzy. I flailed out a hand and grabbed on to the balcony, letting Ian help me to my feet.

As he zipped himself up again and I did my best to rearrange my hopelessly crumpled clothing, I looked for the spark in his eyes that would signify we'd reached some new kind of understanding. I didn't see it. To be honest, I hadn't really expected to.

"So does that pay for the breakages, then?" I asked, as he turned on his heel and stalked back into the bar.

When I turned up for work the next morning, Cameron and Jean were back. They gave no indication that they might have found a stray pair of knickers in the beer garden, so I reckoned Ian must have retrieved them sometime before he'd finally left the pub for good. I wondered if he'd kept them as some kind of warped souvenir, to wank into as he relived our fuck on the balcony. I couldn't ask him: he'd left no note for me, no message of gratitude for the hard work Gill and I had put in for him, no phone number.

I don't know where he's working now, but the brewery owns several pubs in the area, and it's safe to assume he will eventually find himself filling in for the landlord in one of them. I'm not a barmaid at the Red Mill anymore; I finally got my act together and went back into retail management, and now I have a staff of six working beneath me, a respectable, responsible woman once more. And yet on Friday nights I frequent the pubs where Ian might be working, my skirt a little shorter than is decent, and my tight top making it clear I have no bra on beneath it, in the hope that one day I will bump into him. God knows I don't need the aggravation he brings with him, but it seems there's no one else who can quell the heat he left raging in my pussy....

CHILL

Kathleen Bradean

I could have gone home, but they had my six hundred dollars.

Even though I could have told them that I changed my mind, I could imagine the lifted eyebrow, and the apologetic, "Very well, madame, perhaps we can accommodate you another time," but it was the last time I would visit the spa to indulge my fetish. There was no sense in canceling what had already begun, though. I would use it up. Then there would be no more. I wouldn't give myself any more.

Outside the room, three stories down, I heard cars drive through slush. I pushed aside the heavy drapes to look at the busy street below. Windshields on the cars were fogged as heaters ran full blast. People fled home, to bars, to fireplaces and central heat, to life, to warmth.

The discreet townhouse masquerading as a spa for wealthy women was old. Cold air seeped past the windowpanes. I pressed my hands to the flawed glass that made the brake lights look like smeared lipstick.

If I listened, I could hear the elevated trains one block away. And if I peered just right through the narrow slit between the buildings across the street, I could see the darkness of Lake Michigan, inviting me under.

In the room assigned to me, the bed frame was wrought iron. A crimson coverlet hinted at lurid delights, but it wasn't my fantasy to be fucked in velvet splendor. The Victorian trappings seemed pathetic, even cheap, although the wallpaper was probably authentic and the antique chairs were worth more than my car.

I'd searched the drawers of the Chippendale dresser earlier. Masks, handcuffs, paddles—the props of theatrical fantasies. I was disappointed that given a chance to explore the unthinkable at the spa, most women opted instead for a hack rehash. Or maybe I was jealous of how harmless it all seemed. How comfortable. After a third martini, confessing to a spanking and a ride on one of the legendary cocks of the spa was probably de rigueur for the ladies who lunched.

"Antonio? Dear, you absolutely must try him. His dick curves a little, but it hits exactly the right spot when you're bent over the bed, taking it from behind. Trust me."

"If you pay extra, George won't bathe for three days. Get your nose up against those balls and take a whiff. I swear you can smell his boyfriend's ass."

I'll teach myself to crave such tame moments. I'll learn to clutch raw silk between my fingers and marvel at the texture. I'll develop a taste for opulence.

I used silver tongs to pick five ice cubes from the bucket. They clinked into the highball glass, each one making the crystal sing a slightly different note.

It was a matter of degree, really. Kink was candy coating that made sex tastier. Fetish was bittersweet, dark chocolate, straight up, the kind that made your teeth shrink against the intensity of undiluted flavor.

Fetish was sex deconstructed. Removed from my body to my mind. The rites of worship worshipped. The fetish was for the details. Someone once said that God was in the details, but others said that it was the devil. A devil I knew intimately.

I went into the bathroom and turned on the cold tap. The edge of the claw-foot tub made an uncomfortable seat. I set the highball glass in the soap dish and dropped the thick terry robe to the white tiled floor.

While the bath filled, I pulled back my hair in a severe pony-tail high on my head, revealing every line on my face to the unflattering light at the makeup table in the boudoir.

First, I did my nails: hands, and feet. Light purple traced a thin line near my cuticles. Pale blue made a half-moon at the base of each nail. Blue-tinged varnish sealed it. For the last time, every single thing had to be just perfect. That way, if I felt myself sliding back, wanting it, I'd be able to remind myself that for once everything was right and exactly the way it should have been, and I could never hope to duplicate such perfection again.

No one I knew would recognize the brand of makeup in my bag. I used a thick, oily base, a shade paler than my natural coloring, and spread it thickly so that it left an obvious line under my chin and by my temples. Every wrinkle around my mouth and eyes showed like sidewalk crack. Blue lipstick made my mouth looked bruised. I drew another set of lips, slightly smaller, in dark pink on top of that, so that the edges of blue showed. Cherry rouge started as circles on my cheeks and then faded in a slight upstroke.

The first step into the tub was always hardest, like swimming in a mountain lake at camp. My foot ached and I wanted to pull it out, but I stepped in with the other foot, gritted my teeth, and sank into the deep, frigid water.

My skin pulled tight on my arms. Gooseflesh made every hair stand on end. I bent my knees. Gasping, I got my shoulders under the surface. My poor nipples hardened and ached. Fighting the shock, my heart pumped hot blood under my skin. My teeth chattered, uncontrollable. I reached for my highball glass.

My cunt tightened, refusing to take the ice cubes, but I pushed four in anyway. I felt my heat flee to my core. My toes and fingers throbbed and then burned.

"I hate this." My voice echoed off the bathroom tiles. *I hate this, and I'm never going to do it again. If I'm tempted, this will be the part I'll make myself remember. The part I hate.*

Cold. I was so fucking cold. My pussy longed to push out the cubes tucked into it, but every time one floated to the surface of the water, I pushed it back in, deep, until my knuckles pressed against my clit.

The shuddering came next. It exhausted me as no workout with my personal trainer ever had. I clamped down, refusing to let my muscles create more heat. The ice that worked out of me melted to such small slivers that I couldn't find them in the water. My fingertips were leaden as they clumsily tested my internal temperature. There was heat, but only deep inside. My clit was tight. It hurt to touch.

I should leave now. I should drain this freezing water away and pour scalding water over my skin until the burn hurts as much as the cold, until my skin is mottled pink. I should pick up the phone and tell them I've changed my mind, that I want a different fantasy this time, something red and violent, a fuck that will leave my pussy raw. Something normal.

I tipped back my head and let it rest on the folded towel on the back of the tub. The walls of the bathroom had a bluish cast, like icebergs. White seemed a final color, but like black, it had shades, tones, subtleties. When I stared at it long enough, flecks of green, red, and blue danced in the center of my vision.

A drop fell from the silver faucet into the bath, a hollow, metallic sound followed by a rich plop. Ripples pushed across the surface of the water. The water lapped at the underside of my chin.

Ah, well. What was done, was done. I was there. It was in motion. I picked up the highball glass and let the last cube clink from side to side, sweeping out time. Then I plucked it out and shoved it inside me as I exhaled.

I rose from the water, letting it drip, before carefully blotting it away with the thick towels. It took several conversations to convince the house staff that I didn't want heated towels waiting.

When I was dry, I dropped the towels on the floor and opened the other door. Air conditioning rushed against my skin. My nipples puckered to hard, erect rouge nubs. Perfect.

Unlike the bedroom, the other room was stark. Three of the walls were painted glossy white. Large stainless-steel drawers seemed to line the back wall from floor to ceiling, but I knew from exploration that they didn't open. Fantasy only went so far.

In the center of the room was one stainless-steel table. A single, thin white sheet sat folded at the foot. On top of it was a tag. I knew that underneath the table, there were stirrups. The one drawer on the side of the table held enema nozzles. With few alterations, any medical scene could be played out. I hated to think of anyone else using my sterile room, but I doubted the spa kept it just for me.

The floor tiles were cold against the bottom of my feet. The table was a chilled slab and my fingerprints made brief appearances on the brushed surface before disappearing like ghosts. I climbed awkwardly onto it.

I took the tag and placed the loop over my big toe before lying down with my legs spread wide so that Devon's legs wouldn't touch mine when he knelt between my thighs. The overhead mirror was unkind, so I only looked in glances at my pale skin, my carefully positioned body, my death mask. Then I unfurled the crisp sheet and pulled it over my body until it covered my face.

I could see the four bulbs of the overhead light fixture through the sheet. I closed my eyes tight and hoped he'd hurry. We didn't have much time. Every detail was perfection. It would never be this good again. Never.

At the soft click of the door, I opened my eyes again. Every breath was smooth, shallow, measured. I willed myself to relax, to give up control.

Devon was well trained. Although I stared at the ceiling, I knew that he gave my face only a glance as he folded the sheet down to the swell of my breasts. The bare warmth of the sheet escaped as he lifted the sheet from my feet and folded it above my waist, exposing the spider's veins on my calves, the cottage cheese texture of my outer thighs, the fluff of pubic hair carefully confined by waxing to a strip on my outer lips. Only then did he pull on examination gloves. He put his gloved hand on the table.

Would he jump if I moved?

Devon climbed on the table. I stared past the overhead mirror, but I saw he was dressed in white scrubs. He lowered the waistband and freed his cock. Carefully balancing so that no part of his body touched mine, he pumped generous lube into the palm of his gloved hand.

My nipples ached in the cold air and my toes throbbed. So

cold. I wanted to shiver. My skin pulled tight against my bones.

So many shades of white, like textures, all of them different.

I heard the wet slide of his fist over his cock.

Shame rose in a warm glow in my cheeks. It wouldn't show through the thick base, but it was there. Heat.

It wasn't healthy, this thing, this need. I'd go for months without it, and then I'd be on the phone with a client, or at dinner with friends, and I'd yearn for the cold. Thinking about it would make my breasts ache. I'd cross and uncross my legs, and fidget in my chair. Sometimes, I'd take an ice cube from my drink, put in into my mouth, and excuse myself to the ladies room, where I'd rub the cube against my clit until I came. Then I'd smooth down my clothes and take my seat, and no one would ever guess. But it was never a really good orgasm. It was a shadow, a knockoff, a little something to see me through.

When I first came to the spa, the entire staff was displayed for me. One by one, the nude men entered the room and showed me their bodies, their hard-ons, their secret tattoos. My purse sat in my lap and my hand rested on top of it until the last man joined the lineup, discreetly waiting for approval. In their own way, each one was perfection. Cute, handsome, pretty, pouty, tough, nasty, clean cut, muscled, slim, slight, towering, hairy, smooth—they were all ideal.

"Which ones take direction well?"

"All of our—"

With a simple movement of my hand, I cut off the flow of words. "I don't want a sexual submissive, or a man who pretends to be one. I want someone who can correctly follow very detailed instructions. Intelligence is a plus." I turned my head. "And he must consistently shoot a big load."

Devon was not the best-endowed member on staff, his looks didn't excite me, and he was not the one I would have picked for recreational fucking, but he met my requirements.

He was quiet while he jerked off. A few gasps, the slap of his hand, and the squishy sound of the lube was all I heard. I should have told him that it was okay to make noise. Or maybe all men were that silent while stroking themselves to climax.

Don't blink.

A trickle of water from the melting ice cube streamed out of my pussy and pooled under my buttcheek.

My eyeballs were dry. Halos from the light fixture to the side of the overhead mirror seemed permanently seared into my retinas.

The air conditioner kicked on again, fighting the heat given off by the friction of Devon's hand on his cock. Chill air rasped against my skin. I fought the need to shudder.

Yes, remember this. Remember how much you hate what it takes to get the details right. Next time you're tempted to pick up the phone and make an appointment, remember that it hurts to have ice cubes in your cunt. Think of the pain in your feet and hands. Think about never being warm again.

In the overhead mirror, if I allowed myself to focus, I could see his black curls bobbing and the dip of his shoulder with every stroke. I'd see the purplish head of his dick strangled by his gloved hand, the slide of the foreskin until he was so hard that it wouldn't pass his glans. He'd bowed his head to the task and I was tempted to sneak a glance at his face, to see the concentration, to love him for the utter selfishness, but I refused to look. Everything had to be just right this last time.

He groaned. The table shook as he worked his cock. He knew not to waste time. With his free hand, Devon spread my labial lips. Warmth bled through the gloves to my skin.

Devon whispered something, maybe a prayer, and grunted. He hissed through clenched teeth.

Hot, thick cum splattered against my clit. I bit my tongue to hold back my moan. He came buckets, my Devon did, covering my cunt like boiling water splashed on snow. Another shot, so warm, so full of life, pulsed onto my chilled skin. It slid from the hard nub of my clit down toward my pussy. My clit tingled under it, loving the perfection of the moment, soaking in the heated gift from his body. A third, weaker shot, but oh, so hot from his body, dripped onto the hood of my clit.

Fuck. I loved the way it felt on my skin. That was what I lived for, the perfect contrast of my frigid clit and his hot cum. Blood raced through me. I could hear it pounding in my ears, and my heart, shocked into service, beat against my ribs. I was already throbbing inside.

Devon immediately climbed off the table. He pulled the bottom sheet down to my ankles. Hurrying, he stood by my head. Something he'd never done before, he bent down and placed a reverent kiss on my lips. I could smell his sweat on his neck. Then he gently pushed my eyelids closed, and I felt the sheet cover my face.

Immersed in darkness, electric halos slid across my vision. I didn't move. Everything was so perfect that I didn't dare breathe.

The door discreetly clicked shut.

I flung back the sheet and spread my slit to see the cum oozing there. My hand immediately moved to smear it across my clit in large circles. I furiously rubbed my sex back to life. The slick load clung in thick globs to my pubes.

So warm. Warmth is life.

Everything was perfect. Perfect, that time. Better than fantasies.

A spasm shot down my legs. I drew my knees up and spread my legs wide. Pinching and pulling, I overloaded my clit with sensation—hot cum, cold fingers. My hands made tighter circles.

Yes. Yes.

In the overhead mirror, I watched the cum trickle down to my hole, felt the slow, pendulous drop spread. Blood engorged my clit. The muscle hardened under my fingertips.

Fuck.

My lips pulsed.

My hand was almost a blur. Hard peaks hit short plateaus but built. My shoulders lifted off the table. Inside, my pussy clenched tight.

Perfect.

A furious orgasm more intense than any other shot though me.

God or the devil, it was fucking perfect.

I collapsed back onto the table. The headache started almost immediately. I rolled on my side, gathered the sheet around me, and eased off the table.

My legs ached with every step. A cramp threatened my toes. Feeling years older, I opened the door to the bathroom.

By the time I hobbled down to the foyer, static vision made my left eye useless. Two fingers of whiskey, neat, and Vicodin only took the edge off. I wrapped my scarf tight around my throat.

Devon hailed a taxi for me, stepping out bravely into the onrush of night traffic while I waited under the awning. He opened the door and smiled at me as if I were simply a lady, and he, a gentleman. When I stepped off the curb, his hand was immediately at my elbow, but I stepped into a pothole of slush that splashed inside my black pumps anyway. Before he closed the door, I slipped the neatly folded bills into his hand.

"Thank you, ma'am."

It was a hundred more than my usual tip, but he deserved it.

Christ, I was sore. Once the chill got into my muscles, it seemed to take days to coax warmth back into them.

I told the cabbie my address on Lakeshore Drive.

The headlights of oncoming traffic were like daggers in my brain, so I closed my eyes and tipped back my head. I exhaled.

Perfect.

No need to ever do it again.

I could go home and crawl in bed and shut out all the lights, sounds, feelings, and immerse myself in darkness. The pain would go away. My thick blankets would be so warm, and my sheets would be like silk on my skin. I could sleep soundly, knowing that I had touched perfection.

The cold trickle of slush inside my shoe slid under my toes.

Except that he kissed me.

I rubbed my forehead, as if that could bring relief. The static in my vision slid to my right eye. I didn't want to vomit in the cab, but I felt the nausea rise. All I wanted was perfect black, without shade, without texture, without noise. I wanted the world on the other side of that darkness, far away, and warmth coating me like cum hot from a man's body.

Except that I felt the warmth of Devon's hands through his gloves. It would have been so much better if the only warmth I ever felt was his cum. That would be truly perfect.

I opened my eyes. Every streetlamp sent a prick of pain through my skull. My legs ached.

Heavier gloves. Maybe if he didn't touch me at all. Or maybe I could get him to chill his hand too. Of course I could. I paid for it, didn't I?

I pulled my coat around my neck and stared out at the black expanse of the lake as the cab traveled north. We drove and drove, but never seemed to get any closer to it.

PENALTY FARE

Jacqueline Applebee

It was supposed to be my punishment. I'm sure the train guard thought it was only right and just that I should introduce my lips to his hard-on, as penalty for traveling on the railway without a valid ticket. He had given me a simple choice; I was either to pay a week's wages as a fine, or I was to give him a blowjob the next time we met.

I guessed he didn't know how little I earn.

That's why I found myself on the 8:30 service from London Paddington to Bristol Temple Meads the next Friday morning. I waited quietly in my seat by the aisle as the train pulled out of the station in a series of long slow jerks. At first I wanted to find him, to try to keep control of the situation, but I couldn't move; I was far too nervous. As the onboard speakers crackled to life, I wondered if it was his smooth voice that I heard, welcoming everyone to the train, telling us all to observe the safety notices and that no smoking was allowed.

Ten agonizingly long minutes passed before I saw him at

the other end of the narrow swaying carriage, checking tickets, collecting money and pointing the way to the buffet car in an efficient manner. Dressed as he was in his dark uniform, the crisp pressed trousers, jacket and tie made him look severe, almost intimidating. He seemed taller, more solid than before and for a split second, I was hesitant that I could really do this. Then I started thinking that he wouldn't even remember our sordid agreement; he probably wouldn't remember me. And as if he had heard my thoughts, he looked ahead and he saw me; the only black woman on the train by my estimate. I stood out from the pinstriped suits around me and amongst all the stiff uniforms of gray and white, I was like a big black target, dressed in my colorful West African outfit, chunky silver jewelry and a headwrap topping it all off. If I couldn't move before, I was frozen to the spot now.

Once our eyes met, he zeroed in on me, marching quickly through the carriage and ignoring the other passengers who held out their tickets for him to check. He slung his portable ticket machine over his shoulder as he reached my seat and he yanked me out of my chair, without even breaking his stride.

His big firm hand clamped down as a solid weight upon my shoulder and I half stumbled ahead of him. Other passengers looked at me with sympathy; they were probably thinking that I was going to be thrown bodily off the train for breaking the rules and I kept my eyes averted, not wanting to look at anyone we passed. I was directed in hurried silence to the front of the train, to the first-class carriage where no one sat.

As we reached the private toilets there, I saw a sign on the door that almost made me smile. OUT OF ORDER was taped up in big red letters. I suppose that what we were about to do could be considered out of order, but I was just too horny to dwell on it.

You see, this was my choice, my dream; to be so naughty

that I simply had to be punished. It had taken three trips to get into trouble and believe me when I say I had tried. But no one checked the tickets on the first journey to Oxford, the train guard on the second trip to Bath Spa took pity on me and said he'd overlook it. It was only on the third journey that I got lucky at last; this guard actually took me aside, leaned over me and told me that there was more than one way to pay for my crime. He had stared at my chest the whole time, with twinkling blue eyes lapping up the sight of me as if I were completely edible, and then he said he'd always wanted to try out a black girl.

I almost came on the spot.

Don't get me wrong; I think of myself as being reasonably smart. I know I'm not supposed to like things like this, but I do. I like them an awful lot. And just the thought of what was about to happen made me feel so damn hot! Because even though I can look as exotic as you like, I've never ever felt it.

Really, not ever.

I was born and brought up in East London, talk with a Cockney accent when I get excited and the closest I've got to the tropics is buying a tin of pineapple chunks in my local super-market. So when my need to be bad gets tangled up with my need to feel like a sultry dusky maiden…well, it's not too hard to work out why I jumped at his yummy proposal. He might have some island beauty stereotype floating around his head and tugging at his groin, but I have my stereotypes too and they make me hunger for firm pink skin, blue veins snaking around hard muscles and hair that is soft and straight. Big strong men who look like Viking warriors make me gaga with desire. Getting them to notice me is something that I've worked long and hard at.

Back on the train, I inhaled deeply as the guard reached around me. I could feel his hot breath against the back of my neck, making me shiver with anticipation. His scent caught my nose; his cologne was crisp, masculine and it underlined his attributes.

He used a little funny-shaped key to open the door to the restroom and then ushered me inside with a firm push. I glanced around nervously; the room was not large and neither of us was small. I looked back at him with a hint of uncertainty; he was a big handsome man and my layers of bright African cloth hid my voluptuous curves. I didn't know if we were going to fit, but he smiled at me—a lazy crooked grin that let me know that he'd done this before—and then he promptly squeezed in behind me.

As the door shut, I caught a glimpse of the bright green countryside as it blurred past the window outside; I saw the freedom of open spaces that I didn't want. I'd much rather be locked up, thank you very much.

We finally made it in, although we had to dance in a tight awkward shuffle to get the door fully closed. For a moment, we both stood there in the confined space, looking at each other. Then his hands moved to his thick belt and he quickly undid the silver buckle. I took it as a cue to sink to my knees and lifted the hem of my bright yellow dress as I stooped down. The stale damp smell of the toilet was worse down at this level but I tried not to notice. I heard the slow metallic slide of his zipper and I forgot everything else as the sound hypnotized me. His dark uniform trousers dropped to the floor, pooling around thick strong-looking calves, with a mass of fine blond hairs decorating his ivory skin. He was more than ready for me and as I caught my first sight of his cock, it seemed as if there was even less space in the room than before. His large thick crimson dick radiated heat that I could already feel against my lips. It bobbed with the trundle of the train, standing in front of my face like it was a third person in the room.

I pressed my warm face to his burning cock, rubbed my cheeks and lips over the smooth surface until I felt a hand on my head, stilling me. I heard his low voice; it was the first thing he'd said to me.

"Train's due at Reading station in five minutes."

I got the hint—make it quick, no fancy stuff. I could do that.

I looked back up at his cock and opened wide. I conjured up the taste of salt and placed my lips against a bead of his juice leaking from the tip. He shivered against me and I smiled as I descended on him farther. I sucked steadily and slowly on his length and he gasped, almost stepping away from the intensity.

The weight of his hefty cock made my tongue bend beneath it. He felt immense inside me but I wanted it all. I licked the head with short urgent laps and the train began to shudder with me, keeping pace with my tongue. I closed my eyes, breathed out and swallowed him deeper in slow wet gulps just as we entered a tunnel. The only reason I knew this, was because my ears popped and when I swallowed again from instinct to relieve the pressure, he made a strangled noise. I felt his strong wide hands fisting the fabric of my headscarf and he pulled me forward even more.

My gag reflex is something that I have learned to live with; I've practiced on bananas and jumbo hotdogs, pushing them against the back of my throat, half swallowing them and then pulling out before I choked. So when I relaxed my jaw muscles and drew every last inch of him into me, I was as prepared as I could be. I sensed his surprise at this and he surged inside, growing impossibly harder against the roof of my mouth, stretching me to the limit.

I cupped his heavy hot balls and he went up on tiptoes, straining in the swaying room. Both of his hands were now buried in the cloth that covered my head and they were no longer guiding me, but rather he was using me to steady himself. I was half glad that he lost control so quickly, half proud of my abilities.

My slow in-and-out motions made him grunt like a bull, my nibbles made him pant like a horse and quick twists of my swollen lips made him gurgle low in his throat. He was making so many appreciative noises and seemed to be enjoying the experience so much that it was only when we felt the pull of the brakes that he suddenly stiffened against me, swore out loud and practically popped himself out of my hungry mouth.

I was amazed at the speed with which he moved; he was tucked in and dressed almost before I could pull off the blueberry condom that I had sneaked on with my first kiss to his cock.

He disappeared out the door and within moments I could hear his breathless voice announcing the next station, warning passengers to please mind the gap between the train and the platform and reminding them that we were due in Bristol at ten o'clock.

Even though the train was stationary, I still felt the strange swoon wash over me; the feeling that I was still moving, still roaring through the countryside on this pleasure train. I felt my knees start to ache, but I wasn't about to move from my position. I wrapped the purple condom in a tissue and fished just under the edge of my headwrap for a strawberry flavored one instead. That just left the mint and vanilla ones scratching at my scalp, reminding me of the possibilities.

The jerk of the train as it got going once more sent a sudden welcoming jolt to my clit. The strong series of motions as the locomotive gathered speed threatened to pull my orgasm from me, from my overexcited body and right down to the thundering wheels below.

Within seconds he came back into the room, looking at me

with surprise, as if he'd thought I wasn't going to be here when he returned, but I wasn't done with him yet.

"Drop 'em," I said cheekily and he laughed and lowered his trousers once more.

This time I was fully relaxed and eager to have him in my mouth again. My previous actions had made me even more of a slut than before and I was very pleased at my progress. I was determined to suck this man dry, to have my fun.

He seemed more desperately horny than earlier and after a few enthusiastic kisses, his cock grew back to its rock-hard status, gliding into my mouth smoothly and deeply.

The guard became more vocal as he reached his peak, grunting out garbled words and curses as he thrust into me, using my mouth for his sweet sordid pleasure. I was torn between reaching up to pull him down by his dangling tie and staying where I was, to get off on the rumbling between my legs. I thought briefly about how my brain got addled when I was horny but it was worth it, as being bad felt so much better than I could have ever imagined. Every part of me tingled and vibrated with the train and I gripped the base of his cock and felt him almost topple over.

My decision was made and I lowered myself down farther until my pussy was directly atop the shaking floor. I came quickly with a muffled shout around the cock in my mouth, the orgasm rattling my body with a pounding, roaring sensation that thundered through my bones, like the speeding train I rode in.

The guard's ticket machine was still strapped to his back and it made a noise as loud as both of our cries as he jerked against the door, his jagged movements accidentally pressing the buttons on the device while he rocked into me. I sucked hard, drawing out his come in full strong motions and he groaned long and loud, flicking his hips in sharp shudders. I felt the condom swell within my mouth, tasted strawberry milkshake; he withdrew after a sweet blissful moment.

I banged the back of my head against the washbasin as I clambered up stiffly; my knees were killing me and I was damp in places even I was surprised at. He sighed out loud and looked completely spent, but was quick enough to see me put the second condom in some tissue. He reached down and gripped the head of his cock, swiped a drop of come that had leaked out and held it up to me as if to dare me to lick it from his thick fingers, but I had other plans. I wanted a mark from this event, apart from the bruise to the back of my head. I wanted a reminder that it hadn't all been my sex-crazed imagination, so I offered my hands to him and he knew what to do; he smeared a white dribble of his come across my wrists, dabbed a drop behind each ear and stroked the last of it into the cleavage of my breasts. We both smiled in a conspiratorial way as he adorned me; we both knew that I would wear him like perfume all day, would carry a part of him back home to the East End of London.

"That was cracking," he exclaimed in a lazy satisfied voice. "God, I could get into so much trouble for this, could get myself fired..." He paused and then winked at me, smiling broadly. "But you're worth it sweetheart!"

He turned to the door and was about to leave when suddenly a long beep rang out. A concertina strand of tickets ejected themselves from his machine; four singles going all the way to the end of the line.

Maybe we'll do that next time.

THE BITCH IN HIS HEAD

Janne Lewis

I arrived an hour ago at the London flat that Dimitri's company keeps for business guests. I have unpacked my suitcase and changed into the light blue silk and lace teddy Dimitri bought for me in Paris. I am wandering around the bedroom holding a bouquet of butt plugs in assorted sizes and a tube of lubricant trying to decide where I can hide them.

The phone rings.

Corbin, Dimitri's assistant, wants to know if the flat has been arranged to suit his boss's needs.

"I think everything is okay." I scan the room. Dimitri has a long list of domestic requirements. "The flat looks immaculate, the bed linens look fine." I lift the neatly tucked corners of the expensive Frette linens. "The plastic cover on the mattress is in place."

Dimitri cannot sleep on a mattress on which others have slept unless it is swathed in a protective layer of plastic.

"The duvet looks new and appropriately silky." I open the

closet. "Silk dressing gown, silk pajama bottoms. I think you've covered all the fabric bases."

There are many fabrics and textures Dimitri cannot abide; chief among these are wool, polyester, and latex. His position with a multinational pharmaceutical company requires him to wear latex gloves. He manages to do this for brief periods but the thought of putting on a latex condom makes him nauseated.

"I brought new glasses and his favorite whiskey," Corbin tells me. "There's some champagne in the fridge for you, ducks, if you survive your night with Mr. Hyde."

"Is he that bad?"

Corbin lowers his voice.

"He's vile. He made two senior sales managers cry this morning and then tried to sink his fangs into me. I told him that if he wasn't nice to me, your flat would not be priss perfect which would probably make him impotent, or he'd have to fuck you in his own flat, in which case it would no longer be his sterile haven." Corbin snorts. "He turned purple and left me alone. His need for your pussy is my employment protection plan."

"Charming."

"Sorry, ducks, but it's true. Work your magic, and send him back to us nice and lamblike."

I laugh.

"I'll do my best, Corbin."

Poor Dimitri. The Bitch in His Head has been riding him hard.

The Bitch in His Head is my secret name for Dimitri's mix of neurotic tendencies and obsessive-compulsive disorder. The Bitch isn't a nasty dominatrix in leather boots and corset; She is too suave for that get up, too elegant. She is beautiful and cruel like the queen in Sleeping Beauty or the evil White Witch in the Narnia stories. She is my enemy, but I know without Her in control, the brilliant, sophisticated, charming Dimitri would never have settled for someone as ordinary as me. Still, there are many times when I wish the Bitch would take a long vacation from our ménage à trois and leave Dimitri and me alone.

I put the handset down. It rings again.

"Yes, ducks?" I say, thinking it is Corbin calling back.

"Don't use that inane phrase, Alexa." Dimitri's deep voice betrays his irritation. "You sound like a fool."

My pulse instantly quickens when I hear his voice.

"Hello, Dimitri. Lovely to hear from you. Did you get my latest test results?"

Blood samples and oral and vaginal swabs are now part of my weekly routine. The Bitch in His Head would not let Dimitri near me without them.

"Yes."

"Are we off to the races?"

"I need you, Alexa," he says. His voice cracks. He is obviously not in the mood for jokes. "It's been three shit-filled weeks. I need you so badly."

"I know. Corbin told me you've been rather unpleasant."

"Corbin is an idiot. This office is full of idiots. I hate every stinking inch of this city and everyone in it. The only place I want to be is in bed with you and deep in your cunt."

Heat floods my body. My nipples harden. I want him as much as he wants me.

"That's why I'm here, love."

I hear him sigh.

"I'll be there in ten minutes. I'm rock hard. Be ready for me."

The Bitch in His Head does not let Dimitri masturbate himself to orgasm. She keeps him agonizingly frustrated. Usually Dimitri is a sensitive, gentle, generous lover. When we've been apart for a while and She's been torturing him, he will grab me and throw me on my back and bend me into a ball so my knees are by my ears, and he'll fuck me so hard I'll have to use deep breaths like a woman in labor to withstand his onslaught. He'll pound me over and over until I'm praying for him to come. Finally, when tears have started to leak from my eyes, he will roar and tremble and shoot his wad into me. After, he will wrap his arms around me and tell me how grateful he is to me, how much he depends on my understanding, how much he loves me.

I can't help thinking that this kind of fucking is mostly about the Bitch in His Head and has little to do with me. Maybe the Bitch is whispering in his ear, urging him on. Maybe Dimitri is trying to fuck the Bitch into silence. I have thought long and hard about how to avoid that situation this weekend. That is where my bouquet of butt plugs comes in.

I push the butt plugs and the lubricant under the pillow on the right side of the bed. It is not the most ingenious hiding place, but I'll risk it. I put the handcuffs and the coils of silk rope under the duvet.

I lie on the bed with my head on the pillow disguising the lumps I've left. The sheets feel cool and smooth on my bare skin. I raise my wrist and smell the delicate scent of violets, a scent Dimitri has specially made for me. I am not sure if it is the fragrance or the change Dimitri and the Bitch have made in my wardrobe but in the year and a half I've been fucking Dimitri, I've had more propositions from men and women than in my previous thirty-four years combined.

I run my hands over the silk teddy and feel the heavy weight of my breasts in my hands and squeeze them. Dimitri told me it was the combination of my large breasts and serious expression that attracted him to me the night we met at a party. When he found out that I was a tax lawyer—careful, methodical, trained to give meticulous attention to detail—he decided to risk asking me out, hoping that one day, he'd be able to explain himself to me.

I run my fingers down the silk on my belly to where the teddy's lace hem rises over the bush of my pubic hair. The insides of my thighs and the skin on my legs are freshly waxed and silky smooth. I splay my legs open and stroke the soft insides of my thighs, just grazing the tender folds of my labia. When I fly home to New Jersey, I'll have purple marks on my thighs from Dimitri's hands.

I hear the flat door open and slam shut.

The sound makes my heart race, but I don't move from the bed. I close my eyes and gently stroke the edges of my labia. The inside of my cunt passage spasms. I press one finger down the center of my cunt and feel my heat and moisture. I think about Dimitri's muscular tongue, his thick cock, the tight anus he has not yet allowed me to explore. I let the tip of my finger enter my cunt. I am slick inside. I groan with longing.

"You'd better be thinking of fucking me while you're doing that."

I open my eyes, turn my head, and see Dimitri standing in the bedroom doorway.

He is such a beautiful man.

He has taken off his jacket and is unknotting the silk tie around his neck. His green eyes flick over the room. The arches of his black eyebrows are perfect counterpoints to the high curves of his cheekbones. His black hair is thinning, but his mustache is a thick black bristle, like a neon sign proclaiming his virility.

I am still stroking myself with one hand. I take my other hand to my breast and pull the top of the teddy down so one of my nipples is exposed. I rub my nipple, and stretch it slightly, waiting for the Bitch in His Head to be satisfied with the room and let Dimitri look at me.

Dimitri unbuttons his shirt, his eyes still moving around the room. I wonder what the Bitch is looking for.

"Actually," I say, my voice a low purr, "I was thinking about this guy on the plane."

Dimitri drapes his shirt on a chair. He walks to the foot of the bed, and reaches for his belt. I love his broad chest with its pale skin and pink nipples and curly black hair.

"What guy?" His lips hardly move under his mustache, but his green eyes are now fixed on me.

"The guy sitting next to me. He looked at me like he was a cat and I was the proverbial bowl of cream."

I hear the *ssh* of the leather as Dimitri slides the belt out of his pants.

"He said he would love to show me around London. Told me he would make it well worth my while to change my plans." I laugh. The guy was not bad looking and before I had Dimitri, I would have been thrilled with his attention.

Dimitri holds his belt in one hand and scowls at me. I can well imagine him reducing his employees to tears.

"Did he touch you?"

I don't know if it is jealousy or the Bitch in His Head asking.

"Does fucking count?"

I get up and kneel on the bed facing him. I pull the teddy over my head and drop it on the bed. I caress my breasts. It feels so lovely to be touched.

"He did me in the aisle, Dimitri. Then he held me down so all the other passengers got a turn, too. You should have seen the dick on the captain."

"You're a fucking cunt, Alexa."

His hand clutches the belt so hard his knuckles have turned white.

I laugh again.

"You know my cunt belongs to you, and no one else, Dimitri. You know what a good girl I am."

I am a good girl. I am absolutely faithful to him and meticulous in my hygiene and I comply with all the Bitch's dictates, but loving him is hard work and sometimes I can't help teasing him.

His jaw is working like he is trying to hold the lid down on the steam that is boiling inside him.

"Tell me you know it, Dimitri. Tell me you know my cunt belongs to you."

His green eyes bore into mine.

"Your cunt belongs to me."

He drops the belt and reaches for the zipper on his pants.

There is always that moment before we fuck when Dimitri has to summon strength to trust me. After all, those medical tests were performed days ago. The Bitch might be whispering *what if*s in his ear right now.

He drops his pants and his cock stands out from his body as stiff as a steel girder. I don't know how he gets his socks off with it in the way, but he does.

He grabs my wrists in his big hands. He pulls my right hand to his nose.

"I smell your cunt on your fingers."

I spread my fingers wide for him, and he takes my pointer finger in his mouth.

The feel of his warm, wet mouth on my skin and the sight of my finger going in and out between his lips sends a lightening bolt to my cunt and makes me gasp.

He pulls me to him; his hand goes to the base of my skull, and he crushes his mouth against mine. We both groan. I press my breasts against his chest. His hands run down my back and dig into my ass, lifting me against him, the hard muscle of his cock sandwiched between our bodies.

"Oh, god, Dimitri, I've missed you!"

All my resolution leaves me, my veins are filled with mind-numbing desire for him. We kiss urgently, digging our fingers into each other's flesh.

He pushes me down onto the bed and presses my legs apart. He looks at my cunt, then dives into me with his tongue. I grab the sheets on the bed and hold on as he sucks me, bites me, fucks me with his tongue. He squeezes my thighs and pulls my skin still wider so that my labia are stretched. The pressure of his tongue is so delicious I whimper with pleasure. Thank god the Bitch likes the taste of my cunt.

Dimitri rises, his face wet with my fluid. He grabs my legs and rolls me back so that my knees are by my ears, my cunt completely open to him, ready to be penetrated. I know what is coming, but I don't care. All my planning means nothing now. He can pulverize me if he wants. I ache to feel his cock inside me.

But he doesn't enter me. His green eyes are not looking at me. They're focused now on some point past my head. I twist and try to see what he is staring at. He is squeezing my legs so hard it hurts.

"What is it?" I whisper.

"The sheet." His voice quivers. It doesn't sound anything like his normal voice. "The sheet is untucked."

The fucking Bitch in His Head is talking now.

He lets go of me and pulls away. He stands up. His cock is still rock hard. He is trembling.

"The sheet..." he repeats. He looks dazed.

I sit up. I want to cry.

"I did that, love. Corbin asked me to make sure the bed was done up the way you like it. I'll fix it."

I roll to the side of the bed. I am shaking with anger at the fucking Bitch.

"I'll tuck it in. Don't worry. Everything will be fine."

I stand up and tuck the sheet in.

Dimitri's cock still makes a hard right angle, but there is a look on his face that unnerves me. He is only three years older than I am, but he looks like a weary old man.

I will do what I planned to do and I will fuck him and make him come, and the Bitch can go screw Herself.

"Shut your eyes and hold out your hands, Dimitri."

He scowls.

"No stupid games, Alexa." His voice is hoarse. "Get back on the bed and let me fuck you."

"If you don't shut your eyes and play nice, Dimitri, I'm leaving."

I have not threatened to leave him before. I'm not sure why I said it except the Bitch made me so angry. Dimitri stares at me. My threat has clearly startled him. He is much bigger and stronger than me and could easily force me to do what he wants, but he does not move.

"Please, Dimitri. I promise you that after we play my way, you can do what you want to me.

His mustache trembles. He shuts his eyes and holds out his hands.

I reach under the duvet, pull out the handcuffs, and snap them in place.

Dimitri stares at them like he can't believe what he is seeing. His cock, I am happy to see, is unfazed.

I fall to my knees and grab his hips in my hands and take the head of his fat cock in my mouth. I love sucking him. I lift one hand to play with the tender area under his balls, the other I move to his ass to push him deeper into my mouth.

Dimitri moans. The sound of his moaning, the way his eyes narrow with pleasure, is enough to raise the heat in my body and bring the juices back to my cunt. I pull my mouth away and stand up. His cock glistens with my spit.

I take hold of the chain that links the handcuffs and pull him to the bed.

He lies down in the center. He is breathing hard. His cock sticks up like a flagpole.

I take out the ropes.

"All silk," I assure him.

He arches one beautiful black eyebrow.

"After this, we play my way." His voice is normal now, but tense.

"Yes, I promise. Anything you want."

He watches with apparent detachment as I pull his arms over his head and tie the handcuffs to the brass rail of the headboard. I run my hands over his broad chest and belly. I kiss him deeply, our tongues slipping over and around each other like mating otters. His cock twitches. He stretches out his legs, no doubt anticipating my tying each ankle to the footboard, but that is not what I have in mind. I bend his left leg and bind his ankle to his upper thigh. I do the same for the right. Then I run ropes from the top of each thigh to the headboard.

I stand back at the foot of the bed and admire my handiwork.

"Do you like what you see?"

"Oh, yes, Dimitri. You're beautiful."

His cock rises up from his thick black swatch of pubic hair. The pink-colored cleft between his buttocks and the deep rose of his anus are exposed.

"Hurry up and do what you want so I can fuck you!" His voice is petulant.

I see the gap in my plan. The Bitch is lurking and could start issuing orders at any moment. Just as suddenly, I see the solution. I pick up Dimitri's silk tie from the chair and grab the panties that match my teddy. I will make sure I can't hear Her.

"Don't!" Dimitri says. He sounds panicky.

I ignore him and shove the panties in his mouth. He tries to spit them out but I hold his nose so he is forced to open his mouth. He snaps at me and tries to bite my fingers. I laugh and wrap the tie around his mouth.

His eyes bulge out slightly but he stops fighting me and lies back, trussed, silent, and compliant. He is all mine.

I stretch out on top of him, enjoying the sweet sensation as I rub my nipples against his chest. I turn his head and lick his ear and nibble down his neck and along his arms past the black hair in his armpits. I love the scent of his sweat.

I run my tongue down his belly, circle his navel, and push my tongue into it. His belly arches. He does not like this sensation, but I don't care.

I inch down his body until my mouth is at his cock.

I flick my tongue along the head of his cock and around the shaft and down around his balls. I would love to go farther and lick the tender skin around his anus but I'm afraid the Bitch in His Head would not let him kiss me later. I have to content myself with sucking his cock as hard and deep as I can.

I can hear groans and noises through Dimitri's gag. I stretch and reach under the pillow and take out my butt plug bouquet and the tube of lubricant.

"Surgical steel and brand new," I tell him. "Satin smooth and completely safe. Each has a nice wide handle at the end so it can't get lost inside you."

Dimitri utters some protests under his gag, but again I ignore him.

I take the smallest butt plug, not much wider than my pointer finger, and lubricate it. I squirt more lube on his tender pink puckered skin.

I have such a thrill watching the silver metal penetrate his ass. It slides in so easily. While I play with the plug with my right hand, I wrap the fingers of my left hand around the shaft of his cock and pump him like I am jerking him off. His cock is so engorged it is almost purple.

I pull the small plug out and drop it on my discarded teddy.

The next plug is a little thicker. Maybe the size of my two pinkie fingers combined. I can hear Dimitri's muffled groan when I push it in. I have a little bit of the sadist in me; his groan excites me so much I have to lean down and nip the tender skin of his inner thigh.

I suck his cock deeper down my throat as my right hand thrusts the plug in and out. Dimitri's legs tremble with each of my thrusts. I push the plug in and leave it there.

I pick up the largest plug. It is narrower than Dimitri's fat cock, but wider than three of my fingers combined. It is a hefty piece of metal.

I kneel between Dimitri's legs so he can watch me. I rub the head of the plug against my cunt like a dildo.

"It feels so good," I tell him. "Playing with you has made me so wet. I can slide it into me easily, Dimitri, but I don't want to be selfish. I got this for you. Besides, I'd much rather have your cock in me."

I drop the plug onto his belly. I move over him and straddle his waist. I hold the base of his cock with my left hand and rub it in circles against me.

"I want you so much, Dimitri. My cunt aches for you."

I am panting. I press the head of his cock hard against me. I would like to hold off longer, but I can't. My cunt is begging for him.

"I can't stand it. I have to put you inside me."

Dimitri's eyes are narrowed slits. He grunts through his gag.

I hold his cock still and push it into my body. I cry out when it fills me.

"Oh, that's good!"

I rock against him, enjoying the friction of his cock against the walls of my cunt. Waves of pleasure fill me. I look down and see the butt plug bouncing on his belly. I can imagine what it will look like stretching his skin, forcing open his narrow opening, and driving deep into his dark hole. I pick up the tube of lubricant and squirt the plug while it is still on his belly, drenching it and him.

I reach behind me and pull out the middle-sized plug from Dimitri's ass and drop it onto my teddy. I lift up the big plug. My hand is trembling. I look at my lover stretched out before me, his eyes shut, his head tilted back, his mouth slightly open beneath his gag, his chest rising and falling with his rapid breathing, his arms straining against his bonds. I can see the thick base of his cock where he enters me.

I realize that for the first time today, it is just the two of us in bed; the Bitch is nowhere in sight.

"I promise you, love, I will make you feel so fucking good. I promise you."

I reach back and position the big plug between his buttocks. I push gently against his anus.

I shove the plug into him in one hard push.

Dimtri throws his head back. I hear his muffled cry and see his jaw move under the gag.

The power I feel is like a narcotic flooding my veins. I pull the butt plug back and shove it in again. Dimitri's body strains and bucks under me, his head tosses from side to side, and he utters deep muffled cries. Nothing matters to me but fucking him like a wild thing. I dig my fingers into his waist and lean forward, pistoning my hips, and grinding my swollen clit against his pubic bone. Every thrust brings me exquisite pleasure. There is an explosive spasm that begins in my clit and spreads heat up the length of my cunt and makes my cunt muscles clutch Dimitri's cock and forces high-pitched cries of pleasure from my mouth. I am shaking like a rag doll and my cunt spasms again and I am still rocking my hips back and forth trying to sate my body's need.

"Uhh!"

Dimitri's face is contorted like a power lifter struggling to raise a tremendous weight above his head. Every muscle in his body is tense with his effort.

"Come!" I urge him. "Come!"

I churn my hips as hard as I can.

He grimaces and bellows and his head is thrown back and his mouth opens as wide as it can under the gag and his body trembles. I can feel his cock explode inside me. I rock against him until his trembling subsides and his animal cries stop.

I fall on him, resting my head against his chest for a minute. I'd like to stay there, but I know I can't. I have to clean up first.

I slip off of him and reach with shaking hands between his legs for the plug. His contractions have pulled it deep inside his body, and the wide handle is tight against his ass. I pull it out as gently as I can. Dimitri groans.

I wrap all the plugs in my teddy and carry them into the bathroom and put the bundle in a plastic garbage bag. My legs are unsteady, but I wash my hands several times with the antibacterial soap Corbin has supplied. I pick up two fluffy towels from the towel warmer and carry them to Dimitri. He is lying perfectly still with his eyes closed, his chest rising and falling with his shallow breaths. I untie his legs as quickly as I can and wrap his body in the warm towels. I untie the tie from around his mouth and pull out the wet wad of my panties. He doesn't say anything.

I unlock the handcuffs and tuck his arms under the towels. I slip into bed next to him and pull the duvet over us both. I rest my cheek against his forehead.

He pulls me close. He sighs deeply.

"That was good."

"Mmm," I agree.

"Next time, we do what I want."

"Yes."

"I'd love to fuck you in the ass, Alexa. I'd make you scream."

It will not happen. The Bitch in His Head will not let him.

I stroke his head until I hear the deep even breathing that means he is asleep.

Poor Dimitri. Lucky me.

BECKY

Kay Jaybee

Regardless of my warnings, she had applied for the administrative assistant vacancy at the office where I work. Perhaps I was wrong to be wary. Becky had always listened eagerly to the tales I told, before dismissively saying, "Don't be ridiculous, that sort of thing doesn't really happen," quickly followed by, "So what happened next?" Maybe I shouldn't have told her anything. It's too late now.

Becky's face looked as if it would remain in a state of shock forever. Her gray skirt was hunched around her slim waist and her thong lay in tatters after its surgical removal with the boss's scissors. She stood stock still as the correction stool was placed reverently in its familiar position in the very center of the office.

She kept repeating over and over again, "It was an accident, an accident. I never meant to spill the coffee. An accident." I felt for her; she blinked in disbelief as her fellow workers followed their boss's instructions and came to stand around her and the stool.

"Bend." It wasn't a request. Our aging but terrifyingly fit boss was ordering her without even raising his voice. I willed her to do as she was told, for her own sake.

"Bend now." Becky could feel the danger of refusal in the air; we all could. It was almost tangible. Our colleagues were barely breathing as they focused on the stool. Most were thankful that it wasn't them; some had been so broken by submission that they wished it were.

Unsure of exactly how to position herself, Becky clumsily lowered her waist over the wide wooden seat, holding herself steady by grabbing the legs with her outstretched arms. With his usual economy of movement the boss shifted her farther onto the stool so that her ass was deliciously exposed, while her legs balanced precariously on her high heels. Then he fastened her taut limbs in place with thick black bootlaces, carefully designed to cut into the sinner's skin should she wriggle too much.

Then he paused, turning his back on the young woman, who was still battling to comprehend how accidentally slopping a mug of coffee could result in such chastisement. The boss went to the closet in the corner of the room. When he returned, he was holding a long, thin, white cane.

Becky's eyes never left the cane. Her face had taken on the pallor of a ghost as the final shred of hope that this was all some sick initiation ceremony dissolved. What the hell would have happened if she'd spilled the whole cup of coffee?

The sound of the first crack across her tight pale buttocks was drowned out by her shocked scream. *Yes, it really is happening. I warned you.*

The second, then the third, left smart red lines as the cane connected with her prone ass. Becky's screams were reaching epic proportions and the boss was obviously getting bored with the noise. Stopping to undo his tie, he wrapped it into a makeshift gag and swiftly tied it around Becky's flushed face.

The fourth lash, the fifth, and Becky was biting for all she was worth into the thin strip of material. The humiliation of her situation would surely be going around and around her confused mind, as the silent workforce watched her enforced submission. By the sixth stroke she was hardly making a sound, her concentration on simply surviving the ordeal. On the eighth stroke it happened. We all heard it.

She whimpered. Her reaction was changing; she was reaching the crossover point between unwanted pain and desired pain. Perhaps I'd been wrong about Becky. Perhaps this wasn't her first submission. How well did I know her after all? No one here had ever responded that way the first time before. She had seemed genuinely shocked and frightened by the situation, but suddenly I began to suspect she had her own motives for being here.

Her buttocks, now scarlet, bruised, and striped, gave off a throbbing heat as the boss hesitated. He'd heard the subtle alteration in her voice; he waited just long enough for a tiny sigh to escape her moist lips before bringing the cane down with precision onto the exact spot where the previous stroke had hit.

Then it stopped. She was left there shaking and unfulfilled, as the whip was lovingly returned to its home. All the workers returned to their desks, once again mindful of the consequences of making a mistake.

This was the worst stage. During my first humiliation, I had been sure the lashing itself would be the worst thing that could happen. I hadn't counted on the shame factor. Surely Becky would be feeling it now as the air-conditioning wafted across her stinging flesh. Would she be grappling with her thoughts? *How did this happen? Why don't they let me go now? How will I ever look anyone in the eye again?* Maybe she hadn't yet noticed that the people here do not look each other in the eye. In this office the safest option is definitely the meek one.

The blood would have rushed to her head by now. She'd be wondering if there was more to come. I had warned her, and she hadn't believed me. Or had she? I looked furtively across my desk as she remained motionless, either too scared or too sensible to speak. Even if she was stupid enough to ask how long she would remain there, we couldn't have told her. It depended on how long the boss and his assistant took in their separate office.

I saw them once. The boss had rightly sensed I was beginning to enjoy my punishments, and had decided a further level of correction was required. My ass burning from a thorough paddling, I had to watch, helpless, bound to the desk, as the boss received relief from the arousal my disciplining had obviously caused him.

I have never heard his assistant speak. She is simply referred to as Miss Harriet, but I have no idea if Harriet is her first or last name. I do know that she loves her work, and I suspect she fears that he will grow weary of her one day. Perhaps that's why she never speaks—to keep an air of mystery. All this went through my head as I lay there naked, my weighty tits crushed against the writing surface, my aching legs dangling over the edge, not quite reaching the floor, and my ass smarting as I was kept somewhere between agony and ecstasy.

He hadn't said anything to Miss Harriet. Just a look at his face seemed to tell her exactly what to do. First she stepped neatly out of her immaculate A-line skirt, then she slipped off her crisp white blouse. I tried to resist drawing breath as her beautiful bodice and stockings revealed her pantiless, heart-shaped pussy. Not that this was on view for long, as she bent, without prompting, across the arm of the large black leather armchair in the corner of the room and waited.

I couldn't take my eyes off her. She had placed herself in a position of humiliation with every shred of dignity intact. Her buttocks, however, told their own story. The dark-pink welts that neatly crisscrossed her regularly bronzed flesh looked angry. They obviously rarely had time to heal between assaults.

Her master had already taken off his clothes, revealing a well-toned figure for a man of his years, his hard dick showing just how much he had enjoyed my correction. The new paddle he selected for his work had four hard rubber studs encased in a smooth black cover. I was just imagining the agony it might inflict when I saw for myself. Although my view was partially obstructed by the boss, I strained against my bonds so I could see this fascinating creature take punishment simply because she was there and his hard-on had to be dealt with. My boss's skill with the chosen weapon was evident. One, two, three, the paddle came down with speed. I could see indents appear in her flesh as the nodules cut in. Yet, despite her already damaged skin, she shed not a drop of blood.

All that time, Miss Harriet had made no sound. Her concentration must have been incredible as the vicious strokes lashed her rose buttocks. I counted each stroke as I felt my own helpless, wasted, liquid ooze down my thighs onto the desk's conveniently placed blotting paper. The assistant's steady breathing had become shallow and urgent by the tenth lash, and the boss's own had turned into an animal grunt as suddenly, on the twelfth, he dropped his weapon, grabbed her hips, and pulled her toward him, thrusting his painfully hard cock into her waiting ass. Her cry was more one of relief than of pain as he hammered into her.

I lay there, desperate for attention, imagining what it would be like to hold the whip hand for a change; to be able to counteract my corrective measures by touching her soft skin, licking her engorged nipples, kissing her panting lips.

Then it was over. He growled his release as she rubbed herself against the chair to bring herself off. Miss Harriet, silent once more, turned and passed him a handkerchief to clean himself up before dismissing herself with an incline of her delicate head. I was left there for another hour. No one touched me. It was a worse agony than the lashes.

Becky stayed. I wasn't sure she would turn up the following day; many before her hadn't. However, as she sat at her desk her eyes weren't cast down like her peers'; they had a defiant glint to them that I feared could be dangerous. It wasn't that much of a surprise to me when, two days later, Becky dropped a pile of recently sorted filing on the floor directly in front of the boss's door. "Nerves," one of my colleagues whispered. I wasn't so sure. I couldn't help wondering if she had done it deliberately, to see what might happen next.

Just as before, the stool was positioned in the center of the circle. This time, however, Becky positioned herself, with no word of prompting, on the hard surface. She revealed her own, still slightly bruised, rump and offered up her wrists to be bound.

The boss watched her with interest and shook his head. You never got what you wanted here. Becky was left, standing there, ass exposed, as he put the stool away again. Waiting. No one got the upper hand in this office.

He opened the closet and, without a word, beckoned her to approach. I held my breath, already turned on by the prospect of what was to come. To my eternal shame, it is why I've stayed here. This place had changed my tastes. There was no going back. I watched.

It was an unusual closet. From floor to ceiling in height, it had an increased depth hidden behind its gray metal doors. The shelves along the walls were set well back, so that at least two people could occupy the remaining space with the doors closed. On every shelf there was a collection of instruments: canes, whips, paddles, nipple clamps. There was all the necessary material to keep a correction freak going for years: ribbons, ropes, cuffs, chains, gags. The more you looked, the more your heart froze and your eyes widened. Becky looked. Her face revealed nothing.

Miss Harriet had silently come out of her office. Without a word she stood behind Becky and helped her off with her remaining clothes. Becky was so beautiful. I realized I hadn't really looked at her properly before. I already wanted to touch; I began to imagine her beating my breasts with a short stick and then soothing them with her tongue.

I came back to reality. Such feelings must not be displayed here. Becky was now just inside the closet doors, facing her audience. She seemed to shine. How had she got to this point so quickly? It had taken me many beatings before I had learned to enjoy it, and even after nearly eighteen months I could never be so open about it. I still have the shame. Maybe I need it.

Becky stared through us as she looked straight ahead. Miss Harriet had taken one of her slim wrists and was tying it to a conveniently placed hook on one of the shelves with a silk cord. Then she secured the other wrist, then the ankles, and finally she snapped a thin silver collar securely around Becky's neck, its long leather cord dangling provocatively between her breasts.

Miss Harriet stepped out of the closet and looked to her boss for approval. He nodded. I could clearly see, when I dared to glance, that his dick was straining against his suit trousers. They shut the doors of the closet, and we all heard Becky gasp. She had expected pain, arousal. They had given her nothing.

No one could concentrate. Returning to our work was impossibly hard.

An hour after the doors had been closed, our boss came out of his office, his slightly creased clothes revealing that Miss Harriet's services had been called upon once again. As he walked between our desks, the tension was intense. He wanted to punish someone. Any excuse would do.

He signaled to Miss Harriet, who brought the stool forward. "Congratulations," he said. "Despite events," (he gestured to the closet) "you have all managed some work. Not much. But something." He paced around the stool, like a panther waiting to pounce. "Like me, I suspect you have all been rather turned on by recent events. Some of you," (he looked straight at me) "will be literally wetting your underpants with anticipation. Just waiting for the crop to strike. Others are still torn between running and staying." He paused and surveyed his workforce. "But you will all stay. Every day I wonder who will fail to turn up for work, but each day you all come."

No one dared to speak. I could feel my breath scratching my throat as he continued. "It is not in my nature to give rewards, but in this case I think it would provide an apt lesson for our newest recruit." He again gestured to the closet. "Becky cannot hear us through those doors, although she can see around her. The light inside is sufficient for her to be able to examine at close quarters all the instruments that she so unwisely volunteered herself to experience."

"For one hour only she will be your slave. I will open the doors and she will be yours to do with as you like. Do not waste this experience. It is very unlikely to ever happen again."

My eyes must have lit up, because he bestowed upon me one of his rare and rather unnerving smiles. "Yes, I thought you'd like that. But I am also sure that you would benefit from your own ass being warmed. I know I would enjoy performing the task for you."

I glanced at the stool. Was I that obvious? I wasn't like Becky. I could never have engineered a situation like this, but he was right, and I could feel my nipples harden at the thought of the tingling pain that would spread across my buttocks to my already damp pussy.

"Strip," he ordered, and I obeyed. My hands shook slightly as I fumbled with my blouse buttons, and the slightly bent clasp of my bra. Finally naked, I cast my eyes down. Yes, I needed the shame. The wood felt cold beneath my skin as I offered up my ass, hands unbound, holding on to the stool's sturdy legs. I could see the closet doors, now open, as I watched between my legs, my head hanging down. Becky's legs were still bound, quivering slightly. Being shut in the closet for so long had obviously taken away some of her bravado. Doubt had had time to creep in, just as our boss had intended it to.

He was in the closet. Was he selecting a weapon for me or for her? Would I be gagged this time? It appeared that I was to be trusted to be still, and would not be bound.

"Becky." The boss was clearly speaking to her, but addressing the whole office at the same time. "As you can see, you are not the only one who has chosen to feel the sting today." He was standing behind me. There was something in his hand, but I couldn't see what it was. How much pain? Was it a cane or a whip? My question was answered by the crack of a leather strap as it made contact with my tensed skin. Despite my determination not to, I automatically flinched and a shocked cry came from my lips, instantly resulting in a harder slap, then another, faster and faster.

I couldn't keep still. Without the usual bonds, the desire to wriggle after each lash was incredibly strong, and by the fifth hit

I could feel two pairs of cold masculine hands on my inflamed flesh, holding me firmly in place. The result of their touch was almost enough to tip me over the edge.

Becky was beginning to whine. I opened my eyes and saw that she was receiving some attention of her own. I could just hear a faint smack over the crack of my own punishment. My head was full of pictures of Becky's torment, which must have been doubled by the act of watching mine. I wanted her very badly.

It ended as quickly as it had begun. The extreme burn that had spread across my ass was tingling as my brain slowly registered that the pain had stopped. The hands that had been pressing into me slipped under my arms and pulled me upright. My head spun as my stiff body became accustomed to standing, and for a moment I rested heavily on my captor's arms.

They brought me before Becky, and I watched as the boss took over from Miss Harriet, who had clearly been driving Becky to distraction by alternatively slapping her distended tits and rubbing her nipples with a silk handkerchief. The tears that had been silently pouring from Becky's face had dried, and she collected herself for whatever was to follow. I wanted to remind her that she had started this, but all I could do was look at her.

The boss took one long, hard swipe at her engorged nipples with the belt he had so recently used on me. I couldn't decide if the scream that left Becky's lips was one of relief, sheer frustration, or pain.

He released her feet and wrists before taking the leather cord that hung across her chest and pulling her out of the closet. He gave the cord to me and said to us, "She's all yours. One hour only." He left then, grabbing a couple of chains before pushing Miss Harriet rather too roughly toward his office door.

I didn't move. Becky and I were still naked, but no one

else was. The silence lasted for about thirty seconds until the spell was broken and the men who had been holding me down snapped to attention. Both ran to the open closet and grabbed what they wanted. Before I could think, the biting claws of a pair of cruel silver nipple clamps were making Becky cry out in agony as her tortured breasts flushed in response. Her arms were held by some while others watched, fascinated, as canes, whips, and paddles were grabbed from their hooks. Becky's eyes were wide. She began to suffer an assault that was evidently the result of months of pent-up frustration from my fellow workers. Her breasts, arms, thighs, and buttocks all took a simultaneous lashing as she stood there. She screamed and yelled, but her eyes clearly shouted *Don't stop!* and she relished every stroke. Sticky liquid was seeping out of her wet snatch as I watched, transfixed by this amazing creature. She looked at me beseechingly and I could not deny her. I let go of the cord, pushed past one of my colleagues who was pinching the underside of her swollen breasts, and kissed her. I had never kissed anyone like that. It was as if I was saving her, taking her beyond the agony of her deliciously pain-wracked body. Her anguish was silenced by my hungry lips, and I moaned into her as the lashes began to crack across me as well.

An hour later, I gently removed the clamps, kissing the damaged nipples to make them better, and slipped her crumpled blouse back over her warmed chest.

Then we all returned to our desks to work.

There was never any question that I would go home with her. How I didn't come as we simply held hands on the walk to her flat I shall never know.

No sooner had we got through the door than our clothes were in a heap and Becky pulled me into her bedroom. She laid me down on her soft coffee-colored duvet and pulled a large battered suitcase from the corner of the room. It was full of every type of sex toy I had ever seen. Even our boss would have been envious of such a collection.

As I allowed myself to be gagged and bound by this pale beauty, I finally understood why I had been unable to talk her out of applying for the job. This was what she had desired from the very beginning, and for that I will be eternally grateful.

PAID FOR THE PLEASURE

Adrie Santos

I couldn't believe I was doing it—responding to an ad at all, never mind such a strange one. I listened to his introduction one last time: "I am looking for serious replies only…" His voice was monotone—almost cold. "I am a fifty-two-year-old, average-looking man with a fetish for giving oral pleasure. I am seeking women who will allow me to come into their homes or a hotel to pleasure them orally and I expect nothing in return. I am also willing to compensate." That was it. It wasn't a particularly dynamic pitch, and not even remotely sexy by normal standards, yet I was drawn to it.

I had started using this telephone dating service one drunken night with some friends as a joke, and would on the occasional late night get on to kill some time and sometimes reply to ads with a message at best. Never had I dared to chat live.

My heart raced as I pressed ONE to request a live connection. I was nervous and incredibly excited at the thought of what I was about to get myself into. My being an attractive girl with everything most people would want—a great job and a beautiful place—might lead one to wonder why I would respond to such an ad, but I was wet at the mere idea, and determined to follow through.

"Thank you for getting back to me," he began. "Let me tell you about myself; I am fifty-two with an average build. My hair is gray and thinning. I wear glasses and consider myself to be very average looking. I am a business professional who has a fetish for giving oral pleasure. I am looking to meet ladies who will allow me to come over and eat them out with no strings attached. I have done this before and am told that I do it well. Our sessions would last approximately one hour. I enjoy licking not only pussy but ass as well. I am serious, clean, and safe and assure you discretion. I do not like to waste my time. Are you interested or not?"

I sat there for a moment stunned at his cut and dry speech, at the same time my clit was so hard and excited that it hurt. "I'm very interested," I finally said.

We went on to agree that we would meet at my place the following Wednesday afternoon. He didn't ask for a description, stating that age, race, and looks were unimportant, but I insisted on letting him know the basics; that I am a petite, long-haired blonde with an ample bottom and bosom. I figured that would help make the whole thing feel a little less impersonal.

Wednesday finally rolled around and I stood looking in the mirror, wondering what to wear for such an occasion. I couldn't exactly call up a friend: "Hey Deb, what should I wear for my afternoon of pussy eating?"

I decided on something simple: a black V-neck top—he hadn't mentioned a cleavage fetish, but I figured it couldn't hurt—and a knee-length denim skirt with black boots. I didn't bother with panties—it seemed kinda pointless.

When he rang from downstairs, I did a quick primping of my long hair and touched up my lip gloss, making sure that my lips looked pink and wet—perfect for the occasion. My body trembled as I turned the doorknob. There he was, looking exactly as I had imagined, maybe a tad older. He was only a bit taller than I was and resembled my old science teacher. He was not someone that I would ever give a second glance to. He was old enough to be my father.

His hand was cold when he shook mine, barely cracking a smile. "Let's get started. Shall we stay here?" He pointed to the sofa in my living room.

"Sure," was all I could get out as he led me to the sofa and instructed me to sit down.

Almost clinically he told me he wanted to begin with my pussy. It felt so dirty: having this old, generic man in a respectable shirt and tie getting down on his knees in front of me using words like *pussy* and *cunt*. It was inappropriate and utterly exciting at the same time. I lifted my hips and ass off the sofa just enough for him to raise my skirt. I felt like a patient about to be examined by her doctor. I looked down and could see my clean-shaven cunt already glistening—had I ever been so juicy? He ran his hand over my damp, smooth skin, expressing his approval of my clean, bald mound. My knees shook as he pushed them farther apart and leaned in closer. I could feel his hot breath on my skin for a moment, and then he finally placed his open lips on mine. First some kisses all around my inner thighs and outer lips, then his fingers pulled at my delicate skin, parting my cunt lips until I could feel my pussy open wide—ready for his tongue.

I lay back with my eyes closed and just enjoyed the feeling of his tongue running up and down, all over my hot pussy. As he began sucking my clit, I sat up just enough to watch him. Every now and then he would glance up at me with his glasses steamed, his mouth and chin drenched with my juices. His expression was almost trancelike. I could see he was loving every lick.

Just as I would start to quiver, feeling myself ready to come, he would pause and change technique to put off my explosion for just a little longer. I could feel my hard nipples under my top as I watched him suck on my clit, squeezing my inner thighs with his fingers digging into my flesh, completely unaware of how rough he was being—but I was enjoying every second of it, more than anything I had ever experienced before.

I was mesmerized by the sight of this seemingly uptight man going at my cunt with such skill. I couldn't take it anymore and was about to explode when he took his face out from in between my legs and wiped the juice from his face.

"Have you ever had your asshole licked clean by a man's tongue?" he asked in that now familiar dry tone.

Before I got the chance to fully reply no, he instructed me to kneel down on the couch facing away from him. He raised my skirt again and used his hands to guide me into position, lifting my bare ass higher into the air. He spread my cheeks apart and quickly placed his mouth in between. His hot, wet tongue ran up and down my crack, his saliva running freely down toward my wet pussy. It felt amazing. I reached down with one hand and rubbed my clit as he slid his tongue into my asshole. It darted in and out quickly, and though I had never had anal sex before, I began to long for a hard cock to push into me. My whole body was on fire. I pushed my ass against his face, trying to get his tongue farther into me, at the same time fingering my cunt like mad. My insides began to tremble; I knew I was about to come, but it wasn't anything like the other times. It wasn't just my clit that was ready to explode; it was all of me.

He reached for the hand that was pumping in and out of my cunt and pushed it away, whispering into my ass, "Just let go...," and I did. My entire body trembled as I came, hard and fast. I could feel my buildup of juices flowing out of my cunt as my knees buckled and I collapsed downward, his tongue quickly moving to my cunt hole and lapping up everything that was coming out.

When the frenzy of my climax was over, I glanced lazily over at him and saw that his cock was out of his pants and he was wiping away his own come, some of which had gotten on his pants. I had been so sedated by my own pleasure I hadn't realized what eating my pussy was doing for him.

"That was amazing," I marveled, my cunt still throbbing from my climax. "Would you like me to do anything for you?" I asked, to show my sincere gratitude. "No, thank you. You gave me what I needed," was all he said.

I sat and watched him zip up his pants and get himself together; my legs were still open, my swollen cunt exposed. He stood up and thanked me, his face somber, and in that dry tone, he told me to give him a call the following week to arrange our next session. He disappeared through the door, leaving behind fifty dollars next to my telephone.

CRUISING

Lee Cairney

When I'm getting ready to go out on the prowl I often get a feeling like the excitement of being sick but without the nausea, like my stomach lining is trying to peel away. It feels good in the same way that inhaling sherbet up your nose feels good, and believe me, I do mean good. I pull on my heavy, steel-capped biker boots, tucking them under my leather trousers, and sling my battered black leather jacket over my white vest. One large silver spike rivets my ear. My hair is dark and cropped short, snug against my head. I was once told that I had eyes like flakes from an iceberg—whatever that means. I'm wearing bondage cuffs, tight confections of soft, supple, leather and stainless steel, around both wrists for the constriction and sheer pleasure of it. I know I'm looking good.

I bang the door behind me and stroll down the hill from my apartment. I live in an ancient cathedral city where small, beautiful medieval churches cluster and old flint-faced walls run into each other. Beautiful, but it's difficult to find the sex I need in this small, provincial place. I walk to the riverside, leaving little trails of iced breath in the dark air behind me. Dirty water slaps against the moorings and a line of grubby white cruising boats. I slouch my shoulders forward just a tiny bit and check that my jacket covers my small tits. It does. I step across the toll bridge and into the wooded park that marks the beginning of the local cruising area for gay men. I've become used to getting my kicks vicariously. I enjoy the ambiance. Strange men stalk between the trees, crunching leaves underfoot. Some of them walk dogs and feign nonchalance. I've even seen a few round here in business suits—no doubt, their wives are left waiting at home as they sully loafers in the mud and snag holes in pinstripe, rubbing against the rough bark of a tree as they're taken brutally and swiftly by a faceless man they met twenty seconds ago.

A whole new language of looks and come-ons develops. Rejection is as subtle as the tilt of a head. Tonight the air is spiced with the smoky tang of autumn and a sharp, slowly trickling sense of muted danger. Dark parkland, bushes, and trees lie ahead of me. Often I catch men fucking and stand and watch them—on their hands and knees, being shunted hard from behind, or half hidden by a bush having a thickening cock rammed into their warm mouths; even sitting on one of the forgotten park benches stroking each other's dick.

Walking soundlessly, I reach the center of the park, continually checking the shadows and real obstacles that appear in my path. My clit is tingling. It aches from the recent sight of a youngish-looking man being fucked in the arse by a blond, heavy man in biker's leathers, whilst twisting his head around at the same time to service the throbbing, red-tipped erection of another kneeling man. I had to force myself to steal quietly away before they shot down his throat and up his arse, worried I'd forget myself and betray my presence by some involuntary noise of lust and jealousy mixed together. Now just ahead of me I see the outline of a tall, slim shape leaning against a tree. I prepare myself to walk past casually but my heart is bumping in my chest cavity. For the first time tonight I feel like I'm on display. The man is dressed in dark clothes, jeans and a jacket perhaps, and is leaning with one foot up against the tree. Something dangles from his right hand—oh, it's a dog leash. I relax slightly. I'm close enough to see that his hair is cut even shorter than mine. I look around but can't see the dog.

"Hey," the figure murmurs softly and I follow the sound without any real thought. I'm standing opposite now, face-to-face. For all my five feet seven I feel short. A kind of pleasurable sensation freezes my brain as the dog owner reaches forward with leather-gloved hands and manipulates me so I'm facing the tree. I'm pushed so hard against it that I can feel the patterns of the bark pressing into my cunt. Hypnotized, I stay pressed against the thick trunk while the leash is used to fasten my hands together around the other side, securing me tightly to the tree.

"Cuffs—convenient," a concentrating voice mutters from the other side of the tree. The burning, stretching sensation in my arms as the final knot is tied restores some of my sense to me.

"What are you doing?" A pathetic and useless question. The dog owner suddenly slams against me from behind, shoving me hard and nearly winding me.

"You should be quiet. I'm going to expose you...play with you...do what I like with you. If you want to be freed at the end don't make it necessary for me to use a gag or blindfold."

I stop squirming and trying to turn my head to see over my shoulder. That and my heavy breathing are taken for assent. All I can think is how I can now feel breasts against my back, and something harder, lower. The voice, although gruff, isn't quite low enough to be a man's, I realize. I can't believe it.

A cold, gloved hand reaches round and flips open the buttons of my trousers. Then my trousers are dragged down round my ankles. My assailant—whom I now know to be a woman—hoists my vest and jacket into a bundle around my shoulder blades. The chill air is like a slap to my whole body. My skin creeps up into gooseflesh. I'm naked, exposed, tied to a tree. I wonder how many people can see the luminous white of my flesh in the darkness, watching me just as I watched them. Leathermen, big daddies, bikers, circling around me with their cocks out, stroking themselves to hardness.

I can feel the zip of her jeans and hard metal of her belt buckle pressing into my bare arse and burning with the cold. Her hands reach round and grab the erect tips of my nipples as my legs are kicked apart—as wide as the trousers shackling my ankles will allow. She just spreads me wide and helps herself. My nipples are being plucked and pinched and teased into aching points of chafed skin. Then the pressure against my arse recedes and all my thoughts are concentrated in my nipples being worked so hard and grazed against the rough skin of the tree.

My cunt is dripping wet as I feel the cold tip of something long and very thick pressing tantalizingly against it. I try to open my legs wider but fail and I let out a visceral grunt of frustration. The freezing silicone head is rubbed up and down across the opening to my cunt, nudging up to my erect clit and slowly back down again to rest against the tight pucker of my arsehole.

"Maybe I should take you right here," she says, "like the little gay boy that you are, cruising around in the woods, looking for sex. Well, you've found it."

The head of her dick pushes against my clenched arsehole.

"No," I hear myself saying, "I've never been taken there." Can't she read the signs? I'm a top. I do not take it up the arse.

"Forbidding me, are you?" she croons. "We'll see."

Before I can reply she slams the thick dick she's packing into my cunt. Opening and stretching me, she gives my tight hole no time to adjust to the length and thickness. My cunt aches as she rams against the top of my cervix with her blunt, thick head, pulling nearly all the way out of me before thrusting back deep inside me. All I can feel is her in my cunt and her leather and metal bruising my buttocks. Anger at my enforced and unusual passivity and the sheer force of her cruel and energetic pounding begins to warm me.

I'm spread-eagled, wrapped around a tree and helpless. The muscles in my arms and stomach are being pulled to unbearable tautness as she works on me. I simply have to stand, spread and open, and let her impale my cunt repeatedly. I feel like I'm actually going to split down the middle but, despite myself, I can't help trying to push against her insistent, plunging dick.

"Oh, do you want some more?" She grabs me by the half-inch of hair on my head. "I'll give you what you want."

Slicked wet from my cunt she pulls her dick back and then pushes it into my virgin arse. It hurts like hell, more than sherbet up your nose. This is definitely a boundary. I feel like I'm going to dissolve, that I can't possibly bear her plunging in and out with long, hard strokes, or that I'll explode. But my sphincter tightens around every move she makes.

"That's right. Milk my good, big dick."

I'm just about to start screaming when her hand works its way round and insinuates itself against my clit. The cool leather strokes against my hard clit as she fills my arse again and again. I can't hold back and with my arse and clit being worked hard and my cunt empty and swollen to the night air I come so hard that all I can see is the rushing of red blood tissue before my eyes. It feels like she's come inside me, violating me further, flooding my walls, but I know this can't be true as it's only her silicone dick that is now being edged slowly out of me.

I sag against the tree as she plays the point of a knife up and down, up and down over my exposed flesh, before placing the handle in my hand. With difficulty I saw through the binding holding my wrists. Freed, I turn quickly round, rearranging my clothes. There is nothing but shadows and trees and bushes, a severed piece of leather and the rushing of the cold night air.

REAR WINDOW

Scarlett French

Maria paid the guy and shut the door to her new apartment with a sigh of exhaustion. Leaning against a pile of boxes, she cast her eyes over the small flat, and considered the unpacking ahead of her. She threw open the huge sash window and put her head out to feel the breeze on her face. The air was warm and let up very faint smells of salt beef and garlic. The sounds of cars and horns below, and the wafts of the delicatessen, somehow made her feel that the city was welcoming her. Maria found excitement rising in her belly at the thought of this new beginning. She turned to face the unboxing of her life.

After a couple of hours of emptying boxes in no particular order, newspaper and bubble wrap flying, she realized it was growing dark. Deciding it was time to call it a night, she grabbed one of the glasses she'd unwrapped, rinsed off the smudges of newsprint, and loped through to the living room. She found the bottle of wine she'd bought to celebrate her first night in the new place, and flopped down in her huge overstuffed swivel chair, right by the floor-length window.

The merlot was full-bodied and rich and she took long sips, letting it hit her taste buds before swallowing slowly. Finally relaxing, she leaned back into the chair and put her feet up on the windowsill. The cooler night air flowed in, replacing the balmy stuffiness of the day. The sun had gone down now but she made no move to get up and switch on a lamp: with the lights out she could keep her curtains open and still have privacy. It was a perfect way to explore her new view. She lit a cigarette and inhaled deeply. The smoke whipped out the open window and curled off into the night.

Hers was a typical high-rise view: an equally tall block opposite, lights from windows dotting the monolith in an irregular checkerboard pattern. As usual, there were the curtained windows—the muted squares on the board—and the brightly lit open windows of the people who didn't seem to mind that their lives were on display to at least ten flats in the building opposite. The view from their building would be a similar configuration. Maria sat cloaked in her big comfy chair, one of the black squares. She took a sip of the velvety merlot and dragged on her cigarette. There was something daring about watching other people's windows.

Directly opposite was a very white bedroom with its curtains wide open. It had the look of a showroom bedroom in an interiors store—white walls, white furniture, puffy white duvet and pillows. As she scanned the other windows, Maria suddenly caught movement out of the corner of her eye. She followed it back to the white room to find two men kissing in the doorway. Either they didn't realize that the curtains were open or they didn't care, because they made no move to draw them. Her first response was to look away from this private scene, but she found herself drawn in. Maybe just for a moment, she thought.

They were maybe in their midthirties. One of the men was very toned and had dark hair. He wore tight jeans and a black top and was rather perfect in his appearance, like a Calvin Klein model. The other was much less preened, in faded jeans and a plaid shirt. It was obvious to Maria that it was the Calvin guy's flat. Maybe Calvin liked a bit of cowboy rough? Calvin peeled his T-shirt off like a second skin while the cowboy wrenched open the snaps of his western shirt, letting it fall to the floor. Maria could see what the deal was here—these two men probably didn't know each other very well, and they wanted it. Bad.

With both their shirts off now, they immediately grabbed one another, their kisses forceful, their tongues sparring. The cowboy clutched Calvin's arsecheeks with both hands and pulled him in tight, pelvis to pelvis. Calvin began to kiss the cowboy's face and neck, working his way down to his nipples where he settled for a while. Maria saw the cowboy throw his head back in response to the teasing of Calvin's tongue. She also saw now the hard bulges in both of their jeans, and silently urged the two men to release them. Calvin continued his way down the cowboy's body until he reached the waistband. He licked his way along the cowboy's stomach, just above the belt, as he rubbed at the bulge in his own jeans. Maria heard an exhalation of breath and realized that it was her own. Her cigarette had burned down to the butt and the ash was sagging, about to fall away. Her glass was tilted, moments from spilling. She also realized she was getting wet. Collecting herself, she stubbed out her cigarette, then drained her glass and put it on the floor.

When she looked up again, she found Calvin tonguing the cowboy's crotch through the denim and attempting to unbuckle his worn leather belt. Words were exchanged and Calvin got up and pulled down his jeans and underwear in one quick movement. His stiff cock sprang out as he pulled them down past his thighs. Maria was suddenly self-conscious. What if they saw her? She slunk down a little in the chair and scooted it back into the shadows, just beyond the light of the streetlamps.

Calvin stepped out of his trousers and underwear and kicked them aside, then stood before the cowboy, waiting. The cowboy curled his fingers around his belt buckle and pulled hard. The belt flew through the loops and leapt into the air. Maria felt her clit twitch. She knew the sound the belt would have made, cracking in the air. She wanted to touch herself but held off in favor of keeping her full attention on the two men. Her pussy throbbed as the thrashing began. Supporting himself on a set of drawers, Calvin was bent over, proffering his arse to the cowboy. The folded belt came down hard on Calvin's bare skin and he jolted as the leather bit his flesh. His hard cock extended away from his body, twitching in expectation between blows. Even from a distance, Maria could see that Calvin's arsecheeks were reddening with each strike, showing welts of pleasure. There was something about the way the cowboy stood, legs firmly planted on the ground as he administered the belt, that triggered memories of some of the more butch lovers she'd had. Her cunt twitched and flexed, demanding attention.

When the cowboy decided that Calvin had been strapped enough, he flung the belt aside and pulled Calvin's striped arse toward his still be-denimed crotch, where he held him in place with muscled arms, thrusting and rubbing in Calvin's crack. Maria was sure she could see precome shining on the end of Calvin's cock. The cowboy dropped to his knees and began to lick Calvin's cheeks and inner thighs. Calvin spread his legs farther, bending right over and raising his arse up. Maria could see his balls from behind—something the cowboy hadn't missed either—and watched as he took them in his mouth. Calvin's face fell into a gasp and his body writhed. Maria wished that she could hear the cries of pleasure, but settled instead on the sound of her own breathing, which grew heavier still.

Calvin turned and faced the cowboy, who devoured his throbbing cock immediately. Maria watched as the cowboy took it all in, all the way down to the base and back up again, leaving the shaft glistening with saliva. His head bobbed back and forth as he knelt, working Calvin's dick with fast, sure strokes. Calvin began to thrust back, fucking the cowboy's mouth. Maria was mesmerized; watching the cowboy, who clearly couldn't get enough meat, made her mouth water. The sheer desire between them was electric and Maria felt herself drawn in, willing Calvin to come. The cowboy grasped Calvin's arse, pulling him forcefully into his mouth, his lips sealed around his target. Calvin was panting and crying out something when he suddenly threw his head back and closed his eyes as his pelvis began to spasm on the cowboy's mouth. The cowboy gulped and swallowed, his Adam's apple moving in time with the spurts of Calvin's come. Maria's cunt clenched and throbbed, so she shut her legs for a moment to calm herself. *Watching is one thing*, she thought. As Calvin's orgasm began to slow, the cowboy pulled his face away and Maria saw a droplet of come shining in the corner of his mouth. He made sure Calvin was watching as he licked his lips greedily and smiled. In the apartment above, an old woman stood at her kitchen sink, moving her arms to place sudsy patterned china onto a dish drainer.

The cowboy rose to his feet and they began to kiss and shuffle backward toward the bed. Calvin finally pushed the cowboy who fell back onto the bed then looked up at Calvin, smirking. Calvin leapt on him and pulled roughly at his jeans, finally wrenching them off. To Calvin's obvious delight, the cowboy wore no underwear. His cock stood up proudly, uncut, and Calvin took it firmly in his hand and stroked it admiringly before straddling the cowboy. They kissed and clawed at each other as Calvin's cock, stiff again, banged against the cowboy's. Calvin licked the cowboy's whole body, progressively giving him a tongue bath. When he reached the cowboy's cock, he hesitated. It seemed that he had a tease planned, but he couldn't help himself—he gulped the cowboy's rod and gave it several luxurious mouth strokes that sent the cowboy arching backward. Despite herself, Maria found her hand had slipped into her underwear and was stroking away at her now rock-hard and very slippery clit. She didn't care anymore. Her pussy was engorged and every finger-slide through and up to her clit sent shivers coursing through her whole body. She paced herself; she wanted to come with the cowboy.

Still on the bed, Calvin directed the cowboy to get on his hands and knees and then got behind him. Leaning into him, he reached around for a while, sliding his hand up and down the stiff shaft, his own cock pressed hard between the cowboy's cheeks. He dropped back finally and pushed the cowboy's legs farther apart. The cowboy's arse was slightly hairy and Calvin smoothed the hair down with broad tongue licks before spreading his arsecheeks wide. Making his tongue a point, he began to tickle at the cowboy's arsehole. The mirror beside the bed reflected the cowboy's eyes as they flickered closed and his facial expression became one of beatific pleasure. Maria could see that both of their cocks were throbbing as Calvin rimmed the cowboy with enthusiasm, licking and tonguing his puckered hole.

Maria watched mesmerized as Calvin rolled on a condom, then added lube and slid his dick up between the cowboy's spread arsecheeks. Holding it at the base, he slowly rubbed it back and forth over the cowboy's lubed-up hole. Nudging just the head of his cock in, Calvin stopped and waited for the cowboy to take the lead. They were still for a moment, then gradually the cowboy began to back up onto Calvin's cock. Calvin held him by the hips and met his speed, thrusting slowly and deeply. Maria fingered herself at the same speed as the men's thrusting, wanting desperately to fuck herself with something hard. Not prepared to leave the moment, she looked around her for anything suitable for penetration. There on the windowsill lay the big screwdriver she'd used to reassemble the bed and the dining table. Grabbing it by the metal part, she kicked off her shorts and knickers and began to tease at her slippery hole with the smooth ribbed handle as she watched the cowboy being fucked, Calvin's sheathed cock sliding in and out of him at a steady pace. Finally, Maria slipped the handle end into her throbbing pussy and began to fuck herself rhythmically, her knees in the air and her feet curled around the armrests of the chair.

To Maria's delight, the fucking seemed to go on and on at a steady rhythm. She could see that both men were aching to come but were holding it back for as long as they could. Both of their faces expressed in turn the beautiful and the animal elements of sexual pleasure. She continued to match her own thrusts with theirs, pausing when she felt like she was about to tip over the edge. Suddenly the men began to pick up speed. Maria followed suit. Calvin began to slam his cock into the cowboy's arse. The muscles in his own arse were coved with tension and his whole body glistened with sweat. As the cowboy pushed back to meet him, Maria fucked herself hard with the ridged handle and vigorously rubbed her clit. Then, wanting a little of what the cowboy was getting, she discarded the screwdriver and used her now free hand to tease at her arsehole. She sighed deeply as she inserted a wet finger just inside her arse and began to stroke her sphincter while shallowly thrusting. She was pushed beyond the edge as she watched the cowboy's orgasm—his face contorted in ecstasy, come shooting out of his cock and landing on the other side of the bed. In turn, Calvin shot his hot load as he was milked by the muscle spasms going on in the cowboy's tight hole. Maria's arsehole began to clench around her finger and she responded by rubbing her clit faster and harder. As she came, her whole body shuddered and a grunt forced its way out of her mouth. She felt a surge in her pussy and gasped as a stream of ejaculate shot from her spasming cunt. She felt the release through her whole body. Her orgasm began to slow, and Maria watched as Calvin finally collapsed, leaning on the cowboy's back. It was as though the three of them had let out a collective sigh. The men slumped down together on the pristine bed and Calvin brought his arm around the cowboy's waist and pulled him close.

I think I'm going to like living here, thought Maria, as she sank back in her chair and lit a cigarette.

LOST AT SEA

Peony

Has it been that long? The clocks and the calendars are conspiring once again. Surely not? Have I been wandering, trapped in this haze, paralyzed by the thought of you? What day is it?

I shuffle to the bathroom amidst the chaos of the house. Things don't seem to be where I left them, nor do they seem to be the same. Nothing seems to be sane either, anymore. My reflection in the mirror stares back at me with shiny glass eyes. I am no longer seeing through these strange holes in my head and navigate mothlike and by memory, hearing and feeling for the last traces of you.

Showering mechanically, I scrape at my skin and the nest of my hair. The hot water trickles out and turns cold. I stand there as my rubber flesh changes from pink to white, and my veins shrink from the surface and nestle closer to my bones. I suppose it must be very cold, for my skin is prickled and protesting. I hazily ponder the idea that my brain might have severed its ties to my body and is bobbing listlessly, without anchor, in the sea of my skull. I used to hate cold showers.

Of their own volition my feet find their way to the bath mat, my hands to the towel and I'm rubbing robotically. I'm temporarily distracted by the absurdity of my joints sticking out at peculiar angles. Was I always this disjointed and bony?

Emerging from the bathroom I survey the damage. The house is littered with remnants edged with the feeling of emptiness, like a fairground after the circus has left town. Even the sound of my exhalations is loud in comparison and swells out into the room in ragged clouds. My leaden feet slide onto the shards of the glass long since shattered; I suppose it must be somewhere, somewhere down there.

I wonder how long I stood there, naked in the midst of the aftermath, blood collecting under my toes, staring blankly at the enormous hole in the shell of this decaying house. It loomed large and imposing, a porthole to another dimension, the name hanging rustily on hinges holed in my head. It's a door. The front door.

I stopped trying to make sense of it and decided to surrender. If I just give in, maybe I'll find a way out. There's no sense in fighting an irrepressible tide. Perhaps I'm walking in circles following reddened footsteps on floorboards that will probably never end.

You. A synapse fires inside my head. Somewhere near the surface I can see a faint glow fractured by surface ripples. I must be a long way under. We shouldn't have. We did. It's done and cannot be undone. We're on the other side of that which had grown so large between us, the lust that devoured us, swelled fat from the absurdity of it.

You again. Brighter now, refracting like strewn crystals from an exploded chandelier. You. The thought of you burns into a focal point with a brightness that is piercing. I'm rapidly ascending with no time to adjust, chest contorted from the pressure as I struggle to acclimatize. There is a roar in my ears as I rocket to the surface in an explosion of gray water and torn foam.

You again. I am awkwardly floating as I suck air through the cracks in my clenched teeth. I'm suddenly painfully aware of the dimension of space beneath and around me; it is terrifying being without the comfort of corners and walls.

You did this to me. With your hands that carved channels in my skin as you twisted my limbs to your pleasing and fed the burning inside me with pieces of you. You did this with words that pierced my insides with hooks that pinned me open, splayed and inviting, all yours for the taking. And yes, you took all of it, what I gave and what I didn't, you took it all and left me nothing save the taste of your skin and the weight of my heart in my hands.

I let you do this to me. At first we'd adhered to the rules and the rituals. The long lingering contact and words loaded and coated, then sitting so close you could smell the reek of the need burning under my skin. You'd played a deft hand and forced me to spread all that I held, faceup and exposed. There is nothing more dangerous than one with none left to lose and though you might have won, being defeated was sweetened by the sound of my name on your tongue.

I'd read the words in your eyes and the space between lines as I took my last look at the shore before diving headfirst. It was with such little tenderness that you pushed me beneath you and spread my limbs with your hands. These weren't lover's lips that stretched tight to expose my teeth that sank deep in your skin.

The pace was frenetic, fueled by the burning and the wheels sprung loose in my mind. There was no turning back or slowing the rhythm of the pounding both within and outside of my head. Skin flayed and breath burnt from the anger inside us, there is little to exchange when conquest leaves bodies ravished and broken. I had known it would be like this. I had hungered for the taste of it, flesh throbbing with the want of it, the want of you, to be taken, submerged, and surrounded, drowned and destroyed.

You were relentless and I was remorseless, for a time, just a short time, and then.

And then, it was over.

Laid beside without touching, silent and spent, I'm facing away from the fact of your face, from the sight of the redness of my nails on your skin. You've turned from the image that's too much like another's, the other, another, the one I was not.

WORTH IT

Alison Tyler

As the ring slid onto my finger, I knew it was all over. The sparkle of diamonds glinting in the dim candlelight. The pink tourmaline shining like a flame. Those jewels foretold our demise as clearly as any fortune-teller could have. I knew the end was inevitable, even if I didn't know why. Well, that's not altogether true. I knew, sort of. I knew in a half-assed, bitchy kind of way.

A week before, Byron had taken me on a dream shopping spree to Tiffany & Co., had told me to choose the ring I desired the most. "Go for it, Gina. Pick out the one you love." What girl wouldn't melt at an opportunity like that?

Flustered, flattered, I'd landed on this one after nearly an hour of breathless searching.

Or, at least, one damn near like it. Dramatically dark pink stone in the center, two perfect diamonds on either side, a classic platinum band. Admittedly, the price was astronomical, but Byron had the money for the ring. And I was worth it, right?

Apparently not.

This ring did not come in the pretty pale blue box that makes all women's hearts skip a beat, but in a knockoff lavender velvet container, from a knockoff jewelry store in West L.A. *This* ring cost five hundred dollars instead of twelve thousand dollars. And I should have been happy with whatever Byron gave me. I know that. But like a bossy five year old who throws a tantrum at her own birthday party, I was not happy at all. Because it was clear to me from the look in his watery green eyes as they carefully appraised my reaction that I wasn't worth it.

Like I wasn't worth a lot of things.

I wasn't worth kissing in public. ("PDAs are *so* revolting.") I wasn't worth risking potential shame or embarrassment in the back row of a movie theater. ("*Stop that,* Gina. People might see.") I wasn't worth trying something new in bed, even though Byron had dabbled in adventurous sex with girls before me. But no matter how I cajoled, he wouldn't travel uncharted territory on our California King.

Velvety handcuffs? No.

A leopard-print blindfold? No f-ing way.

He'd had *anal* sex before me, twice, with a girl he met in New York City. I knew this because early in our relationship, when we'd been in that cozy sharing place that happens prior to going long term, he'd confessed. I'd told him that I'd lost my virginity to a frat boy whom I chose to do the honors because he put his arms around me on a balcony during a party to keep me warm. Chivalry had gotten him where no man had before. We retreated to my dorm room twin bed and he'd made me come twice while sixty-nining.

Byron had countered with his tale of debauchery in New York City. He'd bragged about the act, as if it were something he did every day. But as the story continued, I deduced that playing this way had been entirely the girl's idea. He'd simply gone along with the concept, taking down her jeans, bending her over the hotel bed, fucking her *there*. I don't actually think he enjoyed the act—too dirty for Byron, who liked things antiseptically clean, from missionary-style sex in our king-sized bed to the grout between the white tiles in the bathroom. Still, he held the experience close to his heart, like a badge of courage. It was a medal of sexual adventurousness for a Boy Scout like him.

Whenever we made love after that, I thought of the girl. She had blonde hair, cut short and spiky. She wore sunglasses even inside, and she liked to chew Double-Bubble gum. There were pictures of her in his scrapbook, black-and-white photos of her blowing bubbles, of her winking at him, of her with her hand in the belt loop of her jeans, looking oh so cocky.

What did she have to look cocky about?

Simply this: she'd had Byron in a way I couldn't.

In truth, I hadn't had sex like that with anyone. I was only nineteen. My experiences were limited. Even frat boys who are willing to sixty-nine for hours don't always broach the taboo topic of anal sex. I wished I'd done it, though. Knowing that Byron had ass-fucked someone else made me feel uneven with him, as if he were winning. As if he'd *always* be winning.

So I asked him to do it to me. To take down *my* jeans. To bend *me* over.

"Uh-uh," he said, shaking his head. "You won't like it."

Why? Why wouldn't I like it?

"It'll hurt."

"We can use K-Y."

"It's—it's dirty, Gina."

He said the word in a way that made me know he thought *dirty* was bad. But to me, the thought of getting Byron to do something dirty couldn't have been sexier. Mess him up. That's what I wanted to do. Rumple him around the edges. Untuck the hospital corners on his highly starched personality.

"Come on," I urged him. "You've done it before. You know how."

"Kiddo," he said in his most condescending voice. "Trust me. It's not for you."

Byron was nearly thirty. You'd have thought he would enjoy introducing me to new things, but aside from training me in which brands he preferred for toothpaste (Crest), mouthwash (Scope), and soap (Dial)—the types his mommy always bought— he claimed that he wasn't much of a teacher.

Yet I desired knowledge. I craved experience. Now that Byron wouldn't even consider having anal sex with me, it was all that I wanted. I started to think about my ass in a way that I never had before. To consider my behind as a sexual object in its own right.

Although I'd always been in favor of hipster panties, or (at the skimpiest) bikinis, I now bought myself a rainbow of thongs, and I twitched my ass in them when I walked, feeling that ribbon of floss tickling me with every step. Opening me up.

When I took a shower, I took great pleasure in using the pulsating massager between my rear cheeks rather than over my clit. The rush of water there had me breathless and shaking as I'd never been before. And when I touched myself solo, I'd finger my ass simultaneously, and my orgasms intensified in ways I'd never imagined. Nobody had told me. Nobody had explained.

Maybe, I thought, Byron needed to see what it would feel like. Maybe nobody had told *him*, either. The next time we made love, I tried to touch him back there, but he swatted my hand away, and the lovemaking stopped abruptly. How could I consider that? How could I dream he'd be into *that*? When I went down on him soon after, something he *did* like, I tried accidentally-on-purpose to kiss him back there, slipping lower between his legs than normal, but he pulled me back up to his cock, horrified that I would even consider rimming him.

The more he denied me, the more I craved what I couldn't have.

How strange that something I'd never known I wanted now consumed me. I dreamed about him taking my ass. I wanted him to pound into me. I felt as if I were on fire all the time, felt as if the curves of my ass were a beacon, a neon sign, pulsing. Throbbing. And was I just imagining things, or were other people suddenly realizing how cool my ass was? I wore tighter jeans. I wore shorter, flirtier skirts. Byron's best friend, Joshua, seemed to notice. On a day when I wore Daisy Duke cutoffs, he couldn't keep his eyes off me. But Byron was oblivious.

I was determined to wake him up.

Whenever I felt the mood was right, I'd try to perk Byron up to the concept. I'd ask him to play with me the way he'd played with Vacation Girl, the trippy little blonde-haired minx in the Vuarnet shades who'd let him take her from behind.

But what did I know? Maybe she'd taken *him*. Maybe she'd fucked him from below.

"Come on," I begged yet again one evening after a party. We were both tipsy, but I acted a little more drunk than I really felt. "Come on, Byron, let's try it."

By then he knew exactly what I meant. We'd had this conversation often enough for him to know what "it" was. His face squinched up. He shook his head. He looked as if he'd just taken a bite of something rotten.

"I want to," I told him, giving him my most desirous look. Lashes fluttering. Bottom lip in a bitable pout.

"No," he said, in a tone that let me know he was gearing up for a fight. "No way."

Although I hadn't given the concept of anal sex much thought before Byron and I got together, now I had discovered that I really *did* want it. Men had been complimenting my ass for years. Since high school, even. Boys who suddenly realized that they weren't breast men, but ass men, took an extra look at my derriere when I walked by. Did anything come between me and *my* Calvins? That's what the boys wanted to know. Byron had that ass in his very own bed, and he wouldn't glance at it twice.

How crazy it is that I begged. How pathetic that I had to go that low.

He'd fucked *her* that way. It was all I could think about. *She* got him to do it. She wouldn't take no for an answer.

I got drunk again. Drunker this time. But I was prepared. I'd purchased a bottle of glistening lube. I unfurled a fresh towel and spread the blue terry cloth out on the bed while Byron was in the adjoining bathroom, brushing his teeth. My body, ass included, was squeaky clean from a shower. I was Crested, Scoped, and Dialed, as tempting as I could possibly manage. Somewhere in the back of my head, I knew that most men would have dived at the opportunity of doing me the way I craved. Young chicklet on the bed, ass up, ready for sex.

Byron said no.

He didn't want to do the act with the girl he would marry. That's what it all came down to. He tried to make it seem as if he were sparing *me* an indignity. Really, I could tell the truth was a different story entirely. I wasn't worth it. The fight that followed was groundbreaking. Byron didn't like me arguing with him about anything, and he punished me by leaving the apartment, storming out to have a cool-down walk in the night air.

All by myself, and drunker still, I looked at the photos from his vacation in New York, the one he'd gone on with Joshua after finishing graduate school. The one where he'd met the girl. I saw her gazing from under her shades, saw her daring me.

I took that dare.

What I did was indefensible. What I did was wrong, wrong, wrong. What I did wasn't actually a *what* but a *who*—Joshua Sparks, Byron's best friend.

I didn't start up with the "fuck my ass" request immediately. I simply began responding to the flirtatiousness in Josh's dark brown eyes whenever we were together. I held his interested stare a beat too long. Whenever we talked, I put my hand on his shoulder, or thigh, or the inside of his wrist. At parties, I stood too close. At dinners, I always sat across from him, and my stockinged toes did naughty things between his legs under the table.

Josh started calling when he knew Byron wasn't going to be around. "Hey, Gina, is Byron there?"

"No, Josh."

"Good—"

He wanted me to talk dirty to him when he was at work. "Tell me what you want," he'd demand. "Tell me everything."

"You first," I'd counter.

He wanted me to watch him jerk off.

I could do that.

He wanted me to give him a blowjob in his car, during rush hour.

I could do that, too.

He wanted me every which way he could get me. At least, that's what he promised. "Every which way—and then all those ways again."

But would he fulfill my one true desire? That was the question. Or would he make me beg the way I had begged Byron, my fingers on the split of my ass, ready to open myself up to him? Would he make me beg, and then reject me? I didn't think I could handle that.

When Josh and I finally got together after all those months of dancing around the issue, I didn't know how to ask. I simply rolled over in bed and bumped him from behind.

"Byron won't," I told him. "I've asked, and he won't."

"Why not?" His strong fingertips lingered between my asscheeks. He touched me more firmly and I shuddered all over. "Why, Gina?" I looked at my ring, glinting at me accusingly from the bedside table. I looked over my shoulder at Josh. "Why do you want to so bad?" he asked, amending his original question.

"Because he won't." I'd built the act into something else in my mind. A super hurdle. Something to overcome.

Josh didn't want me to see it like that. He wanted me not to get over it, but to revel in every single second. He didn't want me to beg him to fuck my ass, he wanted me to beg him not to stop. He explained this to me as he touched my naked skin, humbling me with the sensation of his fingers spreading me apart. Making my heart race faster as he inspected me. And suddenly I didn't want him to fuck me there just because Byron wouldn't. I wanted him to fuck my ass because I needed him to. I wanted him to drive inside of me, to make me scream, to make me feel as if he were fucking me all the way through my body.

Josh knew what he was doing. There was plenty of lube and there was lots of stroking. He slid in one finger. Then two.

"Oh, yes," I sighed. "Oh, Josh."

He finger-fucked my ass as he rubbed my clit with his free hand. My body responded instantly. I felt the wetness spreading down my legs as my pussy grew steadily more aroused. He dribbled the shivery cold lube down the split between my cheeks until it rained onto the crisp sheets. He made me come before he even brought his cock to my hole. He made me come again with only the very head of it inside of me.

"Oh, god," I murmured, undone by the feeling. "Oh, fucking god—"

He kissed the back of my neck as he worked me, and when he slid in all the way, I bit into the pillow and cried.

Byron was wrong. Yeah, it hurt, but it hurt in the best way possible. It hurt like nothing else ever had, and the pleasure of being filled was like no other experience. I didn't want it to stop. I didn't want it to end.

I thought about Byron denying me this. I thought about the spiky-haired blonde and her "I dare you" stare. And then I came again, as the diamonds made dizzy, drunken rainbows from my knockoff ring on the bedside table.

I tried to make myself feel bad for leaving Byron. I told myself I ought to have at least a twinge of guilty conscience over it. But the truth is this: he simply wasn't worth it.

MERCY

A. D. R. Forte

Picture the cast of characters: Rhys—dark hair just a little too long at the neck, tie loosened slightly because it's hot here at the hotel bar, pretty-boy mouth set in that unintentional but totally fuckable pout so at odds with his seriousness; Kyle—half a head taller than every man in the room, blue eyes, wearing the power suit to end all power suits; charisma and control in different ways.

And me staring at both of them over my glass of cabernet, my mind so deep in the gutter I'm afraid I'll need scuba gear to find it and drag it out again. Although with men like these to look at, why would I want it out of the gutter?

Tonight at least Rhys is smiling, glowing with success over his promotion. Between the three of us, we've polished off one bottle of cabernet already and we're almost through with the second. Kyle is telling us a story from a past life—this one about catching a couple of employees in the act, and how we ended up on the topic I'll never know, but I love it. Rhys's face is red; he's trying not to glance my way as Kyle foreshadows the denouement; failing because I'm sitting right at his elbow and he has to be able to feel the heat of my body.

"So we finally use the manual override to unstick the dock door, get the damn thing open and I go over to the control room."

Kyle pauses to take a sip of wine and chuckle before he goes on.

"And mind you, there's half the night crew and the entire morning crew standing there. So I open the door and there's this girl with her big, juicy ass—forgive me Lauren—her ass propped right on top of the dock controls and one of the techs is just bangin' the hell out of her."

Kyle pauses for dramatic effect before delivering the punch line with a wicked grin, and Rhys's face is redder than the wine stain on his napkin.

"And so while I'm standing there trying my damnedest not to laugh, one of my crew supervisors looks around my shoulder and goes 'Guess we weren't the only ones tryin' to deliver a load.' "

"Wh...what did you do?" I ask, when I can stop laughing long enough to breathe and wipe my eyes. Rhys still can't talk, but damn he's irresistible when he relaxes that adamantine composure and laughs. I want him like that; without restraint.

Kyle shrugs. "Suspended them both for a week. I figured the embarrassment was punishment enough."

"You're the very soul of understanding, Kyle."

He meets my gaze across the table and grins. "I always try to take care of my people," he says, and it's my turn to blush.

How well I know. Kyle plays the VP part so well it's enough to make you cry. He says all the right things and none of the wrong ones. When he took the job a year ago, Rhys sang his praises almost daily: Kyle was the best we'd ever worked for; he was who Rhys wanted to be in ten years. I listened and smiled, and since our fearless leader didn't raise any eyebrows, I just agreed with Rhys. Thought nothing of it.

Until a certain party the October after he started with the firm. At first, I didn't even recognize him. That could have been partly due to the leather mask, but Kyle has an unmistakable voice. Like Rhys's voice, it's deep and rich, but his inflections are lazier, Southern, educated. He can captivate listeners when he talks, whole boardrooms and conference rooms of them.

So when I overheard him talking, I almost choked on my egg roll and had to put it down and turn.

"Kyle?"

"Lauren?"

We stared at each other through our masks for a few awkward seconds. Then it hit us; we were both equally compromised by being there. Or equally matched; whichever way you want to look at it. I think we were both simply surprised at the meeting. I laughed and took his arm. He admired my dress, cut low to the waist as it was. I admired his leather trousers and boots. We danced and drank lots of wine and by the end of the night, I knew the stuff our VP was really made of. It was all hard and male and utterly, completely depraved.

He left the hotel room before I woke up, but on Monday morning there were red roses on my desk when I got to work, the card unsigned. He never said anything, and I had to respect the man for sheer class...and for other things. We never so much as hinted at it however, until the day he caught me staring at Rhys with hopeless longing on my face. Desire so naked there was no denying it. Kyle had lifted his eyebrows and I'd blushed.

"Is that what you want?" he'd asked later the same afternoon, and I nodded.

I've wanted for three years, but Rhys has old-fashioned notions of honor. We had coffee on the very first day we met; friendship was a given. He let me be his confidante, he let me into his world, but ultimately he told me no. Told me he wanted me more than he'd ever wanted anything in his life, but he didn't dare. "What if?" he said. "What if it turns into more than one night?"

I didn't have an answer.

I think he's read far too many historical novels or maybe played too much D&D. It adds to his charm, the way he strives to live by his code of lawful good no matter what, all the while looking just like a fantasy slut out of any girl's wet dream. Me, on the other hand, I just want what I want, and Rhys's recalcitrance does me no good. So when Kyle said he would think of something, I chose to believe him. Working together, Kyle and I are capable of plenty, both in the office and out of it.

"Well I don't think I've got anything to top your story," I say now, reaching for the wine bottle to refill all our glasses. "The most interesting one I can think of was the time we found two guys in the exercise room shower 'working off some steam.' "

I catch Rhys's gaze and smile. "I was actually sorry to have to break that one up. It was worth watching."

He looks away quickly and takes a swallow of his cabernet.

"And what did you do?" he asks.

I shrug. "One was a team supervisor so I had to let him go."

"No mercy from Lady Lauren," Kyle teases.

I grin and lean back, and with my jacket off, my silk power-blue shirt pulls tight against my chest and the lacy bra beneath. Rhys turns to me, serious as always, but the alcohol has done its job. He looks and looks and doesn't look away. Across the table Kyle shifts, and as I meet his gaze an unspoken message passes between us. My heart starts to beat a little faster.

"No, no mercy whatsoever," I say.

When the bar closes an hour later, we grumble and whine and polish off whatever's left in bottle number three.

"I'm so not ready for bed yet," I say.

"Neither am I," adds Kyle. "We need a nightcap."

"Champagne to celebrate," I suggest, and Kyle nods.

"Perfect." He turns to the bartender and asks him to put the order through to room service. A bottle of the good stuff to his suite.

Rhys looks from one of us to the other and shakes his head. Maybe some instinct warns him.

"You guys are kidding right?"

"No we aren't. We haven't properly celebrated you tonight," I say.

Kyle agrees as he turns back to us, ignoring Rhys's token protest that it really isn't necessary.

"So...my room?" he says. "You okay with that Lauren?"

Smartass.

"I think I'll be fine with that."

I take Rhys's arm.

"Come on, you don't need sleep. The night is still young."

He laughs as we leave the bar. He doesn't resist.

Kyle closes the door behind the bellboy and holds up the bottle with a smile.

"Champagne. Lauren"—his gaze moves down my torso—"maybe you'd do the honors for us?"

I guess his intent and my heart starts racing again.

"Absolutely."

While he goes to work on the cork, I stand up. I start with my pants and Rhys, sitting across the room flipping through a magazine, glances up and freezes like a trapped deer. He looks at Kyle who is busy with the champagne bottle and then his gaze swings back to me in disbelief.

My shoes aren't particularly sexy, sensible work pumps with three-inch heels, but I slip them back on after I wriggle out of pants and trouser socks. I keep them on as I slide my panties down my legs and take those off one leg at a time. Rhys's lips are parted. He watches silently, holding the magazine strategically in place while I take my shirt off. Then my bra. And I see him take a deep, slow breath.

"Perfect." I turn to find Kyle looking me over with an approving smile. "Now your hair," he adds.

I pull the clips out; tousle my curls a little as they fall free.

"Messy enough for you?" I ask, looking sideways at Kyle, and he laughs.

"Actually, I'd prefer it just a little messier." His gaze goes to my crotch and I nod.

Smiling at Rhys, who hasn't moved a muscle, I sit on the edge of the coffee table, legs apart, one hand behind me for balance.

"Kyle likes me messy, Rhys." I run my hand down my stomach, between my legs. "How would you like me?"

He shakes his head slowly, side to side. Incredulous. In denial. This can't be happening; I can't be doing this and he can't, shouldn't, mustn't look. But I see him giving up his good intentions, and I smile as I spread my legs a little wider.

My pussy lips are already wet with need as I slide two fingers between them and trail glistening moisture up over the soft, shaved flesh, up over my bare mound. My clit tingles at the touch, wanting more, and Rhys swallows. I watch his face, imagining how hard he is behind that magazine, under those microfiber slacks, and I tease my clit, rubbing it between the sheltering folds to either side so that my touch is diminished and I'm even more frustrated. So that I'm even wetter.

Kyle has stopped fiddling with the bottle entirely, watching too now as my fingers enter my soaking pussy. My muscles clench around them and I rub hard, moaning as sweet pressure fills my cunt. I lean my head back and arch my hips upward, the wet sound of my fingers moving inside me filling the room. I don't think my gorgeous boys can so much as remember how to breathe. Even Kyle's never seen me this way; this wanton and hungry for release.

I'm so hot. I'm burning up. I'm so close and I need to come, but I stop. Panting. Straining to resist the insistent throbbing between my legs, I draw my fingers up to my chest. I rub my juices all over my hard nipples and then look at Kyle, waiting.

He fumbles into action, popping the cork on the champagne and looking at me with a dirty, dirty smile as white fizz cascades down the side of the bottle. I smile and lean farther back on the coffee table. Kyle beckons Rhys over and like a sleepwalker, a man in a dream, he stands and walks over to the table.

"Ever done a champagne body shot?" Kyle asks. Rhys doesn't take his eyes off me as he shakes his head. Standing above me, he shrugs his jacket off and I see a glint in his eyes that I've never seen before.

"Never," he replies. "But that's about to change."

He smiles as he takes the bottle from Kyle and leans down, and I'm mesmerized by that smile; distracted by this new, intense, lustful Rhys. I gasp when the cold liquid hits my navel and trickles down my belly, but a second later Rhys's mouth is moving hotly down my skin, sucking and licking, stopping just before his lips touch the sensitive folds of my pussy.

I whimper in frustration, but it's Kyle's turn. He lowers me to my elbows, stretching me out across the table while he pours and licks his shot from between my breasts. Licking all around my soft curves without so much as brushing against my aching nipples.

I hate them both.

"Your turn," Kyle laughs. He's unzipping his pants, and I sit up, but I feel Rhys's hands on my waist pulling me backward. "Up on your knees," he whispers against my neck. I look over my shoulder to see him on the other side of the coffee table. His tie is gone, the first three buttons of his shirt are undone, and the glint in his eyes is brighter, wilder, more arousing than ever.

I'm shivering a little as I kneel and turn to face Kyle again. He's waiting, lazily stroking his long erection and watching me. I open my lips an inch from his magnificent cock, and he pours the shot for me. My timing is near perfect; only a few drops spill to the carpet. I catch the rest in my mouth and suck it all down, suck it off his warm hardness, and he groans. Closes his eyes.

Still sucking on Kyle, I see Rhys take the bottle from him. When cold drops hit my back and run down between my asscheeks I gasp, choking on Kyle's dick as Rhys sucks all the way down my back, biting the tender flesh on the undersides of my ass, and I moan my appreciation as he spreads my cheeks. Rhys's tongue flicks back and forth over my clit, his face pressed into my cunt and ass, and I taste Kyle's precome, salty on my tongue. I suck greedily at him, loving his taste, but he pulls out of my mouth and I look up, confused.

He pinches my cheek and mouths the words "bad girl" as he kneels so that his head is level with my chest. Then he drapes my arms over his shoulders so that I can support myself as he and Rhys suck and fondle my soft flesh. Making me moan and whimper. Making warm wetness trickle down my legs as their fingers and tongues roll and twist my nipples, invade my pussy. As their male kisses and rough male hands cover my skin, back and arms and thighs and belly.

I feel their tongues lapping at my clit, twisting over each other in their eagerness to drive me insane and I wonder how much it turns them on. I know Kyle's tastes; but I know Rhys would never, ever admit such desire in a million years. Yet here he is, swapping spit and pussy juice with another man.

And thinking of how far he's fallen, how much we've already corrupted him, is the last straw. My pussy tightens around Rhys's finger and I grip Kyle's shoulders hard, my knees pressing painfully into the table surface as I come; sweet, messy and sticky enough for even Kyle.

Every girl should be this lucky.

Rhys is the one to scoop me up and take me to the bed. He strips naked while I finger my still-throbbing clit, and then he bends over me, his lovely mouth open and hungry to kiss me as he parts my legs, pushing my hand away and urging the head of his thick cock against my wet opening. I squirm and arch under him, wanting to fill every inch of my pussy with his hardness, squeezing him tight as he thrusts against my aroused flesh, and over his shoulder I smile at his boss. My boss. My partner in crime.

I see Kyle, naked now, putting his own condom on and I know what comes next.

Thrilled with anticipation, wanting it because it's my pleasure as much as his, I watch him slather lube across his cock and then reach out for our beautiful boy's ass. My own buttocks tighten as Rhys's whole body goes tense and he falters, almost pulling away. But I'm looking into his eyes; I won't let his gaze slip away. I run my fingers through his hair and press my hips up into his while Kyle presses his erection to his ass, and Rhys knows he's trapped.

But then he's known it all along, somewhere deep inside. He is one of us after all.

Kyle works a lube-covered finger into him and Rhys closes his eyes, shaking his head. Willing this not to happen. I'm thrusting gently upward under him, kissing his lips, his cheeks. Comforting him with my femininity. And he protests, but he knows it's futile.

He's saying 'No' but Kyle's dick is widening his hole, easing into him. Waiting while he tenses, and then moving again as his terrified muscles relax. I can feel every thrust with our bodies joined like this—Rhys inside of me, Kyle fucking me by proxy— and my pussy responds. I'm still wet and soft and Rhys is still hard. Even though he doesn't want to be.

The tears only escape when the head of Kyle's dick slips full into him and Kyle's length follows. All the way in. He groans and his cock spasms in me, but I lick the salt from his perfect cheekbones. I tell him he's gorgeous and that I love this, as I rub the droplets of sweat and tears on my breasts into my skin. Playing with his nipples; wriggling under him; and his cock, on the verge of going limp, becomes hard again.

Driven by Kyle's rhythm, he starts to thrust into me. His own body takes over, needing more, and I see the confusion tinted with shame on his face as he fucks me. Loving the sensation of fucking me, and being fucked. Loving the soft, sensual pleasure and the brutal pain. Hating himself for it. We kiss his shame away. Kyle runs his fingers through his hair and kisses the back of his neck. I prop myself up on my elbows to tease his lips with my own, and finally, although he's still hurting, he manages a smile.

The force of his thrusts changes. That glint in his beautiful eyes again, he presses me back into the bed and grabs my hips. Holds me in place as he takes his pleasure, and I struggle for air, the breath knocked from me by the double force of their bodies and my muscles clenching hard around his cock. I wrap my hands around his neck and Kyle leans down to suck on my fingers as he fucks both of us. As Rhys pounds into my tight pussy and has his perfect ass rammed in turn. And I've never ever known anything like this before.

I'm moaning and grinding against Rhys; so wet I can barely feel him except for the driving pressure on my clit and in my aching pussy and I don't know where my orgasms start or end. I just know I'm digging my nails into Rhys's back and my fingers hurt, and he's coming, screaming raw and tortured and in ecstasy, his face buried against my neck. Kyle's weight crushing him into me as Kyle fucks him hard, harder. Kyle's face in Rhys's hair as he comes with a desperate cry of his own, his legs tangled with mine, his chest pinning my hands to Rhys's back. Sweet, passionate chaos.

And I think *No, no mercy whatsoever.*

We don't talk about it on Monday morning—and we won't ever talk about it—that's out of the question. But there are two sets of red roses waiting on my desk, both without cards.

WET

Donna George Storey

I'll be honest. I like my sex a little rough. And very wet. Sure, I started out like most women, wanting valentines and sweet words, but all along I was waiting for the right moment, that perfect slap on the ass, to teach me what I really needed. For me, enlightenment came the year after college, when I taught English in Japan—a country that understands pleasure is always sweeter when it comes with a little suffering.

My first months in Kyoto brought hardship aplenty. I'd found myself a one-room apartment above a rice shop in a farming village west of the city. At about forty bucks a month, the rent was right, but the room was so cold I could see my breath when I woke up in the morning. Then I had to stumble outside to the toilet, a squat-style affair located by the stairwell. A bath required a ten-minute walk through the rice paddies to the *sentô*. A long soak in the huge tub was pure luxury, but first I had to endure the gaze of the creepy attendant who watched me undress from his pulpitlike platform with shameless curiosity.

Sometimes I wonder how I put up with it all, but at twenty-two I was a romantic and more than ready to renounce the comforts of my wall-to-wall-carpet childhood for the sake of intercultural understanding. Indeed, each hardship gave me a voluptuous thrill, as if I were sinking deeper into the embrace of a stern and exacting lover.

But the public bath had its pleasures, too. Beyond the frigid dressing room lay a tropical paradise of gleaming white tile. A semicircular tub the size of a small hotel pool filled the entire left half of the bathing room. To the right was a row of faucets, where a line of nude women knelt as if in worship, legs tucked beneath them, their heart-shaped asses resting on their feet, Japanese-style. Sometimes I couldn't help imagining how jealous my male friends back home would be. Wasn't it every hot guy's fantasy to be surrounded by naked women caressing their own bodies with soapy-slick hands, eyes closed and lips parted in pleasure?

I wasn't supposed to have such thoughts in this temple of bodily purification. Bathing was obviously serious business in Japan. I quickly got the basics down, but as I took my place at an empty faucet each night, I still cast sideways glances at my companions for tips on the proper technique. I noticed that they always sloshed a basinful of hot water over their backs and chests, and then went to work with the soap and washcloth, scrubbing each inch of skin with almost religious zeal. Although I tried my best to polish each knee for what seemed like an hour, I could never outlast them.

What filthy things had these prim ladies done to get their bodies so dirty?

This was only one of the forbidden thoughts that swirled through my brain as I sank into the soaking tub at last, my muscles melting to caramel in the steaming water. More distracting still were the sounds drifting over the partition from the men's side of the bath. I tried to keep my thoughts clean, but with all the splashes and sighs and deep male voices gliding through the mist, it was pretty hopeless.

Of course I knew most of those low, sexy voices belonged to farmers I'd seen working in the rice paddies, their faces wizened and brown from decades of hard labor. They were hardly fodder for sexual fantasy. Still at least one or two of the guys had to be acceptably young and attractive. Maybe it was the gorgeous college boy I spotted on the train platform each morning? Or the young office worker with the velvety eyes who kept glancing shyly in my direction at the convenience store?

Before long I was dizzy from the heat, the steam, the X-rated images flickering in my head. I closed my eyes and felt the pulsing water caress my flesh like a warm hand, felt my other lips, down there, plump and ready for him, my lover, so handsome and willing to do every dirty thing I could imagine. Those hungry lips would call to him, silently, through the moist, dripping air.

Come. Teach me. Please.

He rises from the tub, the water falling from his sculpted torso like a veil, and crosses over to the women's side of the bath, heedless of the attendant's jealous scowl. Intent on his goal, he slides the door open and strides right in, although he does hold his towel discreetly over his cock in deference to the other ladies. They titter and hurry to cover themselves with their hands, but he doesn't even glance their way.

He's come only for me.

"Get out of the bath," he orders in gruff Japanese. "You're still dirty. Obviously you need a lesson on how to wash properly."

Heart pounding, I climb out of the water and kneel at the closest faucet, my head bowed.

I know I am a very dirty girl, indeed.

The teacher snaps my washcloth open like a whip and soaps

it to a lather. The first part of the curriculum involves scrubbing my back vigorously from my shoulders to my buttocks. Each stroke finds an answering twinge in my belly. My pale skin is already flushed from the hot bath, but under his scouring, my flesh blushes to a fiery hue. I am red and wet down there, too, because I can feel my own pussy juice oozing onto my legs. When the teacher reaches my hips, he lays the cloth aside and gives my ass a good kneading with his bare hands, then finishes with a stinging slap, one for each cheek.

The spanking shoots up my spine like an electric shock. I can't restrain a low moan, pain mixed with desire.

"I see you're enjoying the lesson," he observes coolly, "but you have much study ahead. I'm going to wash the front of you now, but first you must sit up like a proper Japanese lady. Come now, shoulders back, chin up."

Obediently I square my hunched shoulders, but keep my arms crossed modestly over my chest. Clicking his tongue, the teacher reaches around and grabs my wrists, pulling them apart to reveal my breasts, shimmering with a film of moisture, the nipples pink and erect.

"Let me clean you," he murmurs. "Let me show you how to do it right."

He cups my breasts in his soapy hands and rubs me, circling round and round as if he's polishing two plump apples. My nipples, it seems, are especially filthy for he rolls them between his fingers for the longest time, pinching and tweaking until I'm nearly sobbing with lust. Through half-veiled eyes, I notice the women have gathered around us, their eyes glued to the obscene show. Some even caress their own breasts, mimicking the teacher's movements.

"Now I want you to lie back and spread your legs. I know you need a very good scrubbing down there."

What else can I do but obey? Though I've always been a good student, always gone for that *A*, I have to admit my desire to please the teacher has never been this strong.

Easing back onto the cool tile, I inch my legs open.

Look how pink and swollen it is! It's as juicy as a ripe peach! She is dirty, just like the teacher said....

A chorus of female voices echoes through the steam. Flustered and ashamed, I snap my legs closed.

"No chatter during class time, ladies," the teacher warns sternly. "You there and you, make yourself useful. Hold her legs open so we can continue with our study."

Two pairs of soft hands force my knees open and press them to the floor.

"Would you like the washcloth now, Sensei?" the woman at my right leg asks respectfully.

"No," the teacher replies, "there are too many delicate folds down there for a cloth to get clean. For this part of the lesson, I must use my tongue."

He bends over and gives my swollen slit one lingering lick, like a cat, followed by delicate, probing flicks as he seeks my sweet spot. The way I arch and whimper tells him that he's found it. He cleans me there—the strokes quickening to a lashing—until I groan and thrash against the hands of my captors. I'm just about to come when he pulls away. "Time to rinse."

Before I can protest that perhaps the Honorable Teacher might consider cleaning me like that just a little longer, my exposed pussy is flooded with a basinful of hot water. Tendrils of flame shoot through my belly and I squirm, my body sloshing about on the slick floor.

The teacher seems pleased with my progress, but we have one final lesson.

"It's time to clean you inside now." Grinning, he begins to

soap up his cock, his member growing longer and fatter with every stroke. In the end he is huge, as thick as a young tree trunk, plump purple veins throbbing through the flesh. It's a dick straight out of a floating world print.

"I don't think I can take that thing inside me," I plead, staring at his cock with undisguised horror.

"Even if something is hard," he intones wisely, "you can succeed if you want it very much and you try your best."

I breathe deeply, preparing myself for the ordeal to come. I do want this—very much.

He nods to his assistants who lock their hands under my ass and tilt my hips up to meet him. Nudging my hole gently with the head of his cock, he pushes in with aching slowness.

I can feel him all the way up through my chest, my neck, and my skull. I've never felt so stretched, so full. My teacher begins to move, swiveling his hips to scour and polish every inch of my insides with his rigid tool. Feminine murmurs of approval and envy rise up around me. I open my eyes to see the other women kneeling closer, their eyes fixed on the place where his cock enters my body. I see, too, that they are masturbating as they watch us. The shy ones rub their washcloths between their legs tentatively, as if it's all just part of an ordinary bath. The bolder ones dispense with pretence, their fingers dancing shamelessly over their slits. One lady is even brazen enough to tweak her neighbor's nipple while she strums herself.

I see it all now, everything. We're all dirty. We all want to cleanse ourselves. And this is Japan, where a group effort always gets the job done best. As if they've read my thoughts, the lady on my right begins to stroke my breast; from the left comes a tongue to tease my other nipple. Lips close over mine from above, female lips, meltingly soft. Flesh envelops me everywhere, pulsing with desire, lapping, sucking, pounding into me deeper and harder, until with a cry of release, I am finally clean. And all thanks to his lesson—a little rough, very wet, and just the way I like it.

As I strolled home from the *sentô* in the moonlight, my flesh still warm and tingling, I knew the chances were slim I'd ever really find myself in the middle of an orgy in a public bath. On the other hand, it was reasonably likely that some day I'd meet an attractive young man who'd be willing to give me a hands-on lesson in Japanese bathing techniques.

In fact, my wish did come true in a peculiarly Japanese way— through an introduction by a go-between, like the marriage meetings of old. Early in the new year, I started a teaching job at a pharmaceutical factory in Shiga. The friendly in-house teacher, Sherry, immediately took me under her wing. She was already engaged to a Japanese guy she'd met in the States and was all for setting me up with someone, too. It just so happened she knew the perfect guy, a Mr. Yamada who worked in the main office in Osaka.

Sherry ran down his vital statistics. Mr. Yamada was twenty-six, went to a good college and had his own apartment. (I imagined his bathroom, small but with a luxurious cedar tub and a traditional lantern in the corner, glowing softly.) He was good looking and stockier than most Japanese. (A nice broad saddle would be a plus when I got on top and rode him to a lather.) His English was pretty good. (Not a minus, but how much talking would we do anyway?) And he'd traveled to Europe on his own, not in a tour group. (This showed a hunger for adventure that would surely translate well into wild moves on a slippery bathroom floor.)

"How soon can we meet?" I asked her without missing a beat.

That's how I found myself in a fancy café, gazing into the

eyes of the fetching Mr. Yamada and wondering how many more formalities we had to endure until we could get naked and rub our soapy bodies together. Mr. Yamada was apparently more patient than I was, but he seemed to have similar ideas because three dates later, he invited me to his place.

The first thing I asked for was a tour—an American custom, I explained. His apartment was very different from mine, with all the modern comforts. An electric heater purred softly in the corner, chasing back the February chill. The dining-kitchen had a Western-style table and chairs; the bedroom was equipped with a bed and dresser. Even the traditional *tatami* straw-matted living room was transformed into a high-tech wonderland by an elaborate entertainment system spread out along three walls.

"Would it be too rude if I asked to see your bath? They're so different from what we have in America."

"Of course," he said in his careful English, slightly baffled by the request, but eager to accommodate the foreign guest's wishes.

He led me over to a door next to the bedroom and pushed it open.

My heart sank.

I was expecting it to be small, but I hadn't imagined something this distressingly modern: an all-in-one cubicle fashioned from a seamless expanse of beige plastic. The toilet, sink and shower bath were crammed together so tightly that if we tried to play out my bathing teacher fantasy, we'd be knocking our heads against the john.

"Thanks, it's very nice." I stepped back, forcing my lips into a smile.

Mr. Yamada sensed he'd disappointed me. "Shall we drink coffee? I bought apple pie at the bakery. I hear Americans like such things."

I nodded, blushing at my own selfishness. The kind invitation to his home was my chance to learn more about him as a person, not lure him into some kinky sex game I'd dreamed up to get myself off on lonely nights in my futon. I silently vowed to be the perfect guest for the rest of the visit, pure in thought and deed.

I was doing a fairly good job of it as we lounged on floor pillows on the *tatami* listening to jazz and snacking on apple tart. But then Mr. Yamada put down his coffee cup, gazed into my eyes, and leaned over to kiss me.

At first all he did was kiss me, for the longest time, as if some secret rule of etiquette dictated a good host could go no farther on the first visit. Yet the languid dance of our tongues was having a surprisingly powerful effect on my body, rather like a soaking in a hot bath. Soon every muscle was so soft and rubbery that I collapsed onto the pillow, pulling him down with me.

Now he did use his hands, gently stroking my cheek, my neck, my breasts, and especially my nipples poking up stiffly through my sweater. The fluid warmth, the exquisite care in his touch got me so turned on, my panties were drenched. I feared I'd be leaving quite a wet spot on his pristine straw mat.

"I want you," I whispered.

He smiled and pulled a box of tissues and a condom from the nearby bookshelf—how courteous of him to anticipate his guest's needs before the fact—then undressed us both quickly. He lay back and I straddled him. I was ready to slide right on, but to my surprise he grabbed my hips and pulled me forward so my dripping pussy rested on his taut belly. Instinctively I rocked into him, coating him with my juices. Our bodies made soft sucking sounds as I glided over him, almost as if we were all soaped together in a steamy *sentô*.

Mr. Yamada seemed perfectly content to let me massage

him with my drooling pussy all afternoon. I was the one who finally lost patience. Rising up on my knees, I shifted backward, impaling myself on his cock. The seawater smell of female arousal mingled with the sweet, grassy fragrance of *tatami* straw. I realized, with a delicious twinge of guilt, that I'd been a very bad girl this afternoon. Because I hadn't really given up my selfish fantasy at all. I was reaching out for it, hungrily, in all its liquid pleasure. Hotter and wetter than I'd even imagined, it was almost in my grasp.

By cherry blossom time I was spending every weekend at Mr. Yamada's apartment—I was calling him Shinji now—and the sex just kept getting wetter and better. We hadn't yet taken a real bath together, but I did confess that I liked going to the *sentô*. My fondness for old-fashioned Japanese things always amused him. He laughed and told me that his grandmother still went to the public bath, but young people only did that on vacation at a hot spring in the mountains or an inn by the sea.

"Is that so?" I replied with an innocent smile.

Naturally, from that moment on, my mind was busy spinning out a naughty scheme. Shinji was so sweet about going along with my every whim; I knew he'd easily agree to a weekend at a mountain spa with a rustic coed bath. But I wasn't so sure about the rough stuff I secretly craved—the gruff orders, the spanking, the sweet humiliations. On the other hand, Japanese men were historically known for their lordly, selfish ways and a rather domineering treatment of the fair sex. Perhaps taking Shinji to a traditional mountain inn would allow him to tap into his inner samurai?

I figured it wouldn't hurt to do what I could to nudge him in that direction.

After all, the hot spring was almost a national institution of sensual indulgence. For hardworking Japanese, it provided the perfect chance to shrug off the rules of ordinary life by dining on elaborate gourmet meals in their bathrobes, taking endless baths and, ideally, fucking as much as possible. As soon as we got to the inn, Shinji did suddenly seem more intent on hedonistic pleasure. After our nine-course dinner of fish stew, Kobe beef dripping with butter, and fluffy white rice served with jewel-colored pickles, he claimed he was still hungry. He proceeded to push me back on the futon, spread my thighs and feast on my pussy. When he had me so hot I was begging for it, he flipped me over and took me from behind, slamming his cock into me with uncharacteristic abandon. I came so hard, I wondered if I'd be physically capable of getting off again down in the bath, which of course was the intended climax of the trip from the start.

I hadn't told Shinji the details of my plan yet. I merely suggested, with a twinkle in my eye, that we go for one last soak together before we went to sleep.

The grand bath was deserted when we arrived, just as I had hoped, although in theory, a few willing lesbians would have made for the perfect translation of my fantasy. Still, I couldn't have ordered a more beautiful scene. The water was as smooth as glass; wisps of steam hovered like specters in the golden light of the lanterns glowing in each corner of the room.

Shinji shrugged off his cotton robe and went to the faucet to wash off the lingering stickiness of our lovemaking.

Smiling devilishly, I headed straight for the tub.

"Aren't you going to wash first?" he called after me.

I turned and gave him a bratty smirk. "What if I don't want to?"

"You must." He usually laughed at my lapses of etiquette, but this taboo was too strong for the usual indulgence.

I held my foot over the water as if I were about to step in. "I guess I am pretty dirty after what we did tonight, but I'm just not in the mood to do it."

He frowned. For the first time, I think he was truly angry with me.

"In Japan, you must wash before you get in the bath. It is the proper way."

"Oh, yeah? Well maybe you'll just have to teach me how to do it right."

His frown deepened. I met his gaze defiantly. Then I smiled.

His eyes flickered. I think that's when he finally got it, because in two long strides he was at my side, grabbing my arm and hauling me back to the faucet. With a downward tug, he forced me to my knees. He quickly filled the wooden basin with steaming water and splashed it over my chest and shoulders. I cried out softly. Kneeling behind me, he wrapped his arms around me, but it was more a punishment than an embrace.

I don't think I'd ever been so turned on in my life.

"I will wash you now," he whispered.

"Yes. Teach me how. I'm dirty," I confessed in a low voice. "My breasts, they're very dirty. Maybe you have to scrub hard."

"Is that so?" There was no doubt now he'd caught on to the game. "Why are they so dirty?"

"I let a man kiss them and suck them."

"Yes, then I think you are very dirty." He took the bar of soap and began to rub the flat side over my nipples. Pinpricks of pleasure shot straight to my pussy. A beguiling combination of smooth and hard, it was even better than my fantasy.

"What about between your legs?" he murmured.

"Yes. It's very dirty. I let a man...take me...from behind."

"That is dirty. Like an animal. I must clean you there very well." He picked up the washcloth, draped it over his fingers and pressed it between my pussy lips. His movements were subtle—firm, slow circles over my clit—but the flesh there was already swollen and sore from the earlier fucking. I had to grit my teeth to bear it, but I also found myself pushing into his hand with small rocking motions to intensify the sensation.

"Spread your legs a little. Now we will rinse." He took a basin of steaming water and splashed it vigorously over my slit. It streamed down my thighs, mingling with my juices. My cunt was on fire, my skin a throbbing scarlet hue. When I imagined how it would go, I was hoping this part would last an hour, but now I wanted him inside me so badly I was shaking.

"Shinji? Can we do it here? Now?"

He took me in his arms again, more tenderly, his erection pressing against the cleft of my ass. "I'm sorry. I don't have a condom."

I groaned in disappointment, but I could hardly blame him for the oversight. Still, my primitive life in the countryside had taught me I could adapt to inconvenience when I had to. "Can we go back to the room?"

He paused.

I held my breath.

"No," he barked, in a very passable impression of an imperious samurai lord.

My heart skipped a beat. It wasn't the answer I wanted. And it was.

"I am not finished washing you. This place for example. It is still very dirty." He ran his fingertip between my buttocks to tap the tight ring of my asshole, a caress that sizzled straight to my toes, my teeth, the backs of my eyeballs. This had never been part of my fantasy either—but it would be now.

"No. Stop." In my shame and surprise, the word escaped my lips before I really knew what I was saying.

"No? You don't want this?" he asked, his voice suddenly soft.

The finger pulled away.

My chest was churning with confusion, desire, regret. What did I really want? For so long I thought it was a good, hard fucking on a wet bathroom floor, but I knew now the longing went deeper. What I really wanted was for Shinji to force me to do...exactly what I wanted. Which didn't really make sense. Except here, in the humid warmth of the bath, it suddenly did.

"I do want it, Shinji. Please, clean me there."

I sighed as the finger returned, stroking and teasing my newfound pleasure button. This was exactly what I wanted. Lips grazed my neck, gliding softly over the wet skin, a tender surprise. I discovered I wanted that, too. And then—smack— another surprise, a sharp slap on my vulva, aimed just so to send waves of heat through my tingling clit.

How could it possibly get better than this?

"Yes, oh, god, yes," I moaned, jerking my hips forward to show him I was ready for more.

Shinji made a strange sound, low in his throat. The spanking quickened. On the verge of climax, a weird image flashed into my head: a woman's nude body, poised on tiptoe at the edge of a tub, one trembling foot stretching higher and farther, until she tipped over into the deep water. And then I was falling, too, a soft howl rising from my throat as I came. The spanking stopped, and Shinji held me tight in one arm, while his other hand diddled my asshole until my deepest shudders subsided.

I expected an embrace, the customary conclusion to our love-making, but tonight Shinji had other ideas. Without a word, he pushed me facedown on the wet floor and straddled my thighs. Moments later, my ass and back were showered with a spray of hot, pulsing liquid. It wasn't from a basin, that much was certain.

I hadn't planned on an ending like this, with me facedown on a bathroom floor, drenched with the spunk of my lover, who knelt over me, his dripping cock in his hand. But as with a translation, the exact expression was less important than the meaning. This was my dream come true, a scene as wet and dirty as I could ask for.

But, to be honest, I had never felt so clean.

AMY

Heidi Champa

I turned the mailbox key expectantly. I always loved getting mail. The box was full, packed with bills and junk. It was amazing what had accumulated in three days. The brown padded envelope caught my eye as I sorted through my mail. It had been a while since one had made its way to my door. I could barely think as I ran my fingers over the scratchy brown paper. My pulse raced, my heart pounding like I had been running for hours. I felt like I couldn't catch my breath. I turned the envelope over and over in my hands. It was the same as all the others, no return address, my name scrawled in your thick black writing. I could almost picture you holding the marker in your hand, a smirk on your face as you wrote my address. I pulled the envelope open, and saw the plastic case inside. The DVD was blank except for the name *Amy,* in the same black marker as the envelope. Amy. There had been Beth, Tammie and Jane. Now, it was Amy. I fumbled slightly as I set the DVD on the tray of my machine, my throat tightening with expectation. My hands shook as I pressed

PLAY and the black of my television screen suddenly erupted into color. A young blonde came into view, the camera moving erratically at first, until it stopped suddenly on a close-up of her face.

There she was: Amy. A ball gag was stretching her mouth open, little trails of slobber running onto her chin. I could almost taste the rubber on my tongue, feel the harsh pinch of its latch behind my head. Amy's black mascara had started to run down her cheeks. Her big, blue eyes pleaded with the camera lens. She had the same look on her face as all the others. I knew it well. I had worn it myself many times. I couldn't see you, but I heard your voice, running through my speakers like honey. You were asking Amy if she was ready to take her punishment. Her nodding made her small breasts sway back and forth. I heard a chuckle from you; that satisfied laugh you had perfected long ago. I shifted in my seat, as I was already wet. Amy looked into the camera, lust and anxiety mixing in her eyes. Her small hands were tied to the foot of the bed, which was dressed in familiar-looking blue sheets. If I closed my eyes, I could still feel the sheets under my knees. She was in my favorite position, the one you put me in all the time: knees spread, ass high, my ultimate submissive pose. Now it was Amy's turn to submit to you.

I recognized the room as well as I would my own. I recalled the countless hours I spent there, in front of you, and the lens of your camera. I sometimes wondered how many DVDs of me were out there, being watched by other women. How many people have sat and watched you dominate and pleasure me? The thought of it made my pussy even wetter. As much as I secretly loved watching the DVDs, knowing I had been watched was even more intense. It was comforting to know I wasn't alone in my dependence on you. How many other girls are there in the world, watching another go through the same fate as them?

I heard your hand hit Amy square on the ass almost before I

saw it. Two more blows followed immediately, the sound echoing through the little room. Her cries died quickly behind the gag, a fresh batch of tears pricking the corners of her eyes. Despite her pain, I could tell there was pleasure there too. You asked her if she wanted more. When she didn't nod fast enough for you, you grabbed her blonde hair in your fist and asked again. She nodded fervently this time and was rewarded with two more hard smacks on her already red ass. This time, her muted moans gave her away. She loved it. She wanted to tell you so, but her voice was choked off. I could make out her teeth digging into the hard rubber between her dry lips. I knew the feeling well. I had done my fair share of biting my gag too. Suddenly the camera moved, showing me that you had two fingers teasing her cunt, trying to dampen the pain with pleasure. You fucked her slowly, but hard. If I tried, I could almost feel the rough texture of your skin sliding past my wet cunt lips, the way you would twist as you forced them deeper, pressing into my G-spot with ease. It had been too long since I'd felt you like that. I missed you, even though I didn't want to. Your hold on me was still powerful, even though it was no longer physical.

Amy must have been getting the same treatment from you, as her cries of pain had turned into muffled squeals and moans. I could hear how wet she was every time your fingers came out of her pussy. The wetness shone on your fingers, gleaming in the camera's spotlight. You got on your knees behind her and ran your tongue up the back of her thigh. Your pace increased, as did the moisture running out of her cunt. I saw her tremble, just as I did when you teased me that way. The whimper as you pulled your fingers from her was audible, even with the impediment. She was soon placated by your tongue on her cunt. I missed that sweet, salty tongue, the one that I had sucked on when I couldn't touch any other part of you. You dug into her ripe flesh, releasing another wash of juices from her cunt. You really had this one worked up. She wasn't indifferent like some others had been. Some of them had managed to stay so strong, trying to resist you. But not Amy. Was she as hot and wet as I used to be with you? I wanted to believe she wasn't. I still wanted to be your favorite, your perfect little submissive doll. But I knew I was no longer special to you.

You abruptly stopped what you were doing and the camera again focused on Amy's face. I heard you off camera, your tone harsh. Did she want to suck your cock? Did she want that gag out? She was nodding before you even finished the questions. She wanted you in her mouth, just like I had back then, back when you asked me the same questions. Your hand released the buckle behind her head. Amy sighed and cried all at once as the air hit her stretched, tired mouth.

Let me hear you say it. I spoke the words myself, in the privacy of my own living room: *I want to suck your cock*. I willed you to hear me through the television; to bring me back to you for one more chance.

God, your voice could unnerve anyone. She replied. Her voice was high pitched, squeaky. She wanted to suck your cock right now. Thankfully, you didn't let her talk anymore. The tip of your cock came into view. It looked just as I remembered it, thick and slightly purple. My breath caught in my throat. God, it made my mouth water just looking at it. I wondered if it felt the same to her as it had to me. Her cherry tongue rubbed against it, leaving a wet trail over the flesh I longed to taste again. You let her go on for a bit longer, but I knew what was coming. Before another swipe of Amy's amateur tongue was finished, you grabbed her head and forced the full length of your cock into her mouth. Her shock was overwhelmed by your insistence, and she had no choice but to take it. I could hear her gagging, I remembered the feeling well. Tears left her eyes in hot lines as your thick cock pushed into her throat again and again. The sounds of her moans were again muffled, and a little saliva started running down her chin. Soon, she had loosened up and was sucking as hard as you were fucking. God, you still had a way with women. You taught me how to deep-throat. Your new student was doing even better than I had. My jealousy shocked me, and made me wetter.

Amy had her rhythm now and she appeared to be enjoying herself. You quickly put a stop to her pleasure with a hard pinch of her swinging nipple. She winced at the pressure and your cock left her mouth just in time for a shocked "Ouch!" to leave her mouth. You squeezed again, and twisted, just like I liked it. Amy didn't seem to like it as much as I had. I wondered if that was for me. I wondered if you still thought about me, about what I was willing to do for you. Everything you were doing to Amy, you had done to me. Things that I had loved and begged for, you were giving to her for me to see. You barely made her ask for anything. I had spent hours begging you, pleading with you for my release. I learned to love it, to need your permission. Even though I didn't need it anymore, I still wanted it. My hand was in my pants gently teasing my clit as I thought of the last time your fingers held my nipples like that.

Amy bit her lip to take the pain, until you eased up and gave her a break. Her nipple was hard and bright red when you let it go. Another yank on her hair, and her full lips managed a quick yelp before you covered her mouth with yours, sucking the air and what was left of her fight right out of her. As you sweetly stroked her nipple, she purred into your mouth, thrusting and wiggling her hips back into the air. I had never gotten a sweet kiss from you. You took my mouth like you took the rest of me, with force.

You want to get fucked, don't you? It was an absurd question, but one you asked without a hint of irony. Wasn't that why we were all there in the first place? But you asked, and we had to respond. She responded with the only answer that made any sense. So did I. We almost spoke in unison, choosing the same words to respond to you. Only she was the only one getting what she wanted.

Yes, fuck me please.

With her desperate plea, I knew you had hooked another one. One more soul who couldn't get enough of you; willing to let you document her pleasure and pain, as long as you gave her one more taste. One more earth-shattering, mind-erasing twist of pleasure from you. I had been replaced, just like she would be someday. But for now, Amy could feel the unabashed desire that forced her back into your room again and again. The searing heat of knowing you were there, ready to do your best and your worst. The giving up of dignity, of common sense, of time and space, just to feel your cock in her cunt until she couldn't think straight. I still wanted it, all of it. Maybe someday, when you tired of all of them, you would come back to me. It was my secret hope. But I knew my dream would never come to pass.

I envied Amy, just as I had all the others. I wanted to be her and hated her at the same time. The camera showed her face crumpled into a mass of relief and desire as you finally gave in and filled her cunt. The camera went back to its usual position watching your stiff cock enter and leave Amy's wet and waiting cunt, over and over. My fingers dove into my own empty, lonely cunt. I tried to remember the last time I was with you. The last time I got to be like Amy.

Was it really a year ago? A whole year since I cried out into the darkness of that room, just like Amy, begging for a hard, deep fucking. Needing you so bad that I was willing to let you tie me down, turn my ass bright red and keep my pain, fear and lust all on a convenient disk forever. It had been a long, long year. My desperate cunt craved, like Amy's, to be filled. There didn't seem to be a finger or dildo big enough to fill the void you left when you told me you were through with me.

You promised to keep in touch. The first DVD arrived months later. Another girl, another Amy on your bed, taking your cock deep inside her. Right now, Amy began begging you to fuck her faster, but your pace stayed steady and slow, teasing her with every swirl of your hips. My hatred for her grew as my pussy got wetter. I needed you again. I wanted you again; just like the last four times the DVDs invaded my life. You still managed to turn my life upside down, even though you wouldn't take my calls.

I'm going to come.

Her words made my heart sink, but sent a rush of heat and wetness to my cunt. I knew better than anyone her need. You wouldn't make it easy for her. She didn't know it yet, but I did. I saw your cock leave her cunt, and I heard her moans turn to protests. My fingers transmitted her pain into my pleasure. Two more hard whacks on her ass rang out of my television speakers and went straight to my clit. That was what I wanted to hear. Her cries only made my orgasm bigger and better. My clit throbbed as my cunt tightened around my fingers, all while Amy lamented her current state.

By the time you were back in her cunt, fucking her into oblivion, I was lying back on my couch stroking myself to a second climax. I looked up just in time to see Amy's face twist into a knot and her cunt tighten around your cock. She wept as you made her come harder than she ever had before. She collapsed onto her stomach, her wrists rubbed raw by the scarf attaching her to the bed, the one I had given you so long ago.

Unlike on the other DVDs, this time you looked right into

the camera. Your eyes were looking straight at me. If I hadn't known better, I'd have thought you could see me right at that moment, my fingers wet from my own cunt, my body slowly returning to earth. But I did know better. You winked and the shot went to black. The familiar hiss of static filled the room. Finally, I pressed STOP.

FLY

Valerie Alexander

It's night on Neverland. The Lost Boys sit around the fire. Their war-painted faces glow with the fervor of boyhood delusion. They want adventure; their throats ache with unsung cries of battle and bloodlust. But the night won't begin until Peter arrives. Restless and agitated, the boys open beers and throw sticks into the fire and wait for him to return from his latest girl, his latest flight.

Across the island Tiger Lily also dreams of Peter. Naked on her bed, she toys with her tight amber tits, one fingertip circling her nipples. The other hand surfs down the silky dip of her navel until she cradles her own pussy under the pretence of someone else's touch. She is beautiful but she is ignored. Her clit hardens to the dream of something ambiguous, fantasies of a pointy-faced boy who at eighteen is all swagger and brashness. A boy whose thick golden-red hair is always askew, whose clever eyes are always alive with the possibility of danger. He is lithe and he is pretty, and from spying on him in the lake, she knows he is well endowed. But it's not his cock that haunts her dreams, it is his smile. He's a beautiful boy with a beautiful smile. All the girls want Peter.

Tiger Lily wants to fuck him more than life itself, but she wants more than that; she wants to pin him down and rub her pussy all over his face until he surrenders completely, until his endless taunts and stories are silenced. She wants to break his will and slap his face, wants to subsume his bragging in her sexual heat. Yet mostly what she wants is for Peter to teach her to fly. But he won't. Girls don't fly in Peter's world, not unless it's by holding on to him.

She rolls her clit between her fingers, slowly rubbing as she imagines that she is him. Now she's climbing rocks and scaling pirate ships, a prettier daredevil than he as she levitates with her long black hair flowing behind her like a flag. She knifes through the dark violet sky over Neverland until she sees Peter's last lover walking out of the lake. The girl is naked in the starlight and voluptuous as Peter likes his women to be. She's smiling dreamily as she towels off, perhaps lost in a reverie of that narrow-hipped boy who fucked her so soundly and never returned.

"I'll fuck you better than he ever will," Tiger Lily mutters and swoops down, still in her Peter guise, to push the girl down against the sand. Roughly she spreads her legs and fucks her with Peter's cock, pumping into her with savage thrusts.

"I knew you'd come back, Peter," the girl groans, arching her spine. "Oh, harder..."

But he never will come back, Tiger Lily thinks as her interest in the scene abruptly dies. She changes the fantasy to the last actual time she saw Peter, digging ammunition out of a pirate ship. Cheekbones smeared with dirt, bare-chested in ripped jeans, he talked excitedly of a fight he had won the previous night. She had been wearing her shortest dress, flexing her long bare legs for him. But he was too wrapped up in his story to even look at her.

But if he had. If he had turned and really seen her, the most hot-blooded girl on the island, he just might have knelt between her legs. Pushing her dress up her thighs, he would have pushed his thumb deep into her pussy, making her squirm there on the ship deck....

The thought sends a white bolt of heat ricocheting through her body, her cunt shuddering over and over around her fingers. Wetness soaks her hand, her thighs, as she furiously rubs herself into another flood of contractions. "I'm going to fuck you," Tiger Lily whispers, her legs spread wide for that phantom Peter thrusting into her. "I'm going to fuck you blind."

Collapsing back on her pillow, she licks the tangy, pearly strands of honey from each finger. Then she gets up and throws on her dress and heads off into the night.

The Lost Boys are still waiting to be found tonight by the boy they call their leader. Past the empty beer bottles and the boastful tales of girls fucked and discarded, their thoughts are anxious. They are not warriors or lovers, just followers still.

And then suddenly there he is at the fire with a self-satisfied smile. By the hand he holds his latest conquest: a hesitant-looking girl of about eighteen, softer than his usual girls and doe-eyed, her long brown hair wet and disheveled. She has the dazed and startled look of someone who has flown for the first time.

He pushes her forward for their appraisal. "This is Wendy."

Her wet cotton nightgown sticks to her body. It clings to her legs, is plastered to the hollow of her navel and sucked into the indentation of her belly button. But it's the outline of her nipples, stiff, with large aureole that are unexpected on such a petite young girl, that makes every boy there go hard. From the look in her eyes, they know she's too stunned by the flight to realize this. From Peter's lascivious grin, they know he flew her through a rainfall on purpose.

"Say hi," he urges, dropping his hand to gently cup her ass. She blushes deeply. "Um...hello."

No one says a word. The boys stare at her with a grim and begrudging lust. Then Peter flashes a cocky smile at his tribe and says, "Be back soon," and leads Wendy away into the night.

Concealed behind her rock, Tiger Lily watches, scarcely daring to breathe as Peter saunters confidently to a banyan tree and tugs Wendy next to him. "Sorry I got you wet," he murmurs and kisses her ear, but not before another smug and secret grin escapes him at his own wordplay. Wendy doesn't notice it but only because she's growing suspicious now; she's looking uncertain of this long-limbed devil who shimmied up her drainpipe and crept through her bedroom window. That had to be how he did it, Tiger Lily thinks, his naughty grin appearing at the window like every repressed fantasy of her good girl imagination. For Wendy is definitely a good girl, procured by him in some hushed fancy place full of manicured gardens and teatime and other things Tiger Lily doesn't understand; that's Peter's secret type. Well-bred and easily awed and secretly burning to break out of the nursery. Instead the devil came to the nursery. Of course she let him in.

Wendy shivers now with some theatrics, prompting Peter to go predictable: "Are you cold? I'll warm you up."

So boring, so clichéd, Tiger Lily thinks, she should interrupt and teach them a thing or two. Still she wants to see Wendy's nightgown come off and that is exactly what happens, as Peter's mouth moves across her throat so skillfully that his hands push the nightgown up her hips without notice. Up it rises to reveal oval knees and soft pale legs. Something stirs deep in Tiger Lily's body. Moments later, Wendy's cunt comes into view, a soft mound of hair that doesn't quite conceal her shy cleft. Then her hips, rather wide and narrowing up into her waist, and finally her tits, full and round and creamy with those pink saucer-like nipples. Perfect breasts, the kind Tiger Lily wants to feel bouncing against her own as the two of them fuck each other into oblivion.

She drags her gaze up to check Wendy's face. The girl is scarlet with embarrassment and trembling. She should be spanked, Tiger Lily thinks, turned over my knee and spanked until her creamy ass is as red as her face. Then she'll cry and I'll lick her tears away....

Wendy's body is so pale and soft. This is a naked body that has never seen sunlight, Tiger Lily can tell, and this is a girl who has never felt a man's touch anywhere beneath the neck. That's clear as Peter, too fascinated to bother with sexual amenities now, traces one finger over her slit. Wendy's legs open and her eyes close with shame. "Oh, my god," she whispers.

Tiger Lily's blood grows hot. She cannot bear to watch this a moment longer, Peter with yet another girl, so soft and obedient. In moments he will be playing with her clit and stroking the insides of her pussy until what will possibly be the girl's first orgasm slams through her—and then those soft doe eyes will gaze at him in a way no girl has ever gazed at her....

She scrambles silently through the trees, scales one and launches into her best pirate voice. The warning she calls out is ridiculous—Peter would be stupid to react to it so immediately, they both played pirate a dozen times together as kids, but his lust for war is stronger than his tactician's instincts and he abandons Wendy in a second. "Wait here!" he commands, all boy-man authority, and fairly skips off to the Lost Boys, his boys, who are already creeping toward battle.

Such an idiot, Tiger Lily thinks. Always forsaking the girl for the adventure, that's Peter. But no mind. She runs back through the trees and is at Wendy's side before the girl can put her nightgown back on.

Wendy is sure she is going to be murdered. The girl looming over her is like no girl she's ever seen, barely clad in a tiny buckskin dress, her long black hair alive in the night wind. Even her voice is different and commanding as she hisses, "Shut up! I'm Tiger Lily, I'm a friend of Peter's. The pirates are here, I'm going to rescue you." At the word *pirates,* something blank and primitive tightens Wendy's throat and she can't say a word as the girl snatches down the nightgown from its branch and ties the sleeve quickly and expertly in a gag through her pretty mouth. Wendy chokes a bit but she has been gagged before in her brothers' games and perhaps that is why she doesn't protest as the black-haired girl ties up her wrists with the other sleeve and leads her off into the forest.

Or perhaps she doesn't protest because of the cumulative shock of the night, which began with her tossing restlessly in her bed: too old at eighteen to spend her nights staring at the London rooftops through the nursery window. There was the shock of seeing a beautiful boy her own age appear at the window with a devilish smile, a boy who climbed in to shamelessly appraise her body through the skimpy nightgown before taking her hand and tugging her out the window. The shock of flying away over London, the shock of being stripped naked and spreading her legs as Peter touched her pussy. And now this, being tied up and led off into the woods, a naked captive. Not captured by a man like in her most forbidden fantasies but by a girl—a girl with hard lean muscles and long legs who moves so fast Wendy stumbles behind her.

Dazed as she is, it takes a minute to replay Tiger Lily's words and realize their basic contradiction: that if Tiger Lily is Peter's friend, why did she tie Wendy up? Her bare feet hurt from the sticks and debris of the jungle floor, and the night chill is making her stiff nipples ache. No one knows where she is. Yet soon enough they stop in a clearing, where Tiger Lily pushes her to her knees, before building a fire. She stockpiles a supply of kindling then takes her place opposite the flames.

Now the two girls stare at each other. Wendy can see every detail of her kidnapper's face in the firelight: a fiercely beautiful girl a little older than her with high cheekbones and fiery eyes, and a tough mouth that Wendy can tell will know exactly what to do to her. Everything about her wiry, taut body screams of sexual knowledge. This is a girl who knows what to do.

Then Tiger Lily drops her eyes and draws all that glorious black hair over one shoulder as she gazes into the fire. She seems absentminded, tracing a bruise on one bare thigh—and it is by following the movement of her hand that Wendy realizes Tiger Lily's legs are slightly open and her pussy is on full display. She seems either unaware of this or indifferent.

Wendy swallows nervously. She has never seen another woman's pussy, has never even gotten a good look at her own. She stares at it now, its mysterious pink folds, and wonders exactly where Peter had touched her to make that electric feeling ring through her.

Tiger Lily looks up, notices her gaze, and smirks. Wendy swallows again but doesn't shift her eyes. Yet Tiger Lily bounces abruptly to her feet, ending the show, and is at her side with that terrifying swiftness again. Roughly she pulls the knotted night-gown sleeve from her mouth. "Sorry."

Wendy's tongue, dry and stiff and tasting of cotton, moves tentatively around her mouth. Her knees hurt and Tiger Lily seems especially tall standing before her. "Who—why did you bring me here?"

"Why did Peter bring you to Neverland?" Tiger Lily is staring down at her with blank obsidian eyes, but Wendy can tell from the humming tension of her body that she is feeling far from blank at the moment.

"I—I don't know."

"He brought you here to fuck you, Wendy." Tiger Lily yanks the nightgown still tied around her hands and brings her roughly to her feet. Then she jerks Wendy's arms up over her head and moves her back and forth like a marionette, making her breasts bounce and sway.

Fear and arousal set off a throbbing between Wendy's legs. No one has ever taken such blatant control of her nor treated her so rudely, and it's exciting. As Tiger Lily pushes her back toward a tree, she finds herself turning up her face expectantly for the other girl's mouth. Instead Tiger Lily ropes the knotted nightgown on a branch, imprisoning Wendy's arms over her head. With a dirty smirk, she takes both her tits in her hands and begins to play with them.

"I bet you went to boarding school," Tiger Lily accuses.

"I did…"

"And I bet all you girls got in each other's beds at night."

"No! No, I mean, some girls, yes…"

"But not you?"

"No." Wendy shakes her head too fervently, her damp brown hair falling over her nipples. Tiger Lily impatiently flings the hair away, then slaps her breasts hard as punishment.

"You don't cover yourself around me." She pinches her right nipple, making Wendy gasp. "Understand?"

"Yes." That excitement in her pussy feels like melting honey now. Soon her thighs will be wet with it and Tiger Lily will see it and then she'll really be punished.

"So." Tiger Lily resumes feeling her tits, almost in a detached exploratory manner. "You never wanted a girl to do things to you."

"Well, I..." Wendy can't say the truth of this, which is that the shadow who tops her in her fantasies never has a face, let alone a gender. The shadow only has hands that stroke her, a tongue that licks her, a heat that's sometimes as hard as the hardest cock and other times pillowy as the softest breasts.

"Yes or no, Wendy. It's not that difficult a question."

"Leave her alone."

The rising heat cools in Wendy as she turns to see Peter in the clearing. He's here to rescue her, she realizes with a pang of annoyance, but she's not quite ready to be rescued. His mouth is set in a hard little line but those green eyes aren't quite as angry as his voice pretends. Yes, he's pissed that Tiger Lily stole his prey—his catch, Wendy thinks—but watching her tied up naked as Tiger Lily flicks at her nipples isn't something he's ready to stop just yet.

"You're the one who took her out of her own bed and flew her here, Peter," Tiger Lily taunts him. "Shouldn't you have left her alone?"

She smacks Wendy's breasts together a few times as if they're balloons, then dips her fingers between her legs. "Spread," she orders. Wendy's face burns hot now as she obeys, thighs shaking with anticipation of that first penetration of Tiger Lily's fingers. But Tiger Lily only traces one light finger around her clit in a soft, maddening circle without taking her eyes from Peter. *I am just a pawn to her,* Wendy thinks. The thought only makes her clit harder.

"Come on, Peter," Tiger Lily smiles. "Come rescue your pet."

So he's here at last. Peter looks as confused as Tiger Lily's ever seen him look, rubbing his hair in a way he does when he's thinking. It's rumpled around his face like a golden-red halo, as if he's an angel with a giant cock rather than the arrogant smartass she knows him to be. Once again he's shirtless, his bare chest smooth in the firelight, and two war stripes adorn his sculpted cheekbones. He stopped to paint himself to do battle with the pirates, how ridiculous. Tiger Lily gestures to the erection swelling in his pants.

"This is probably a little much for you so maybe you better just watch."

He flings himself at her with a roar. She dodges him well, with the practice of a hundred mock battles between them, then brings him down on his back. He looks stunned as she straddles him, quickly tying his hands tight with a piece of rope. But he recovers immediately.

"I can bust right out of these knots." He snarls at her in a way that reminds her of defensive animals trying to ward off a predator.

She shifts the heat and pressure of her pussy on his erection. He goes still. Subtly, with a clever smile, she rocks back and forth. His cock swells even bigger until a strangled groan escapes him.

Stupid boy, you don't know what you've been missing, she thinks. But all she says is: "I know what you want." Wendy's impatience and jealousy is palpable by the tree, but Tiger Lily ignores her for now. Staring into Peter's eyes, she opens her knees until she's showing him her pussy. So many times she's thought of Peter reaching for her, asking her, begging her, but now she's controlling him, and his submission is better than any of her dreams.

"Oh, fuck yeah," Peter mutters, his eyes locked on her.

With one quick move she swings up and settles her crotch directly on Peter's mouth. "Do it," she commands, not because he doesn't understand what she wants but because the sound of her own authority arouses her. She is soaked, wet from her clit to her asshole, and she takes pleasure in smearing it all over his nose and eyelids and cheekbones until his arrogant face shines with it.

"Fuck me," Peter moans against her, somewhat illogically as his tongue is desperately seeking her slit. She lifts herself just out of reach to tease him, then relents and sits down on him until the agile heat of his tongue squirms inside her.

Deep euphoria spreads through her. "Just like that," she whispers. She had known this would be good but just the sight of his face framed between her thighs sends an electric power through her body. Peter's endlessly talking tongue finally silenced and fucking deep in her pussy at last, his wrists tied so he can't fly. This is her moment.

Tiger Lily reverses direction on his face, leans over, and takes off his pants. Then the prize is in her hands at last: Peter's hard and straining cock. She rolls his shaft between her hands for only a moment before sucking it into her mouth, all of it, until her nose is buried in his balls. He tastes mustier than she expected, a boyish earthy taste, and his cock is as alive in her mouth as an animal. She pulls back to suck his head hard, tonguing it until he gasps.

Peter's not licking her pussy anymore; his tongue has slid up to frantically push inside her asshole, spearing her tightness over and over. And it's this that really does it for her: the knowledge of his tongue in her ass pushes her over into complete orgasmic mindlessness. Her pussy squeezes over and over as a hot gush of ejaculate floods out of her. Beneath her, he pulls back in surprise, but she sits down on his face and rides out her orgasm, grinding against his mouth until the last waves sputter out.

His hips bang the ground in frustration. "Tiger—"

She doesn't bother silencing him. Instead she returns to his cock, pressing it flat against his belly and wiggling her tongue up and down and around him before sucking him back inside her mouth. He writhes beneath her as if he's gone mad. "Don't— oh, god—don't stop." She keeps sucking him, feeling his balls tighten right up until the moment of no return—and then she does stop, because after making her wait for so many years, Peter really has no right to any kind of satisfaction this early in the night.

He sinks his teeth into the right cheek of her ass with a long, frustrated groan.

Oh, you bastard, she thinks with a mixture of indignation and amusement. She reaches back and feels the bite mark on her ass. Her fingers come away tinged with blood.

"You little bitch," she says and rings him across the face. It only turns him on more, making his hips dance. Her fingertip traces the bite again. Sometime tomorrow she will hold a mirror before her lifted legs and stare at the teeth marks as she fingers herself. But for now she feigns outrage.

"Get up." She yanks him to his feet, a naked and dazed boy looking almost sick with lust. His cock strains toward her as if magnetized. She shoves him against the tree and ropes him next to Wendy. Then she turns their bodies toward each other and begins to play with them like dolls. First she brushes Wendy's nipples against his chest until her face burns tomato red. Then she strokes Peter's cock over Wendy's slit, pressing his head hard against her clit until they both moan.

Tiger Lily laughs. "It's not going to be that easy."

She returns them to their separate positions and begins to toy with them. They look so beautiful, so flushed and horny. Sliding her fingers deep into Wendy's wet and swollen cunt, she rubs her in the way she likes herself, pressing her knuckles against the walls of her pussy. Wendy's pale body steams and shakes, she twists against her bonds and begs to be fucked.

Tiger Lily pulls out to stroke her clit. "Is this what you want?"

Wendy's legs strain open. "No...!"

"Tell me what you want."

"Just fuck me," Wendy gasps, a pink flush spreading across her breasts. She seeks to bring Tiger Lily closer by locking her ankles around her, but Tiger Lily deftly steps out of her way. "Don't stop, oh, please don't."

She fingers Wendy's clit for a few moments longer, then slides in three fingers, deep as she can go. Now she fucks her hard and rapidly, holding Wendy around the waist so she has to take it. The girl's cunt feels impossibly full and wet around her fingers and as a low growl breaks from her mouth, Tiger Lily feels her come; Wendy's velvety heat clenches her over and over until wet aftershocks tremble deep in her own pussy.

Tiger Lily gently withdraws her fingers and smears the glistening juices over Peter's parted lips. His eyes are locked on her, not Wendy, with reverence. *Oh, Peter,* she thinks, *we haven't even started.*

"Kiss me," she says. Her mouth, her tough mouth that has insulted and mocked him so many nights and cried his name alone in her bedroom, covers his. He tastes of Wendy's honeyed brine and then his own surprising sweetness. A sweet boy with a hard cock, captured at last. He's not flying anywhere until she's done with him, and the night has only begun as she presses her cool long body against his flushed and trembling one. Tiger Lily twists her arms up around his neck like a lover, like she dreamed of when she was young and romantic and naïve. But now she grabs his thick soft hair in her fist and twists it, pulling his head back so she can bite his lips.

"Anything you want," he begs in a low voice. "But please, please…"

What I want, she thinks, is to fly. And then it's happening, his cock pushes into the initial tightness of her pussy, demanding and inexorable yet torturously slow. She hooks one leg around his waist and brings him in deeper inch by teasing inch, until the cool sac of his balls rests against her. Already she's beginning to throb as they start to thrust, his heat and his hardness driving her up and up into blinding wet bliss, and then they're really fucking, faster and faster until at last Tiger Lily is flying.

ON MY KNEES IN BARCELONA

Kristina Lloyd

This happened before the '92 Summer Olympics in Barcelona, when the nights were so hot the city couldn't sleep and everyone grew angry and crazy. Zero tolerance was just a rumor, so whores, thieves and smackheads skulked in narrow streets and everyone avoided the docks. I only went to Bar Anise in the hope they'd give me some ice. Had I known what kind of bar it was, I might have stayed away.

It was nearly 2:00 a.m. and I was standing on my dinky balcony, feeling pretty zonked. The fuse had gone in my fan and the air in my apartment felt thick enough to slice. In the street below, a globe lamp hung like a moon on a bracket, adding a sheen of pearl to the facade of Bar Anise. I held a damp cloth to the back of my neck, arms resting on metal too hot to touch during the day. Earlier, the cloth had contained fast-melting ice and my mind returned to the cold rivulets trickling over my shoulders, collarbone and breasts. Like a tongue, I'd thought, the tongue of a lover making whoopee with my skin. How long had it been now? Oh, too many months to count.

Six floors below, footsteps echoed in the dark street. I watched a guy in a white T-shirt stride along with a sense of purpose unsuited to the hour. When he suddenly looked up I was unnerved, feeling a rupture of that odd balance where my balcony is at once part of the street and part of my home. It was as if he'd barged in on my privacy.

I turned away, embarrassed to have been caught watching, then glanced back to see him enter Bar Anise. A relic from another age, the bar's exterior glowed with low-watt tones of honey and oak, its door closed, its windows pasted with faded posters, that globe lamp fuzzed with a halo of white light. As the guy pushed the door, I half expected the structure to wobble like a stage set.

How come I'd never been in before? Generally speaking, I socialized in Barcelona's hipper bars along Las Ramblas, in Plaça Reial or Barri Gòtic, and I only ventured into local bars to buy late-night beers or water. They were down-at-heel joints with Formica tabletops, fruit machines and a TV tuned permanently to the lotto draw. I fancied Bar Anise was different but I'd never set foot inside. Oh, sure, I was curious but the place seemed to exist in a world of its own. It may as well have had NO ENTRY on its door.

At 2:00 a.m., however, it was the only bar open.

I wiped the damp cloth over my face, reminding myself I was lucky to be single and sleeping alone. Along my street, shabby ironwork balconies were cluttered with blushing geraniums, cramped little washing lines, green roller blinds and even a bird in a cage three buildings to my right. In these Spanish homes, behind the old lace at the windows, the occupants probably slept two to a bed, sticky bodies wrestling with hot, tangled sheets. Yes, in this heat, I was lucky to be single. Some ice to see me through the night would be welcome though. Unfortunately, my ice compartment was empty so I had to ask myself: how badly did I want it?

My sandals were noisy in the deserted street, ringing off walls and metal shutters. I hesitated before the door of Bar Anise, disconcerted by the sense of stillness beyond. A sign in Catalan proclaimed the bar open but was it really? And if so, was it open to the likes of me? In those months, I was working as a sub-editor on a weekly expat newspaper called *Gander*. Prior to that, I'd spent three years teaching English in Seville until I'd tired of both the work and a boyfriend who'd kept the fingernails long on his right hand so he could simultaneously learn Spanish guitar and repulse me. Sometimes, I felt at home in that foreign land but when I stood on the threshold of Bar Anise, I felt I'd just arrived from Mars.

I considered quitting, then recalled those tongues of molten ice trailing across my skin. Taking a deep breath, I entered. Cigarette smoke hung in the yellowing light and a ceiling fan turned sluggishly as if enervated by the heat. Half a dozen men sat alone at separate tables, smoking, reading or staring into space. No one paid me any notice and I was grateful. I took it to be one of those places where everyone is a stranger, even people who've been drinking side by side for years.

When I approached the counter with my empty jug, a customer seated there cast me a look of lazy appraisal. He wore a white T-shirt and I took him to be the guy I'd seen from my balcony. Big nosed with dark hair feathering across his forehead, his wrinkles added interest to a strong, angular face. But irrespective of rugged charm, middle-aged men who believe they're entitled to leer unsettle my confidence. I was self-conscious in asking for ice and when my request was met with a frown, I stumbled in repeating myself. The bartender wiped the counter with a cloth, apparently loath to serve me. Behind him, among shelves gleaming with bottles and glasses, a mirrored Coca-Cola clock said quarter past two. The clock's red logo gave me that old jolt of jarring familiarity, making me feel I was on territory at once homely and strange.

"I have money," I said.

With that, the bartender disappeared into an adjoining room, a curtain of plastic strips clattering lightly as he passed. I waited, wondering if the drinkers could see the ice tonguing my skin; if they could see me at night, water coursing over my flesh; if they could see how I tried to kill the heat of my longing, failing as the ice melted away and I climaxed once again.

I felt they could and it troubled me. On the counter, a wedge of tortilla sat forlornly under a plastic dome. I could hear the bartender on the phone in the adjoining room. All this for some ice? When he returned with my jug blissfully full, I asked how much I owed him. Before he could reply, Big Nose interrupted, addressing the bartender in Catalan, a language I wasn't yet familiar with. The bartender poured a large brandy, then set it in front of me.

"*Gratis,*" he said.

Unwilling to risk offence, I accepted the drink while trying to convince myself it left me under no obligation. So bloody English of me. Why couldn't I decline the brandy, pay for the ice conventionally and leave?

"*Graçias,*" I said, turning to the customer, but I didn't smile.

He nodded, lips tilting in wry amusement. The brandy was rough, its heat scorching my throat and blazing inside my chest. The nape of my neck was wet with sweat, my hair damp. I was concerned about the ice melting in my jug and wished I could sip the ice water. The ceiling fan clicked faintly. Nobody spoke and I was relieved. It could simply be this guy was silently extending the hand of friendship. If so, I would silently shake it then shoot off home. The brandy was difficult to drink though, fire when I wanted ice.

"*Ay, qué calor,*" said my new friend at length.

"*Sí, qué calor,*" I replied.

Hot weather. I sipped my brandy. I could feel him watching and his passive interest bugged me. After a couple more minutes, wanting to escape his gaze, I asked for the *lavabos* and was directed down a flight of rickety stairs. I descended toward a basement with scruffy, dark crimson walls, toilets at the far end and a swinging door with a small, dirty window lined with wire mesh. Halfway down the stairs, movement below caught my eye. I paused, looking over my shoulder at the corridor behind me. Beyond an open door was a guy on a chair and a woman on her knees, her head bobbing in his lap. I clutched the banister, immobilized by fear and a sudden, pornographic lust.

My cunt swelled and swelled, blood throbbing there. Oh, Christ, what a picture. The guy's mouth was slack, his head tipped back, as the woman, her chestnut curls fanning over his thighs, dipped up and down, up and down. Had they heard me? Hell, I hoped not. I needed to watch. Until that moment, I hadn't known how much I wanted cock; hadn't known how much I'd missed it since dumping the guitarist; hadn't known that stab of raging desire. Because while I could fuck myself with cock-shaped objects (cool as a cucumber), nothing could ever come close to the overwhelming sensations of a deep, dark, blinding mouthful. I stared, hardly daring to breathe.

The guy was young and lean, a tumble of ink black curls giving him an air of flamenco passion. Transfixed, I watch him grow fiercer, pulling the woman onto him, his fingers snarled in her hair as his pelvis rocked either to meet or defeat her. In her kneeling position, the woman kicked at the floor, squealing in muffled protest, her hands flapping. My yearning for cock was knocked for six by a second wave, a shocking urge to be claimed and used in a myriad of filthy ways.

My cunt flared to a cushiony mass of need, so sensitive I fancied I could feel the warp and weft of cotton in my underwear. I wanted to be where she was, at the mercy of a wild stranger who regarded me as nothing but an object for his pleasure, insignificant and disposable. I wanted to be all body and no mind, a thing made of cunt, mouth and ass, wide open and ready to receive.

Face aflame, I turned, intending to hurry back to the bar. I would put it from my thoughts, pretend nothing had happened, pretend I hadn't seen either the couple or the grubby depths of my desire. Was this because I hadn't had sex for so long? Was I craving the basest sort of action as compensation for those months of lack? Feeling shaky, I clasped the banister, mouth dry as a bone.

My stomach somersaulted. To my horror, at the head of the stairs stood the big-nosed guy from the bar. He grinned, descending in slow, swaggering steps. Panicking, I glanced down to the room. The guy in the chair was looking right at me, smirking as he slammed the woman's head between his thighs. My knees turned wobbly while blood pumped in my ears, roaring like seashells and high fever.

Big Nose was at my side, his forehead gleaming with a film of sweat. He tipped his eyebrows at me. *"Cuatro miles pesetas,"* he said.

Outrage spiked my fear. Four thousand pesetas! He thought I was a whore, thought I would blow him for a nasty brandy and a handful of notes!

"Déjame paso!" I snapped, attempting to sidestep him. He mirrored me, blocking my path. I grew more afraid then,

trapped between these two randy *cucarachas,* and yet my groin was pulsing as hard as my heart.

"*Cuatro miles,*" he repeated, nodding toward the basement room. Then in Spanish he added, "Take it, go on. It is a good price. You know you want it."

And I understood at once that I was to pay; that I was the punter not the whore. I didn't know whether to be more or less insulted. I stared at him, incredulous. He actually thought I was so desperate for cock I would pay to suck off a stranger in a sleazy, backstreet bar!

"Move," I said, no longer bothering to speak his language. Despite being on a lower step, I tried shouldering him out of the way but with swift skill, he jostled me backward. I cried out to realize I was now sandwiched between him and the wall, his chest pressing against my breasts, my arms trapped in his hands. For several seconds we stood there, our breaths shallow and tense.

"*No me molestes,*" I said, a Berlitz phrase I'd never had to use before.

The guy laughed and with good reason. My demand sounded so pitifully insincere I may as well have said, "Molest me." He crooked a finger, resting it in the hollow of my throat, and I turned aside, looking past him to the room below. The woman was watching us. She wiped the back of her hand across her mouth and laughed, white teeth flashing. I was relieved to see she wasn't in trouble but, more than that, I was relieved to see I wasn't the only woman keen on skirting so close to danger.

I turned to face Big Nose with renewed bravery but he trailed his bent finger up my neck. My skin tingled to his touch, tiny shivers of pleasure rippling through my body's heat. I tried defying him, tried steeling myself against his advances, but I caught the sadistic brightness in his bitter chocolate eyes and I melted a little more. I pressed my head back to the wall.

"*No me molestes,*" I repeated, my voice soft and tremulous.

He laughed quietly, his breath tickling my face. I wanted him to touch me in horrible ways, to stick his hand between my thighs or paw my breasts. But he didn't. He just reiterated his price. When I didn't reply, he ground his crotch against me, rubbing his hard-on above the swell of my pubis. The pressure of him there distilled to my cunt, making my lips part and pout.

"*Qué barato!*" he said. A good price.

The basement was hot as hell. Sweat prickled on my back, cotton clinging damply. He knew he was turning me on and every rock of his body was sweet torture, twisting me with what I didn't want to want.

In Spanish, I said, "I just came for ice. I need to go home now. Release me, please."

"You will not sleep," he replied. "It's too hot."

"I have ice."

"You don't want ice," he said. "You want cock."

I felt the color rise in my face. He placed his hands either side of my head, caging me loosely in his arms, his biceps forming swarthy little hillocks on the edges of my vision. A waft of sweat, earthy and masculine, surged into my senses and I wanted to bury my nose in his armpits and inhale him.

"There's cock here," he continued. "Take it, *guapa*. We are not expensive. Take what you want then go home."

His eyes were such a deep brown I could barely distinguish pupil from iris.

"I don't have much money on me," I said.

He chuckled and I flushed deeper to realize I'd betrayed myself.

"Then go get some money," he said. "There's a cash machine—"

"No," I murmured.

"Yes, stop resisting yourself. Do you agree it is a fair price?"

"I don't know," I whispered, and I genuinely didn't. It seemed an amount I'd pay without too many qualms. But fair, good? There was no market value for this; it flew in the face of the usual sexism dictating the flow of supply and demand: women give, men get. Without a scarcity of clean men with hard cocks, why would I pay? And what in the world would prompt a cock-drought? Guys were always up for it. But here and now in the early hours in Bar Anise, they'd changed the world, creating both a need and a scarcity. Demand outstripped supply. A fair price? The thud in my pussy insisted it was a bargain.

I swallowed. "I have money in my *piso*," I said, deeply ashamed. "I live across the street."

He stepped back. "Vete!" he said, gesturing up the stairs.

I wasted no time, striding through the bar, head held high. At that point, I was unsure if I would return. I thought I might come to my senses but the night was sultry and weighted with the city, its heat wrapping me in strange enchantments where Bar Anise's subterranean secrets seduced me away from the prosaic. The man's voice echoed in my mind: Stop resisting yourself.

Gone was the Barcelona I knew where the metro whisked me to work, sunshine poured on mosaic lizards, plane trees shimmered and cathedral spires and scaffolding stabbed a flat blue sky. Instead, lust conspired with magic and menace to lead me as if in a dream to collect money from my apartment and scurry back to the bar.

Stop resisting yourself.

I downed the brandy still awaiting me on the counter and crept downstairs, my sordid hunger flaring at the wine-dark walls and scents of sweat and semen lingering in the shadows. All I'm doing, I told myself, is buying sex much as men have done for centuries. Nonetheless, I felt myself less an empowered consumer and more a desperate, greedy slut, a woman shameless enough to slake her desire in this masculine habitat of beer, cigarettes and sullen, perceptible misogyny. But I liked that these guys probably didn't much care for me except as an object to fuck. The feeling was mutual.

No one was about in the basement so, nervously, I entered the room I'd seen earlier, an underused storeroom with drums of olive oil lined against a wall, boxes under a large wooden table and four towers of orange chairs stacked in a corner. Big Nose was sitting spread-legged on a reversed chair, arms folded on its back. Behind him on the table sat his flamenco-looking friend, one leg swinging back and forth. My heart was going nineteen to the dozen.

"Who takes the money?" I asked.

Big Nose held out a hand. Feigning confidence, I gave him the notes. Stretching, he passed them to Flamenco who bundled them into his jeans pocket as if he were the pimp. There was a brief exchange in Catalan and I understand only that it was about money and that Big Nose was called Jordi.

"*Graçias,*" said Flamenco, relaxing his posture to suggest his work was done.

Jordi stood and spun the chair to face me. Still standing, he said, "On your knees."

I glanced at Flamenco who was making no moves to leave. "It's not a floor show," I said.

Jordi grabbed my face with a broad hand, forcing me to meet his gaze. He squeezed my cheeks. "On your fucking knees."

His nastiness sent shards of arousal to my groin. I felt bullied and debased, even more so because of our audience, and it was everything I wanted but would never have dared ask for. I fell to my knees, the scuffed hardwood floor briefly cooling my skin. Ahead of me, the fly of Jordi's jeans undulated over his boner, the faded denim at his crotch reminding me how much of a stranger he was, the rhythms of a life unknown imprinted on fabric concealing the cock I was about to blow. With a clink of metal, he unbuckled and unzipped, rummaging to release his erection.

My heart gave a kick of joy at the sight of his hard-on raging up from the wiry thicket of his pubes. I'd forgotten how obscenely aggressive hard cocks are and his was a brutish beauty, the color suffusing the head with such intensity I fancied it might seep through his skin to stain the air with a blood violet hue. He gripped himself, fingers thick around his girth, the sea blue vein on his underside peeping as he gently jerked.

"It's a good price, no?" he said.

Doing my best to forget about Flamenco, I opened my mouth to take Jordi but he stilled me with a hand on my forehead. "It's a good price," he repeated sternly.

His balls were tucked up tight and they lifted as he worked his shaft.

"*Sí, sí, claro,*" I replied.

He clasped my head and drew me sharply onto his cock. The sudden fullness of my mouth made me splutter and he held me there, forcing me to inhale his humidity and that smell I'd forgotten, the smell of men, a smell reminiscent of depths and of things discarded, of dark oceans, forest floors, dereliction, old tires and knives left out in the sun.

"*Así me gusta, nena,*" he said approvingly as I withdrew to his tip.

He held my head, adding a slight pressure as I began slurping back and forth, making it seem as if he were the one leading. Perhaps he was. That seemed at odds with me being the paying customer but I enjoyed him taking the upper hand, so perhaps the incongruity was superficial.

"*Qué bonita,*" said Flamenco. How pretty.

Those watching eyes inflamed a shame that fueled my lust. I

swallowed Jordi as deep as I could, my appetite provoking him to greater force. He began fucking my face, driving into my instinctive resistance, making me whimper and cough as my saliva spilled and my eyes watered. I felt sluttish and used, at the mercy of these callous brutes, and it was bliss. My swollen cunt was so fat and rich it barely seemed to have room between my thighs.

"Hey, Àngel," said Jordi, addressing his friend. "Why don't you give her a free fuck? You would like this, *nena? Es gratis!*"

He withdrew from my mouth to let me speak.

"*Sí, sí, fóllame!*" I croaked, gazing up at Jordi through a veil of tears. He sat heavily in the chair, lowering my head to his height. I dropped onto all fours, engulfing his length again while hoping the free fuck would be as hot and rough as the free brandy.

I heard Àngel cross the room. Àngel. What a perfect, preternatural name for this other-worldly scenario. Taking position behind me, Àngel flipped up my skirt, and yanked down my underwear. I groaned around Jordi's cock and his answering groan echoed in my ears. I heard Àngel unzip and I shuffled my knees wider, groaning again when he teased me by slotting his cock to the length of my folds. He sawed to and fro, the upward strain of his erection pressing into my wetness and making me ache for penetration.

Àngel spoke to Jordi in Catalan, tight hard words muttered under his breath. Jordi replied, throaty and urgent. With a sound like an expletive, Àngel slammed into me, hissing as he lodged himself high. He was meaty and solid and he clasped my hips, gripping hard as he began driving into my hole. Every thrust jolted my body, jerking me forward onto Jordi's lap. I felt skewered all the way through, my mouth and cunt both stuffed to capacity. The two men worked together, fucking, pushing, grunting and groaning. Occasionally they exchanged words I didn't understand and once or twice there was amusement and faint laughter.

They had me. They well and truly had me. And when Àngel reached for my clit, I knew I was lost. My climax raced closer and I bleated with nearness. Àngel hissed in Catalan. Jordi growled.

"*Sigue, sigue,*" he said. He grabbed fistfuls of my hair, his cock swelling to its absolute limit in my mouth. I was a rag doll between the two men, so close to coming my limbs seemed to have lost their bones. With a hoarse cry, Jordi came, flooding my mouth with his bitter silk, and the sound of his release tipped me over the edge. I came hard, disoriented and dizzy as pleasure clutched and stars exploded in my mind.

Moments later, my body began to drop with exhaustion but there was no letup from Àngel. He kept fucking me like there was no tomorrow and my pulpy walls, swollen with sensitivity, clung to his thrusts. I held Jordi in my mouth, gasping on his dwindling erection until Àngel's hammering became so frenzied I fancied he wanted to destroy me. He peaked with a long, low groan, wedging himself deep, and I moaned around Jordi's cock, wishing I could melt clean away.

The three of us held still until Jordi stroked my hair, a tender gesture that took me by surprise. Àngel caressed my buttocks. For a minute or two, we rested in silence and in those moments, I felt we shared a tacit understanding and mutual respect. We had all got what we wanted and were grateful.

But I didn't want to stay. I had nothing to say to them, nor them to me. Conversation would have made us awkward and I wanted to leave it there, pure and perfect, a moment out of time devoted entirely to pleasure. Àngel slipped away and I tidied myself up. Jordi asked how I was. I told him I was fine just as Àngel returned with my jug, full to the brim with ice. There was no one in the bar when I left and all the lights were off. Jordi unlocked the door so I could leave.

"*Graçias,*" I said.

"*De nada,*" he replied with a smile. "*Y graçias.*"

Back in my apartment, I tipped half the ice into a freezer bag, stashed it in my ice compartment, and took the remaining ice to bed. I thought I would do my usual routine of rubbing cubes over my skin to cool me into sleep but I must have crashed out at once. In the morning, my jug contained only water and my mind was a fog of lust and filth. Where had I been? What had I done? Did that actually happen?

I slipped on a T-shirt, rolled up my shutter and stepped out onto my balcony. It was early morning but already the heat pulsed like the midday sun. I rubbed my eyes. Below, the street was coming to life, the baker's window lined with breads and pastries, people heading to work, a woman on a Vespa turning left. I could see a couple of bars were open but not Bar Anise. It looked as if it hadn't been open for years, its facade concealed by chipboard, graffiti and tatty fly posters. Of course. Hadn't it always been derelict, just another dump waiting to be spruced up before the Olympics?

Drowsily, I padded to the kitchen. Had it been a dream then, just a crazy dream brought on by the heat? I withdrew the bag of ice from my fridge and went back to bed. I had another hour before work. I broke the ice into the jug, scooped up a handful and cupped it to my skin. Just a dream, I told myself, and I lay back on the pillows, wondering if the heat would transport me to Bar Anise on nights to come.

I smeared the ice over my skin, savoring the trickle of water melting onto my stomach. I murmured softly, imagining the touch was the lick of a lover. Just a dream. Words floated to me as if from a great distance. Stop resisting yourself. And I slid an ice cube up my neck then sucked it into my mouth, closing my eyes as I twirled my tongue around the cube, ice when I wanted fire.

ABOUT THE AUTHORS

VALERIE ALEXANDER is a novelist and freelance writer who divides her time between California and Arizona. She is currently finishing up both a short fiction collection and her first erotic novel.

JACQUELINE APPLEBEE (writing-in-shadows.co.uk) is a black bisexual British woman who breaks down barriers with smut. Jacqueline's stories have appeared in Clean Sheets, *Iridescence, Best Women's Erotica 2008* and *2009, Ultimate Lesbian Erotica 2008* and *2009,* and *Best Lesbian Erotica 2008.*

KATHLEEN BRADEAN's (KathleenBradean.Blogspot.com) stories are in *The Mammoth Book of Best New Erotica 6, Best Women's Erotica 2007, She's on Top* and more. She reviews erotic literature at EroticaRevealed.com and Erotica-Readers. com.

RACHEL KRAMER BUSSEL (rachelkramerbussel.com) is senior editor at *Penthouse Variations* and hosts In the Flesh Reading Series. She's edited more than twenty anthologies, including *The Mile High Club, Do Not Disturb, Bottoms Up, Spanked,* and *Best Sex Writing 2008, 2009* and *2010.*

From East Anglia, England, **LEE CAIRNEY** writes about the imaginative loophole sex creates out of the boring contract of everyday life. "Cruising" is her first foray into the dirty and demanding twilight world, or so she likes to imagine it, of women's erotica.

HEIDI CHAMPA (heidichampa.blogspot.com) has appeared in over ten anthologies including *Tasting Him, Frenzy* and *Girl Fun One*. She's also steamed up the pages of *Bust Magazine*. Find her online at Clean Sheets, Ravenous Romance, Oysters and Chocolate and The Erotic Woman.

ELIZABETH COLDWELL is the editor of the U.K. edition of *Forum*. Her stories have appeared in a number of anthologies for Black Lace, Xcite Books and Cleis Press.

A. D. R. FORTE's erotic short fiction appears in several anthologies from Cleis Press. Her stories have also been featured in Black Lace's *Wicked Words* collections and in fantasy erotica from Circlet Press. Visit her at adrforte.com.

SCARLETT FRENCH is a short-story writer and a poet living in London's East End. Her erotic fiction has appeared in *Best Women's Erotica 09, 08* and *07, Best Lesbian Erotica 05,* and many more.

K. L. GILLESPIE is a regular contributor to *Erotic Review* and *TANK* magazine and has been published in *Best Women's Erotica 2008* and *The Mammoth Book of the Kama Sutra.* Her anthology *Panopticon* is out later this year.

KAY JAYBEE is the author of *The Collector,* a regular contributor to oystersandchocolate.com, and has dozens of stories published by Cleis Press, Black Lace, Xcite Books, Mammoth Books and Penguin. Information about all of Kay's work can be found at http://sites.google.com/site/kayjaybeesite/.

JANNE LEWIS is fascinated by the way desire can turn the most rational and reasonable human being into someone altogether different. Her stories have appeared in anthologies published by Cleis Press, Drollerie Press, Ellora's Cave, and Ravenous Romance.

KRISTINA LLOYD (kristinalloyd.wordpress.com) is the author of three erotic novels including the controversial Black Lace publication, *Asking for Trouble.* She is described as "a fresh literary talent" who "writes sex with a formidable force."

PEONY writes for those who have slept beside her, exhaled her name, been locked inside her, marked her skin, and held her close. She lives alone by the seaside, writing in fits and starts in words that taste like sex and poetry.

TERESA NOELLE ROBERTS' erotica has appeared in *Best Women's Erotica 2004, 2006* and *2007, Best Lesbian Erotica 2009, Lust: Erotic Fantasies for Women, Dirty Girls,* and more. Teresa also writes erotica and erotic romance with a coauthor as Sophie Mouette.

After a long career as a teacher and writer of children's books, **CATE ROBERTSON** is finally living her dream and writing smut. A novel is in progress, of course.

ADRIE SANTOS (adriesantos.com) smiles often because she's once again made the sweet realization that she is doing exactly what many said she couldn't; she is earning her living writing about sex.

DONNA GEORGE STOREY (DonnaGeorgeStorey.com) is the author of *Amorous Woman,* a very steamy tale of an American woman's love affair with Japan. Her erotic fiction has been published in *Best Women's Erotica, Best American Erotica* and *X: The Erotic Treasury.*

ALISON TYLER's sultry short stories have appeared in more than one hundred anthologies including *Rubber Sex* and *Sex for America*. She is the author of more than twenty-five erotic novels, and the editor of more than fifty explicit anthologies, including *Playing with Fire* and *Naked Erotica*. Please visit alisontyler.com.

SASKIA WALKER (saskiawalker.co.uk) lives in the north of England close to the Yorkshire moors. Her erotic fiction appears in more than fifty anthologies including *Best Women's Erotica, Secrets, The Mammoth Book of Best New Erotica,* and *Kink*. Her longer work includes the erotic novels *Along for the Ride, Double Dare,* and *Reckless*.

KRISTINA WRIGHT (kristinawright.com) is an award-winning author whose erotic fiction has appeared in more than seventy anthologies, including the inaugural edition of *Best Women's Erotica* in 2000 and *Best Women's Erotica 2007*.

ABOUT THE EDITOR

VIOLET BLUE (tinynibbles.com) is the author and editor of more than two dozen books. She is a sex educator, blogger, podcaster, GETV reporter, SFAppeal.com reporter, the *San Francisco Chronicle*'s sex columnist, robotic artist, a *Forbes* Web Celeb and one of *Wired*'s Faces of Innovation. She's presented at UC Berkeley (Boalt), ETech, SXSWi, to sex crisis counselors at community teaching institutions and Google Tech Talks. Webnation called her "the leading sex educator for the Internet generation" and the Institute for Ethics and Emerging Technologies named her "America's leading (very) public intellectual sexologist."